Jaci Burton

Kismet
Frost and Fire

ELLORA'S CAVE
ROMANTICA PUBLISHING

What the critics are saying...

❧

WINTERLAND DESTINY

"Lusty characters and erotic customs add searing heat to the story. The sexual tension between secondary characters Roarke and Solara gives the promise of another sizzling story in the future. This is an awesome start to another great series from the talented Ms. Burton." ~ *Sizzling Romances*

"This book is a MUST read in this reviewer's opinion! Once you turn the first page, prepare yourself for Five Star blazing adventure!" ~ *Timeless Tales Reviews*

FIERY FATE

"When the sparks flew as Roarke and Solara touched foreheads in WINTERLAND DESTINY, the first book in this series, I knew they would get their own story and that it would be good, but I didn't expect something this wonderful. Ms. Burton's sequel is absolutely superb. The plot is engrossing, the characters are magical, and the sex is scorching." ~ *Sizzling Romances*

"Once again Jaci Burton takes readers on a journey to Winterland where we catch glimpses of King Garick and Noele (see WINTERLAND DESTINY) and watch Roarke and Solara's story unfold. FIERY FATE is a welcome addition to this exciting series of elves and faeries, and I can't wait to read more." ~ *Romance Reviews Today*

An Ellora's Cave Romantica Publication

www.ellorascave.com

Frost and Fire

ISBN 1843609495, 9781843609490
ALL RIGHTS RESERVED.
Winterland Destiny Copyright © 2004 Jaci Burton
Fiery Fate Copyright © 2004 Jaci Burton
Edited by Briana St. James.
Cover art by Syneca.

This book printed in the U.S.A. by Jasmine–Jade Enterprises, LLC.

Trade paperback Publication January 2005

Excerpt from *Summer Heat* Copyright © Jaci Burton, 2004

Also by Jaci Burton

౭

About the Author

ဆာ

Jaci Burton has been a dreamer and lover of romance her entire life. Consumed with stories of passion, love and happily ever afters, she finally pulled her fantasy characters out of her head and put them on paper. Writing allows her to showcase the rainbow of emotions that result from falling in love.

Jaci lives in Oklahoma with her husband (her fiercest writing critic and sexy inspiration), stepdaughter and three wild and crazy dogs. Her sons are grown and live on opposite coasts and don't bother her nearly as often as she'd like them to. When she isn't writing stories of passion and romance, she can usually be found at the gym, reading a great book, or working on her computer, trying to figure out how she can pull more than twenty-four hours out of a single day.

Jaci welcomes comments from readers. You can find her website and email address on her author bio page at www.ellorascave.com.

Tell Us What You Think

We appreciate hearing reader opinions about our books. You can email us at Comments@EllorasCave.com.

KISMET: FROST AND FIRE

WINTERLAND DESTINY
~13~

&

FIERY FATE
~107~

WINTERLAND DESTINY

ॐ

Dedication

ᔆ

To my editor, Briana St. James, for *cough*
lovingmyfaeries *cough*.

To my Paradise Group…thank you for helping me title
this book. It's always fun having your help. Hugs!

And to Charlie…my destiny, my fate, my heart and my
soul. You are the true magic in my life.

Chapter One

ᔛ

Noele sighed heavily as the entourage approached the elvin castle where she was to make her new home.

Behind lay the forests of D'Naath, her home for almost twenty-five seasons. Ahead lay her future, as uncertain and overwhelming as the castle towers that reached high above the clouds of Winterland.

"You fear the joining?"

Noele turned to her sister. Solara's red wings fluttered in the cool northern breeze. She shook her head and flew closer to Solara, squeezing her petite hand. "Do not worry for me, sister. I have known of this betrothal my entire life. I do not dread what may be."

'Twas true, at least partly. Resigned to do her duty as the new queen of the Winterland, she did not fear joining with the elvin king, Garick. Neither did she feel joy at the upcoming nuptials. It was simply the faerie way.

Their entourage was protected by the elvin guards who'd accompanied them on the trek from the D'Naath forests to Winterland. Somber and quiet, the men concentrated on the woodlands on either side of the trail.

Noele knew what they watched for. Or rather, who. She shuddered, suddenly anxious to reach the safety of Winterland's gates.

She flapped her wings quickly, rushing toward the castle entrance. She only hoped her mate-to-be wouldn't possess the visage of an ogre. If he were moderately pleasing to look upon, she could at least tolerate the union.

The tall gates opened before them. She took a deep breath and peered inside. The common area was filled with people bustling about. All activity came to a halt as they stood at the entrance, awaiting an official greeting.

"M'lady Noele of D'Naath, welcome to Winterland." An old elvin male greeted her with a bow, his gnarled hand sweeping forward as a signal for them to enter the courtyard. "I am Limon, the ancient."

Noele nodded and smiled politely at Limon, ignoring the curious stares of the elvin people assembled there. She turned quickly to glance once more at the deep green forests of D'Naath. She hoped one day to return to her woodland for a visit. She would miss all her family and friends.

Especially her parents, who had bravely sent her on her way with tears in their eyes. But they, like she, knew that this union would provide protection for them all. Hopefully her new husband would allow her to go back to D'Naath and see them. As King and Queen of D'Naath, her parents could not leave the woodland forest, lest it fall under attack by those who wished to harm the faerie people.

They could not even see their daughter marry. Noele fought back the tears. She would cry no more. She had duties. Duties she'd prepared her entire life for. And she would not shame her family by acting like a child.

At least she had Solara and her other sisters to keep her company, as well as the guardians of the faerie and a handful of elders who'd come to witness the union.

Limon spoke, breaking her mental connection to her past. "Garick will be joining you later. He wishes you to have enough time to settle in. He will have the evening meal with you in your chambers."

Grateful she wouldn't have to undergo the inspection rite just yet, she let out a sigh of relief and followed the old man through the castle.

It was certainly spacious, and the doorways and chambers were wide enough that she could keep her wings extended. She was settled in a spacious room with a lovely bed draped in a silver gossamer to match her wings. Waving her wings excitedly at the gray stone hearth near the bed, she anticipated the warmth it would put out on the chilled, northern nights. Large rugs were scattered over the wooden flooring and would ward off the chill at night. . She settled on the floor and brushed her toes against the thick carpet, thankful for its softness against her feet.

A floor to ceiling window nearby overlooked D'Naath forest. An open view upon her homeland, a constant reminder of the place of her birth. The sight brought her great comfort, almost as if she could still feel the warm embrace of home and family.

For a castle that had always appeared so imposing from far away, it held a strange comfort she hadn't expected. Many times she had stood at the edge of the forest and looked across at the great castle, wondering what lay within the walls of Winterland. Knowing it would someday be her home had made her curious.

If only the king would turn out to be as warm and comfortable as his castle.

A young elvin woman appeared, curtsying and scurrying about the room. "I am Isolde, your handmaiden," she announced, curtsying again.

"It is not necessary to curtsy before me, Isolde. I am happy to know you and welcome your aid."

The young girl appeared as nervous as Noele felt. "Thank you, my queen."

Queen. By tomorrow's sunset she would be a queen. Although not her choice, she accepted her fate as did all faerie, knowing their destiny had been decided the moment of their birth. As the first female child of her parents, Noele had known early on that she would some day become a queen and rule alongside her mate.

She'd pushed her destiny to the back of her mind for all these years until the inevitable twenty-fifth solstice approached. Now there was no turning back. Her days of frolic and gaiety were over. No more playing in the woodlands with her sisters. No more spying on the other creatures of the forest. No more basking away the days in the sunshine by the lake.

Why did she equate this marriage with the cessation of everything joyful in her life?

"What troubles you, sister?"

Solara had arrived to help her bathe and dress, as had her other sisters. Elise, Mina and Trista. She introduced them to Isolde. The handmaiden's eyes widened and she said, "You are all so beautiful, and yet so different from each other."

"Thank you, Isolde," Noelle said. They'd often heard their beauty praised by both their own people and strangers visiting their lands. Whereas Solara bore the colors of summer with her hair like the flames of the sun and wings a blood red, Noele was fair, with almost white hair and eyes an icy winter blue. Noele's wings were white as snow and threaded with silver that matched the glittery shimmer of her skin.

The twins, Elise and Mina, bore colors of autumn…burnished gold and sienna, and the youngest, Trista, wore the fresh green wings of a blossoming spring, her hair as darkly rich as the fertile soil of D'Naath. When they stood together they encompassed all the faerie seasons and were quite a sight to behold.

She would miss her sisters greatly when they traveled back to D'Naath after the nuptial period. But they, too, had duties and destinies to fulfill. A sudden emptiness filled her being and she brushed the ache aside with a determined flap of her wings.

The large bathing tub was prepared with heated water. Noele retracted her wings until they were tucked deep inside her flesh. The water was steamy and inviting, and she laid back and allowed Isolde to minister to her. Her sisters remained with her in the oversized bathing chamber.

"My queen, will you tell me of D'Naath?" Isolde broached the question in a whispered voice.

Noele reached for Isolde's hand and patted it. "You do not need to fear me, Isolde. If you have questions, you may ask them. Neither I nor my sisters will do you any harm, nor do we expect you to speak in a servile manner to us. Please, we are all women, although you are elvin and we are faeric. That is our only difference."

Isolde nodded and smiled, the tips of her elvin ears as red as her round cheeks.

"Now, about D'Naath. What do you wish to know?"

"Your cultures, your customs. I've heard stories…"

Noele laughed when Isolde reddened. "You mean stories of our sexual frolic?"

The woman nodded.

Trista fluttered over to the edge of the tub, undressing and sliding into the bath with her sister. "Mostly, they are true," she said with a wicked grin. Trista was the most devious of her sisters, fiery hot and passionate. Many times Noele had to rescue Trista from the arms of a faerie boy intent on enjoying her pleasures. Her ardent nature was bound to land her in trouble some day.

"D'Naath is a land of pleasures," Noele explained. "Many outside our realm come to enjoy faerie delights. Our days are warm despite the northern climate. The wood glen contains a magical heat that keeps out the wintry chill. It truly is a paradise."

"Not to mention the desirable faerie women who live in D'Naath."

Noele nodded at Mina's statement. "'Tis true. Many of the female faerie are quite pleasing to look upon. My sisters, for example, have an unparalled beauty."

"As do you, dear sister!" Elise added. "Why, Noele has been sought after since the day of her birth. Many have tried to capture and hold her, and yet she has been promised to your king and therefore unable to accept their overtures."

Noele laughed at Elise's disappointed face. She had enjoyed enough pleasures without laying with a man, yet to Elise, the fact she had to wait to give herself until now was unheard of. "I am no prettier than my four lovely sisters."

Isolde smiled. "You are all so lovely. And a bond exists between you that I envy. I have no sisters."

Solara fluttered over and sat next to Isolde on the stone bench above the bath. "Then we shall be your sisters."

They laughed and splashed water, playing like children. Eventually, her sisters joined her in the bath, giggling and making Isolde blush with their bawdy stories. Noele knew this would be the last time she would enjoy such closeness with her sisters. Her heart ached at what she was losing.

"I will miss summers in the meadow," Noele said.

"Ah yes," Solara added, recalling their adventures for Isolde. "Lying upon the warming moss and swimming in the frigid lakes hidden deep in the forest glen. Many a warm day we'd lounge upon the rocks to dry, pleasuring ourselves with our fingers and fucking ourselves with the long, sleek tubara until whimpers and cries of delight echoed through the trees."

Isolde's eyes widened in shock. She gazed at Noele. "My queen, are you not to be virgin when you come to Garick?"

Noele laughed, relaxed by the warm bath and memories shared with her sisters. "I am still a virgin, untouched by a man. Your king knows full well of the pleasures faerie partake of, including fucking ourselves with the tubara, which is shaped very similarly to a cock."

"A well endowed cock," Trista added, bursting into a fit of giggles with her sisters.

After Noele's bath, she dressed in a simple sheath of silver and paced the room, awaiting her intended mate.

"Quit fluttering so wildly. You are creating a breeze and I am chilled."

Noele turned to Solara. "Go stand by the fire, then and warm yourself."

Solara stepped behind her and held her wings still, then leaned her chin on Noele's shoulder. "You are nervous. It is understandable."

Noele reached for Solara's cheek, the magical touch of her sister's skin calming her. "I cannot help it."

Trista approached her from the front and held her hands, a merry twinkle in her crystalline eyes. "Elvin men are very virile. I've heard stories of their cocks. They are quite impressive. Long and very hard and they can make love for hours without tiring."

"Yes, I've heard that, too," Solara said, squeezing her shoulders. "You will have a lusty man in your bed, my sister. I am envious."

She had dreamed of so much more than simply fucking an elvin king. Dreams of a magical love, an undying, soul-binding joining that would last beyond eternity. But her dreams didn't matter.

Noele grew more nervous with each passing moment, her mind conjuring up an ugly monster she'd have to submit to tomorrow. Tonight too, remembering the required inspection. Excitement warred with trepidation. If he were pleasing to look upon, the inspection and consummation could be quite enjoyable. But if he were hideous, or mean-spirited, then she would dread the upcoming events.

For many years she had looked forward to lovemaking, tired of pleasuring herself with her own fingers or the tubara.

She was ready for a man, wanted a man's thick cock inside her.

She'd just about convinced herself that she could endure the beast's fucking with her eyes shut tightly when steps sounded outside her door. She sucked in her lower lip and breathed deeply as the door opened, a shadowy figure emerging from the darkness.

Her sisters lined up beside her, eager to view her intended mate.

When he stepped from the shadows, her heartbeat halted.

By all that was magical—he was a beautiful man! Tall, over six lengths at least, and well-muscled. His hair hung straight to his shoulders and was black as a moonless night. Would it be soft to the touch? A sudden urge to thread her fingers into his hair overwhelmed her. His eyes were grey as a winter storm, and yet she felt no chill from their depths. Black breeches covered his muscular thighs. His shirt matched his eyes, the colors making him look imposing.

Dangerous. Virile.

Her heart picked up a frantic pace and her wings fluttered excitedly at the thought of fucking this virile elvin king. If his appearance was any indication, her fantasies of lovemaking would, indeed, be as pleasant as she had imagined.

Perhaps her sisters were right. Thoughts of her and this elvin king entwined in an intimate embrace, his massive body covering hers, doing things to her that she'd only dreamed of, had her pulse quickening and moisture gathering between her legs.

Another man entered the room, equally as tall but not as massive in size. Hair almost as dark as the first, but with eyes like amber ale, he stood slightly behind the first giant.

Noele heard Solara suck in a quick breath. Ah, so the second man intrigued her sister.

The raven-haired man spoke to her. "I am Garick, king of the elvin people of Winterland. I bid you welcome to my kingdom."

For a moment she couldn't move. Then Solara's hand at her back reminded her of her duty.

Noele stepped forward, inclined her head in a bow and tried to stem the nervous fluttering of her wings. "I am humbled to introduce myself as your betrothed, Noele of D'Naath."

Garick's brow arched, his nostrils flared slightly. He strode toward her, seemingly growing taller and taller with each booted step until he towered over her. He reached for her, his hands cupping her cheeks, and touched his forehead to hers. His gaze penetrated her, his magic powerful and nearly overwhelming. Sparks flew throughout her being as he sought to telepathically enter her mind. Not unpleasant, but somewhat irritating that he'd be so bold as to attempt to invade her so quickly after their first meeting.

But she had magic, too, and blocked his probe of her innermost thoughts. He raised a brow, clearly understanding that she would not yet allow him access to her mind.

He motioned for the other man in the room to come forward. "This is Roarke, my protector, my right hand, second in command of the Kingdom of Winterland."

Noele nodded warily, fully aware of the role that Roarke would play in her union to Garick. At least he wasn't repulsive, either. To the contrary, both elvin men would be fought over greatly by the faerie women of her kingdom.

Though nervous about the coming joining, Noele's excitement grew as she envisioned what was to happen between her, Garick and Roarke over the next few days. Would it be as thrilling as she imagined? Her body was already aroused at the pictures in her mind.

Solara cleared her throat and Noele remembered her place. She swept her hand to either side of her. "These are my sisters. Solara on my left, and on my right are Mina, Elise and Trista."

Garick, using the same elvin custom of touch as he'd used with her, brushed his forehead to each of her sisters. Then Roarke stepped forward. He bent his head and touched Trista, then Elise, then Mina. When he made contact with Solara, the sparks between the two of them nearly pushed Noele sideways.

Heaven's magic. There was chemistry between those two. And yet, they were not betrothed. How strange. She'd seen her sister tease and frolic with many of the faerie men, but never had Solara been so affected before.

She both heard and felt the tremors within Solara. Roarke pulled back, his brown eyes darkening as his gaze focused on Solara. Then he quickly moved away.

Garick stepped before her, his gaze boring into hers, his grey eyes like the frosty winter storms of D'Naath.

Would he be as cold, she wondered?

She inhaled a quick breath, stunned when his essence filled her nostrils. Briefly, she closed her eyes and allowed herself to feel him.

Noele's senses were already overloaded with Garick's presence, his scent so like the pine forests of D'Naath that just breathing him in made her ache for home. Yet he didn't smile like so many of the males she was accustomed to, instead seemed to wear a perpetual frown.

"Leave us," he commanded. With a bow, her sisters fluttered out of the room, Solara casting a comforting and warm glance in her direction.

But she felt neither comforted nor warm. She felt alone, at the mercy of this handsome giant who was a stranger, and yet soon to be her husband.

"Roarke, return after you have taken your meal."

Roarke nodded in response and departed, leaving her alone with Garick.

"We will dine now." Garick nodded to the servants waiting in the doorway. They brought in a small table and their meal and he motioned for Noele to sit.

The sight of food made her stomach roil. Why was she so nervous? She'd been prepared for this her entire life, knew it would happen.

But she hadn't expected Garick. Hadn't expected the magic between the two of them to be so powerful. He frightened her, excited her and worried her, too.

Her destiny was in his hands, and she did not care one bit for that part of this entire marriage rite. To possibly be cast aside or given to another was not what she would choose for herself. And yet Garick held that right.

For someone like her who had done exactly what she pleased her entire life, it was a bitter pill to be forced to bend under someone else's will.

Noele looked down at her plate of food and pushed it away. She had no appetite, merely picking at the roasted pheasant and dola on her plate.

"You must eat," Garick said, having already devoured his meal. "You will need your strength."

The thought of why she needed strength wasn't something she wanted foremost on her mind, so she tucked the thought away. "I am much smaller than you, Garick. I do not require as much food."

"Then drink this. It will relax you." He poured her a cup of wiloa, an ancient elvin wine that burned her stomach and fired her blood, heating her from the inside out. She welcomed the relaxing effect of the drink, knowing what would be forthcoming.

"You seem uncomfortable."

She looked up from the table and met his probing gaze. "I am not uncomfortable."

"You do not wish to be here."

His search of her innermost thoughts had not been successful earlier. He was merely guessing now. "Why do you say that? I am where I am supposed to be."

His lips curled in a half smile that Noele found quite appealing. "But it is not where you would want to be."

"Does it matter?"

"No."

"Then why ask?"

"Curious. If the situation were reversed, I would not be happy at all."

"No, I cannot imagine you would be." Garick was not the type of man who would bend for anyone. She already knew that much about him. His will was strong. She had to fight hard to keep his thoughts from invading her.

At least she'd managed to prevent his entry into her mind. She may be forced through official rites to do certain things, but she was not required to give up her thoughts to him.

"Shall we get on with the rite of inspection?" he asked, pushing back from the table.

Noele swallowed past the lump in her throat and stood. Garick nodded to Roarke, who had returned and stood at the doorway. He stepped in, closed the door and guarded silently.

"Must he remain?"

Garick arched a dark brow. "Have our customs been explained to you?"

"Of course," she answered quickly, surprised to hear the nervous rasp in her own voice. "I merely assumed his presence would not be required until consummation eve."

"Roarke is required to view the inspection, but he will not participate."

She nodded. "Very well." As if she had a choice. She could no more change elvin custom than she could change faerie. If she could, she would be anywhere else but standing here right now, about to be stripped bare and inspected by the elvin king.

Chapter Two

ಬಿ

Garick eyed the pale-haired faerie who was to become his queen, unable to believe such blinding beauty existed. He'd been forced to call upon all his magic to mask his shock when he entered the chamber and found the ethereal creature standing before him.

Clad in a simple shift, the flowing garment showed off her long legs and creamy thighs. Her white wings, woven with threads of silver, glittered against the light cast by the fire. She looked to be an angel, pale except for the shimmer of silver that graced every centimeter of her exposed skin.

His hands shook at the thought of taking her as his bride, and he fought desperately for control. He would be no good to his or Noele's people if he couldn't keep his emotions under control.

But Roarke knew his reaction. Knew it and laughed at him telepathically.

"I think you have met your match," Roarke thought to him, a touch of sarcasm lacing his deep thoughts.

"Bah. I haven't fucked a faerie in many a long year, 'tis all. And this one is particularly alluring."

"Your heart pounds for her," Roarke said.

"No, my cock pounds for her," Garick objected. But Roarke was right, Garick thought as he forced his lifelong friend and protector out of his thoughts and emotions. Noele of D'Naath had struck him a fatal blow, and he'd be certain to guard his heart around this one. She may be his life mate, but he did not need to bring emotion into their union. Their marriage was one of his duties as king, and he would perform it just as he had performed all his required obligations. He had not shown emotion since he'd taken the throne upon his parents' death.

Emotion was for the weak. Love was for the foolish. He was a warrior, and had been his entire life. Warriors had no time for such frivolity. His father had shown him that from a very young age. Women were to bear children and oversee the daily activities at the castle.

His father had shown no love or affection to his mother, and his mother had accepted that as her duty as his wife. Aye, she had loved Garick, but she had been just as immersed in her own duties as his father had.

As a result, Winterland held strong to the northern territories for many years. Garick would make sure that hold would continue.

"Retract your wings," he commanded Noele, noticing the nervous flapping of the shimmering wings at her back.

She nodded, her wings folding onto themselves and disappearing from sight. He reached for her, sensing her anxiety and waiting for her to flinch. She stood still though, her chin held high and her pale blue eyes fixed on his face.

He admired her courage, realizing how difficult the ceremonies over the next several days would be. But it was custom and he would do what was required, as, it seemed, would she.

Not one to employ tenderness around females, he surprised even himself when he gently grazed her slender shoulders. At his first touch upon her skin, a shock of pleasure unlike anything he'd ever known knifed through him.

He removed his hands and gazed upon her, fighting for control over the intensity of desire that stabbed at his middle. It would be so easy to take her tonight, to bury his cock within her, and make her his.

But their marriage was all about ceremony and ritual. He could not have her this day. Soon, he would. Once he did, the fire that licked at his loins would be quenched and he could return to his other duties without another thought for Noele.

Breathing in a fortifying breath, he once again touched her, fighting back a groan as his fingers traced her magical skin. She shuddered against his fingers and his gaze met hers. A man could get lost in her wintry blue eyes.

Thankfully, he wasn't a man easily lost.

He slipped his fingers underneath the gossamer gown. He did so slowly, watching Noele's reaction. She shivered, but kept her gaze focused on his face.

His cock throbbed against his breeches, coming to life in a fast and furious way. If she were one of the many willing elvin females that clamored for his touch, he would pull out his rigid shaft and plunge it inside her, immediately relieving his tension.

But she wasn't. She was faerie, his betrothed, and a virgin. He would hold his emotions in check and not violate this fragile creature. "I am going to disrobe you."

She nodded and trembled when he pulled the garment to her waist, baring breasts that bordered on perfection. Nipples, as pale as cream, were surrounded by small, high breasts that shimmered with silver flecks. The buds puckered and hardened.

His heart pounded and he recognized a desire to lick the tips of the globes until they glistened with his saliva.

"It is my right to taste you this eve."

"Yes, I know." Her voice rasped against his senses, flaming him hotter than the burning wood in the fireplace. Neither her words nor the magical essence unique to faerie told him she objected.

Noele's lips parted, her mouth forming a perfect bow. He brushed his thumb against her bottom lip and moved forward, leaning down to capture her mouth in a kiss.

He meant only to kiss her briefly. No more, just a brush of lips, a way to gauge her reaction, to prime her for their wedding eve.

But as soon as their lips met, her pheromones released, assaulting his senses with the sweet scent of the sterling silver roses that grew in the forest. He inhaled, then shuddered and lost all control. He slid his tongue inside her mouth and fit his lips more fully against hers. He couldn't find his next breath as she'd stolen it away from him.

Her skin was the softest rose petal, her body pliant and willing in his arms. Her agreeable response both shocked and pleased him. His erection quivered, his balls tightened and he suddenly wished for release more than anything.

No, not yet. With great discipline he held back, not wanting to crush the faerie with his ardent passion.

A desire to see more of her overwhelmed him. He bent down to draw the garment over her slender hips.

A pale tuft of hair covered her mound, it, too, threaded with silver. He crouched down and reached for her buttocks, drawing her femininity closer to him.

The scent of roses and sweet female nectar assailed him. He couldn't resist taking a taste of her bounty. She let out a moan when he rubbed his nose against her soft fur and inhaled her essence. When he placed a light kiss against her mound, her small hand threaded through his hair.

Needing no further encouragement, he nudged her legs apart and slowly swiped his tongue over her stiffened bud, licking the honeyed drops of desire from her nether lips.

By the gods, her taste was sweet, his desire for her grew and he began to mentally count the hours until he could sheathe himself within her.

This faerie held a dangerous magic. The magic to enrapture him, to release emotions he'd held too long in check. Garick vowed to push back any thoughts of warmth or love where she was concerned.

After consummation, after he'd had his fill of her, he would have to turn her over to Roarke.

For the protection of his own people, of course. A king could not be consumed with his bride. And Garick was fearful that Noele would consume his every thought.

Noele was awash in indescribable sensations. Her body arched against Garick's questing tongue. She couldn't have fought him if she wanted to. By the heavens above, she did not want to! His tongue was magic, his breath hot against her throbbing pussy.

Lick me, she begged silently, hoping somehow her mental message would get through to him.

For a second she'd forgotten he was elvin and telepathic, because he chuckled low in his throat, then bathed her with his long, moist tongue.

Her legs shook. She was barely able to stand with her limbs spread apart and Garick doing deliciously wicked things to her clit. Without thinking, she brought forth her wings and flapped furiously for balance.

Garick reared back and regarded her, then stood. Noele could have cried out at the loss of his burning tongue on her flesh, but kept silent, wondering if he was finished inspecting her. Surely he wouldn't leave her like this, aroused and unfulfilled. Could he not see what he'd done to her?

Please, more. Don't stop now.

She hovered face to face with him, his eyes dark as the night sky.

"Would you like to come, my betrothed?" he asked in a voice so low it reverberated through her senses.

"Yes, Garick, I would." He flamed her sexuality like she'd never been able to do for herself. Even watching faeries fucking in the glen had not excited her as much as this tall elvin had.

"And would you be equally receptive to pleasing me?"

Her eyes widened and she glanced down at his breeches, noticing the huge bulge. So, he was as aroused as she. The thought gave her a great deal of pleasure. His shaft pressed hard and insistently against the material, as if struggling to be free.

She wanted this, wanted to taste a man, to feel his hard shaft in her hand, to stroke him and lick him until he bathed her body with his essence.

Mental images of wrapping her lips around his heated cock almost made her come, but she held back, wanting Garick to lick her honey when the time came.

"Oh, I will, my faerie princess. I will taste every drop of your sweet come." He flipped open the button of his breeches and said, "And you will taste mine."

When he spread open his breeches, his cock sprang forth from the dark, curling bush of hair surrounding it. Thicker and longer than any tubara she'd ever seen, her mouth watered at the sight. Then she looked up at him. Garick's pupils dilated when she licked her lips, and she suddenly realized her power to captivate.

She might be slight in stature, her powers no match for the elvin king. She may be forced by destiny to bend to his will and do his bidding as his bride, but she wielded sorcery of her own...with her mouth, her hands and her pussy. A sudden desire to use what magic she possessed to enrapture Garick had her wondering. Why would she suddenly have such interest in captivating him?

Perhaps because when they met he'd shown very little interest in her? Other than arching his brow, the entire evening had been dictated by custom and Garick had followed through with very little emotion.

Until now. And the thought that he hadn't been immediately enraptured by her stung worse than the bite of the bramble bush.

Faerie were all beautiful, seductive creatures, admired and desired by men and women from every kingdom. Noele was used to being pursued and having lavish praise given to her beauty and her magic. Admittedly, his disinterest had made her wary. She feared he would give her to Roarke after their consummation, as was his right.

What do I care which man keeps me? I will still be queen, and as such my people will be protected. Which was the only reason she allowed this to happen. By all that was magic, she did not care for having no say in her future, and yet it was the way of her people.

She could have run, hidden away somewhere, instead of being forced to marry a man she did not know. A man who had the choice to keep her or give her to another.

But she didn't. Noele was not a coward. She would not turn away from her duty.

So, she would please him and in turn allow him to please her. For the sake of her people, of course. The merger between faerie and elvin in the northern lands was vital to maintain their magical stronghold over the wizards of the North. And that was the only reason she'd play this game of seduction and sex with him.

"Your mind stays busy, Noele. Would you like to share?"

Forcing her thoughts deep inside herself, she shook her head. "I only care to share my body with you, and ask that you let me taste your hardened flesh."

His chest rose with his sharp intake of breath. "Curious?"

"Very."

He offered her the first smile she'd seen, a wickedly sensual curving of his lips that took her breath away. "Good. That pleases me. Let me satisfy your curiosity."

She glanced to the corner of the room to see Roarke staring at them. Rather than unnerving her, it excited her to know he watched. How strange these elvin customs were. Her eyes caught and held his, and he smiled. Roarke's erection was clearly outlined against his tight breeches. His lips curled slowly, so wickedly seductive she trembled. She offered him her own smile in return.

Garick spoke. "If you wish, Roarke will obtain release also."

She kept her eyes focused on Roarke, her senses afire with the knowledge that these two men wanted her. And that, for once, she could make the choice. Roarke's gaze burned into hers, his eyes filled with sensual promise. Oh yes, she wanted to watch him stroke himself to a climax. "Yes, I wish it."

"But he will not touch you. It is not allowed," Garick said.

She must remember to keep her mind closed to Garick, lest he think she desired his protector instead of him. Nay, only one man held her attention, her every desire. The thought surprised her, given she had barely met Garick. And yet he compelled her, enticed her, and she wanted him with all her being. Roarke was merely added fuel to her flame of arousal. She wanted to watch him, and to know he watched her.

"I wish to see you naked," she said, turning her attention back to her betrothed. She pulled at his tunic and breeches, eager to feast her eyes upon his body. Her wings whisked her hair into her face as she fluttered about, yanking at his clothing.

When she had undressed him, she stood back, admiring that which would be hers very shortly. He was magnificent. A perfect body, strong, tapered at the waist and muscular in the thighs. Well muscled in the cock, too, she noticed, her eyes focusing on his jutting erection.

She glanced over at Roarke. He'd opened his breeches and exposed his cock. She licked her lips when she saw it, imagining what would happen very soon. He wrapped his hand around the shaft and stroked slowly, his heavy-lidded gaze trained on her. Her cunt tightened with pleasure.

Garick spoke, capturing her attention with his dark, husky voice. "Come, faerie princess, and wrap your mouth around me before I explode."

She fluttered toward him, intent on dropping to her knees. But instead, he reached for her waist and turned her upside down, her face in line with his cock and his hot breath against her damp pussy.

Her wings kept her afloat even when his mouth came down on her clit and swiped against her pussy lips. She cried out, unable to wait any longer for a taste of him.

Nuzzling the mat of hair at the juncture of his thighs, she licked the twin sacs dangling tight and hard underneath his shaft, rewarded with his groan.

He smelled of the crisp, fresh outdoors, flaming her senses and calling to mind images of the earthy forest. Had he ventured into D'Naath, she would have wanted to take him at the forest glen, where the cool streams would bathe their heated bodies.

But she was here and overjoyed at the prospect of tasting her first man. And what a man he was. She licked the side of his shaft, her tongue rolling over the length of his heavy cock. When she reached the tip, she took him in her mouth.

"By all that's magical!" He groaned when she engulfed him. She lapped at the salty drops of his pre-come that spilled over her tongue.

The dual contrast of his velvety hard texture in her mouth and his soft tongue licking at her folds sent sparks of pleasure shooting between her legs. She moaned against his cock and he thrust harder against her mouth.

Truly this was heaven! This wicked, double sensation of tasting and being tasted. Garick was a master with his mouth and tongue, darting the tip in and out of her dripping cunt, lapping up her juices and eliciting more. She could not bear it! Every time he touched her, she took his shaft in deeply, suckling his cock and reaching for his sacs to gently caress and tug them. In turn, he licked greedily at her throbbing clit.

She might die from the pleasure.

"Pet my cock, faerie," he rasped. "Stroke me and suck me at the same time."

She lifted her mouth from him and wound her fingers around his swollen shaft, sliding her fingers up and down while licking his cockhead with quick swipes of her tongue.

Suddenly, Garick turned her upright and pulled her down on top of him on the carpet in front of the fireplace.

"Now. Straddle my face and suck me."

Without hesitation, she did as he asked, turning herself and lowering her pussy onto his waiting mouth. She arched her back when his tongue licked at her clit, and devoured his cock with her mouth.

This position put her in view of Roarke, who furiously pumped his shaft, his half-hooded eyes watching her. Roarke stroked his cock in rhythm to her sucking of Garick's. When she sped up, so did he. When she slowed, he did also.

Stimulated beyond measure, she fought to hold herself over Garick. He reached for her buttocks, squeezing with his fingers and forcing her hips up and down. Her cunt contracted, the spasms forcing more of her juices into his waiting mouth.

Her body ached for an invasion she had never felt, a man's cock sliding into her wet sheath and pummeling her until she screamed. Yes, she'd fucked with the tubara stick, but it had no life, no heat — it would not burn in her mouth like a fire against her tongue. Garick had life, a flame, a force so powerful she wasn't certain she could withstand the pleasure he gave her. The heat of his cock coupled with his fiery mouth on her clit melted her insides.

His tongue held magic, licking the length of her until she shuddered with the rush of her approaching orgasm. When she whimpered against his cock and began to suck him harder, he thrust forward with his hips. She took in as much of his thick member as she could, his frenzy only adding to her excitement.

Roarke was close to the pinnacle, she could tell. His cock swelled even longer, the head darkening with his arousal. She slowed her movements over Garick's cock so she could watch Roarke. Thoughts of Roarke's imminent release, coupled with Garick's continued assault on her pussy had her nearly delirious.

Roarke gave a long groan, squeezing his cock tighter, and shot a stream of come several feet towards her.

Hearing Roarke's groans and seeing his come spurt forth onto the floor sent her over the edge. Now she could hold back no longer. She sucked Garick deeply as her climax shot magical dust into the air around them, the sparkles falling like shooting stars. She tensed with the rush of her orgasm, her body wound around the magic swirling around her and the intensity of her climax. Garick forced his cock deeper into her throat. Whimpering uncontrollably, she could barely take in his fluids when he let out a guttural groan and emptied his seed into her willing mouth. She swallowed all his tangy cream, then suckled him gently until he removed his cock from her mouth.

She turned toward him and Garick pulled her to him, covering her mouth with his. Their juices mingled on her tongue and set her afire again. She wanted this consummation now, wanted his heavy cock buried deep inside her core until she screamed the walls of the castle down.

He panted against her cheek as he held her close and whispered in her ear.

"No more tonight, my princess." He stood quickly and helped her up, then grabbed for his clothes and quickly redressed. "Soon we shall unite and you will be Queen of Winterland."

He turned and motioned Roarke out of the room, closing the door behind them.

Noele's body shook with the force of her response to Garick. He pleased her in many unexpected ways, and yet she had no inkling of whether she'd satisfied him or not. Yes, she'd done so physically, the evidence of that remained in the salty taste on her lips. But he'd not smiled at her or even stroked her after he'd emptied his seed in her mouth.

He had not told her she would be his tomorrow, or that they'd be mated, only that she would become the Queen. Which could mean she could easily be handed over to Roarke if she displeased Garick.

Roarke did not displease her, at least in his looks and the way he excited her. Yet she did not know him.

But, she also didn't really know Garick. So why did she ache for him to keep her?

Before, she'd always had choices, had always done whatever she wished. She'd been in control of her own life for more seasons than she could remember. Yes, she'd known since birth of her betrothal, but she'd come and gone as she pleased in every other way. Now with the swift turn of the moon, her freedom of choice had been taken away.

Duty be damned, she did not care for this!

Chapter Three

ॐ

"Tell us of his cock. Was it long and thick? And what of the inspection? What happened? Was it glorious? Did he touch you?"

Noele blinked open one eye to spy Solara sitting on her bed, her eyes inquisitive, a grin spreading over her full lips. Her other sisters stood at the foot of the bed with expectant expressions on their faces.

"It was passable."

Solara frowned and held her hand against Noele's breast. "I feel your heart, and it lies to me, sister. Now tell us the truth."

Noele struggled to sit up, wiping the weariness from her eyes. Had she only just fallen asleep? She could swear she slept not a wink last eve, her mind occupied with worry about her future. Worry, and a desire so thick it seemed to spread over the very air she breathed.

"Very well. It was beyond description. He was magnificent. A warrior, a lover, he pleased me in more ways than I could ever describe."

Her sisters screamed with delight, hugging her and pulling her from the bed. She extended her wings and stretched, fluttering toward the fire for warmth.

Isolde brought them the morning meal, and Noele was surprised to discover her appetite had returned. As they ate, she told her sisters of the rite of inspection last eve.

Trista's eyes widened. "And Roarke stroked himself while watching the two of you?"

"Yes."

"And what of Roarke? Is he as pleasurable as Garick?" Elise asked.

"Roarke is very male. Although I could not view his entire body, his cock is equally as impressive as Garick's." Just the thought of last night had her moistening with arousal. She both anticipated and dreaded the evening of her nuptials.

She would definitely look forward to sharing herself in the elvin custom of consummation, knowing it would be like nothing she'd ever before experienced. But what would come after—that her entire being objected to with vehement denial. Unfounded irritation at Garick pricked at her, and she forced the thoughts aside.

"And what of Garick's prowess?" Mina asked. "Do the stories of the elvin males hold true?"

Noele laughed. "I do not know everything. But yes, his tongue is very talented."

"As is Roarke's, I'm certain," Elise added with a laugh.

Solara remained silent, staring into the fire. Noele leaned over the chaise and touched her sister's hand. "What is wrong?"

"Nothing."

"You are silent."

"I am pondering."

"Yes, pondering how she can be the one to fuck Roarke," Trista said with a laugh. Elise and Mina smothered their snickers behind their hands.

Solara turned her sharp gaze on Trista. "I was thinking no such thing!" She stood and fluttered about the room, settling at the window and gazing outside.

"She is quite taken with Roarke," Trista whispered to Noele.

Taken, indeed. Solara's pheromones had shot from her essence when Roarke laid his forehead upon her yesterday.

Never before had Noele witnessed her sister have such a strong reaction to a man.

She dismissed Isolde and her other sisters from the room, intending to speak to Solara privately.

"What plagues you, Solara?" she asked, trying not to hover too close to her sister.

"Nothing plagues me. I miss D'Naath."

Misery clenched her middle, causing physical pain. "I know. I do, as well. I will always miss our home. You, at least, will be returning soon."

"My destiny is the same as yours, Noele. I, too, will be leaving our home soon, only traveling south. Further from D'Naath, further from you."

Noele flew to her sister and pulled her into her arms. Red-flecked tears rolled down Solara's face. She swiped at them and held her sister's hands. "I know. But we have known all our lives that this day would eventually come. It is our destiny."

"Destiny be damned. I wish to make my own choices."

Noele's heart ached at her sister's pain. Yet, she was surprised. Solara had never indicated her feelings about her betrothal to the southern elvin king. "You do not wish to marry him?"

"I do not wish to marry anyone not of my own choosing. Why must we do this, Noele? Why must we give up our freedoms to become slaves to men we've never even met?"

"Because it is our duty." And one that Noele had conveniently chosen to ignore for most of her life. Until just recently, when she knew what was to come. But she'd never complained to her sisters of her fate, had never let them see how much it disturbed her to be taken away from the land she loved.

"Bah!" Solara moved away and sat in front of the hearth. The flames cast a burnished light against her wings, making them appear as if they, too, were on fire.

Solara's sadness emanated from her being. Noele sat with her, loath to admit she felt the same way.

"I know it seems unfair, but we must do what has been preordained. It is the faerie way." The words rang empty in Noele's heart, even as she said them aloud.

Turning pained eyes to her sister, Solara said, "I know. I am sorry. Here it is the day before your wedding and I am only concerned with myself. Forgive me, sister."

She laid Solara's head on her shoulder and petted her wings. "There is nothing to forgive. We have always spoken honestly with each other."

"Have you ever considered what would happen if you wanted a man other than the one chosen for you?"

Solara's question surprised Noele. "No. Then again, I have never been interested enough in a man to wonder." She raised Solara's head and searched her face. "Why? Is there someone for you?"

"No. Maybe. I don't know. I just…there was…something. Something I have never felt before."

"With Roarke." They had all experienced Solara's reaction to Roarke.

"Yes. He frightens me. The way my body responds to him frightens me. And yet, it is more exciting than anything I have ever known."

"You realize that nothing can happen with the two of you. You must remain untouched by a man. You are betrothed, body and soul, to the southern king."

"Aye, I know. Roarke would not be interested in me, anyway."

Solara laid her head back on Noele's shoulder.

This was quite unusual behavior for her sister, who had never showed interest in a particular man. Noele had always thought it was because of Solara's own destiny, knowing she was betrothed to the king of the southern lands. She'd had no idea her sister felt this way.

In many ways, it mirrored her own feelings. Marriage to a man she had never met, did not know, and may not even spend the rest of her life with.

No wonder Solara did not look forward to her wedding. When Solara married, would Garick allow her to attend and support her sister?

So many unanswered questions. She wished this ritual were over so she knew what her fate would be. Would she stay forever at Garick's side? Or would she be given away like nothing more than one of the elvins' horses?

Only Garick knew the answers to her questions. Like it or not, it was the way of her life. She had no choices, could make no decisions. She would simply have to bide her time until after the wedding.

* * * * *

Garick stood in the courtyard with Roarke, overseeing the training of the guards.

Today they prepared their weaponry and fighting skills, combining elvin magic and superior strength. It would take all their powers, both mystical and physical, to defeat the wizards intent on taking over their land.

Garick had spent his life training for this. His father had pounded duty into his head from the moment he could understand language. This was his destiny.

Swords clanged in the courtyard, the sounds of steel against steel echoing off the stone walls. Early morning mist rose above them like smoke from a woodland fire, chilling the air.

An attack could come at any time. Insidious and quiet like a snake in the night, or full-on barrage at the gates by the light of day. One never knew what the wizards planned. Either way, his people would be ready.

"They are well prepared," Roarke pronounced, nodding his head to the captain of the guards. The captain raised his hand and ended the training.

"But will it be enough?"

Roarke frowned. "You doubt we have the strength to defeat them?"

He shrugged. "Their magic is very strong. Wizard attacks are borne of cunning and deception. We have lost several of our people in the night hours, and in unusual ways, as you well know. Our people do not simply vanish without a trace."

"Aye, but you can bet it was the wizards' doing. Finding where they hide will be difficult, battling them even more so, but we are prepared. Fear not, Garick, our people will be protected."

"I worry about tomorrow. The nuptials are a prime opportunity for the wizards. People will let their guard down during the celebrations." If he had his way, this marriage to the faerie princess would not be taking place tomorrow. Too many rites and customs, too many chances for a mistake to happen. One mistake and Winterland could suffer devastating consequences.

"I will not let my guard down, and neither will your warriors." Roarke clasped Garick on the forearm, his steely strength evident. "I will keep my eyes and ears open. I will protect our people."

Garick offered a half smile. "You will also be occupied elsewhere tomorrow eve."

Roarke arched a brow. "Does this concern you, my king?"

"Yes, it does. I worry about attack. I've already told you —
"

"That is not what I meant. I'm referring to your princess and my role in the rites of marriage."

"You think me jealous? By all that's magical, Roarke, that's ridiculous. You and I have shared many women through the years. Why would this be any different?"

"Because this particular woman will be your wife, your queen. And because you feel a connection to her."

Garick refused to even consider Roarke's statement. "I have no connection to her. I feel nothing for her."

"You lie. We are linked, you and I. Have been since our youth. I know what you think, I feel what you feel. Your emotions where the faerie princess are concerned run deep, despite your protest to the contrary."

Garick ignored Roarke's comments and turned toward the great hall, intent on breakfasting with his warriors. Roarke followed silently.

Feeling the need to explain what Roarke might have felt, Garick said, "I think you are confused. My emotions are mixed because I worry about our people, about what would happen if the wizards invade during the ceremony. If I feel anything for Noele it is irritation that this event even has to take place right now. It is such foolishness."

"I think you are trying to deny to yourself that your intended bride sparked something within you. It is no shame to feel emotion, Garick."

"Very little point in it, in my opinion. You have known for years that what I will do as far as marriage has nothing to do with emotions and feelings for a woman, and everything to do with what has been destined since my birth."

He had no choice. Marrying Noele was his destiny, his duty. And he always did his duty.

They sat at the head table and ate with the other warriors. Garick glanced around, filled with pride at the sight of his men. So well trained, so devoted to their people. They would lay down their lives to protect Winterland. These men, along with the rest of his people, had to be his focus, not the wee faerie with eyes like a blue snowflake and skin like the winter snow. He couldn't afford to be distracted.

Noele *was* a distraction. No doubt he would claim his right and turn her over to Roarke after their consummation night. What use did he have for a wife, for children? Any children born of Noele and Roarke would be his heirs to claim, would continue his lineage. Noele would still be Queen of Winterland and her people would be protected. She simply would not reign at his side.

Yet the thought of Roarke lying with Noele every night, the thought of her sweet mouth taking in Roarke's swollen cock and pleasuring him the way she had pleasured him last night, filled him with a red haze that nearly blinded him.

"You see? You *do* feel for this faerie. Your emotions are transparent to me, my friend."

"Get out of my head, Roarke."

"I assure you, I hold no claim on her. She does not have a magical effect on me as she does on you."

"She has no magic."

"For you, she does."

Garick went silent, refusing to lend credence to Roarke's comments.

"I will do my duty to both you and her on consummation eve, Garick. And that is all."

"What will happen will happen. We will see on consummation eve. But my mind is made up. I have no use for a wife."

Roarke sighed and left the table, claiming he had much work to do.

Garick had much to do today, also. But not what he should be doing. Today, he would have to put aside thoughts of battle and preparations, and spend the day with his bride-to-be.

What ridiculous customs. He had no time for lolling around a meadow with Noele and touring her through Winterland. What would they talk of? They had nothing in common. She was faerie and he was an elvin warrior. She would not understand his drives, his ambitions. She would not appreciate his duties, his desire to protect his people.

Faerie only thought of pleasurable things. From what he understood of their lives, they spent days frolicking in the meadow and doing other useless tasks.

So why did the thought of being alone with Noele cause his cock to stir? Why did his mind torment him with visions of silver-tipped nipples and long legs?

Garick clenched his hands into fists, frustrated by the feelings coursing through him.

He stood, drained the last of the mead and slammed his empty goblet onto the table. He stormed from the room, intent on taking out his frustrations by beating Roarke soundly in a game of swordplay.

Feelings! He did not have feelings!

Chapter Four

ଊ

Noele dressed, her stomach tied in knots at the thought of seeing Garick again.

Today he was required to show her Winterland. They would spend the day together, alone. By custom, he was to present a marriage gift to her. Then, they would share the midday meal. After that, they would not be allowed to see each other until the marriage ceremony tomorrow.

She smoothed her dress against her legs, trying to still her shaking. After her conversation with Solara today, she was plagued with more doubts than ever. Always the strong one, Noele had found it difficult to reassure her sister, when her own fate hung on the decision of the elvin king.

No, it did not make her happy to realize she could not choose her own mate. And yet, the thought of lying with Garick did not displease her. Nay, on the contrary, her body remained stimulated and aroused as she thought of last eve's events.

She stood in front of the long mirror and examined her features. A blush stained her cheeks, making the silver flecks sparkle as if on fire. Her nipples beaded and pressed against the silk of her shift.

Arousal thrummed between her legs. She imagined Garick standing behind her, undressing her, touching her breasts, her hips, her buttocks. Would he slide his fingers into her nether region and pleasure her there? Would he want to pleasure himself that way?

She reached behind her and swept her fingers over her buttocks, wondering how his cock would feel embedded in her small puckered entrance.. Her thighs dampened as desire seeped from her. Slowly she lifted her dress, revealing the silvery tuft of hair on her mound. She examined her cunt as if he were examining her. Was she pleasing to look upon?

Her breasts swelled and pressed against the dress, the nipples aching and aroused. Her pussy clamored for attention. Noele chewed her bottom lip, wondering when Garick would appear for her.

She palmed her breasts, sucking in a gasp as her nipples scraped against the silky material of her dress. Moving her hands downward, she stopped at her mound, teasing the fine hairs there with her fingertips.

Shocks of pleasure knifed within her. Her pussy lips opened, juices seeping along her thighs. Arousal took hold of her and she slipped two fingers into her aching cunt, using her thumb to circle her clit.

A moan escaped her lips as she fucked herself, watching her body flush with desire. She spread her legs so she could see better. Moisture clung to her fingers as she moved them in and out of her pussy. If only it were Garick's cock inside her, thrusting hard and fast until she screamed her pleasure.

If only Garick were here, watching her, coaxing her into plunging her fingers in and out of the moistened slit. If he were standing behind her, would he want to fuck her while he watched her pleasure herself? Would he reach for her breasts and tease the nipples, adding to her excitement?

Release loomed ever closer, visions of Garick adding fuel to the fire she'd created. She moved her other hand over her clit. She had no idea it would be so arousing to watch herself take pleasure like this. She could barely stand on her shaky legs, so intense were the sensations running throughout her body.

Garick's visage entered her mind again, his strong body, muscular arms that could lift her easily. His cock would give her much pleasure. Would she only have it inside her once, or would he want to make love to her night after night for the rest of their lives?

No, she would not think on such things right now. Tension coiled deep within her, and she quickly strummed her clit in time to the thrusting motion of her fingers inside her core.

Her orgasm rocketed through her, her juices flooding her fingers as she pumped them harder with her release. She whimpered and let out a low cry of delight, then collapsed onto the nearby chaise, her body shuddering with the aftereffects of her climax.

She was still panting when a knock sounded and Garick walked in. She quickly pulled down her dress, feeling immediately guilty for having pleasured herself. Her body no longer belonged to her. She was his to do with as he willed. And yet she had been unable to stop until she had reached the pinnacle.

Garick arched a brow, watching as she smoothed her wrinkled dress. "Are you prepared to spend the day with me?"

"Yes," she rasped, her throat dry from panting. "I am ready." A few seconds earlier and she'd have been ready to forego waiting for the marriage and would have been begging him to consummate right then.

She had desperately needed the release of her tensions. And yet, one look at Garick and arousal began to build again. Her heart pounded, her body flushed with familiar heat. She craved his touch. When he was near, her body responded by heating with desire. What was it about this man who barely spoke to her that made her want him so much?

Without another word, Garick nodded and motioned her through the doorway.

Curiosity took over and Noele was anxious to see the castle and grounds. Other than her room and the courtyard, she hadn't seen much of Winterland. If it was to be her home, she wanted to know everything about it.

He led her down the wide hallway, pointing to the closed doors on either side. "Up here, as you know, are my quarters. There are several bedrooms. You will sleep in my chambers after our marriage, of course."

She looked at him, wondering what he meant by that statement. Was it a given he would want to keep her, or was he just making conversation?

"You have not yet made claim for me, Garick."

He stopped and turned to her. "Of course. You are right."

When he continued walking, her heart fell. His statement had been made without thinking. Clearly, he did not wish to keep her. It was evident from his somber face.

Did the man have no feelings, no emotions? Could he not see that her very future was in his hands? She walked along quietly, listening to his descriptions of the great hall downstairs, the kitchens, the meeting areas. When they turned to a set of thick double doors and Garick opened them, Noele's mouth fell.

It was a huge room, with no furniture inside. The wooden floors reflected the morning sunlight coming in from the tall windows.

"This is our place for parties, balls, whatever festivities the people of Winterland have at various times of the year."

Noele had never been to a ball, or a party. Faerie life was spent mainly outside in the woodland, although they all lived in small cottages throughout the glen. Her mind conjured up great parties where both elvin and faerie mingled, laughing gaily and dancing.

"Shall we go?"

Loath to leave, she nodded and followed him through another doorway in the back of the castle. A desk and papers were spread throughout the room, and hundreds of books lined the built-in shelves surrounding the room.

"I have a gift for you." He stepped to a paneled wall and pulled it open, taking out a garment and turning to her. "From me, from my people. I am honored that you will be my queen. I present this gift to you in the hope it pleases you."

He handed her an ermine cloak. White with silver threads, it nearly matched her wings perfectly. She was awestruck, never having seen a cloak of such beauty.

"Thank you, Garick. It is truly lovely."

"I hope that it will warm you on cold wintry days. The northern climate here is different than your protected forests."

She nodded, touched by his generosity. Although the gift was customary, the king was required to choose it himself.

"I cherish this gift and accept it with gratitude."

Garick took the cloak and folded it over his arms, then directed her attention to the room.

"This is my place to work, to study. Many of my colleagues also make use of the books of elvin magic."

He turned to leave, but Noele stopped him by placing her hand on his sleeve. She brushed by and fluttered to the shelves, scanning the various titles. Her heart beat excitedly at the sight of so many mystical books. She turned to Garick. "These are wonderful! I have not read a book of enchantment in many years. May I be allowed to read them?"

Garick paused, then inclined his head. "Yes, of course you may. Are you familiar with elvin magic?"

"Yes, very much so. Being faerie, magic fascinates me. Elvin mysticism is quite different from faerie. Much of what we do is instinctive, reactive without thought. Like turning on a lantern when it is dark outside. It's done by instinct, not by conscious thought. The elvin way requires utilizing the mind as an active participant in creating magic. I would love to learn more about your customs."

"Then you shall be allowed free access to the library any time you wish."

"Oh, thank you Garick!" She fluttered to him , intending to hug him in gratitude. Something about his stance stopped her. His body tensed, giving out signals that indicated he would not be receptive to her touch. Her face fell, the smile dissipating and crumbling to the ground along with her ego.

This may be a new and exciting venture to her, but clearly Garick did not share her enthusiasm.

He led her outside the front doors. It was a beautiful winter day, a frosty chill in the air but the sun was a warming overhead blanket. Nevertheless, she shivered.

He pulled the cloak from his arms and wrapped it around her, carefully draping it over her shoulders and wings.

"Thank you." As he stood near her, she inhaled his manly scent. He smelled of the crisp outdoors…the scents of the forest, the glen, all wrapped into one delicious elvin male.

She pulled the cloak around her.

Garick led her through the gardens and out toward the bluffs. She held her breath as they approached the edge, hearing the sounds of the northern ocean crashing against the rocks far below.

Winterland was protected on its northern side by a cliff no man or beast could scale. Therefore, no walls were necessary. The spectacular view of the sea was open and visible.

"'Tis truly beautiful here, Garick. Thank you for welcoming me into your home."

He opened his mouth as if to utter a reply, then closed it. When he spoke, his voice was tight, devoid of emotion. "If you like, we will luncheon in the great hall with my warriors. Unless you prefer we take the meal in your room."

"Of course not. If it is allowed, I would welcome the opportunity to meet your people."

He arched a brow, but once again said nothing. She followed him into the hall, a massive room littered with long oak tables and benches. The tables were formed into a u-shaped pattern, and Garick led her to the center of the middle table.

Within minutes the sound of hundreds of boots smacking the wooden floors nearly deafened her. Loud, male voices carried in the air as the other elvin males entered the room.

Women, too. Unlike many of the other kingdoms, the women shared the tables equally with the men. Many of the women cast glances in her direction, but Noele felt no animosity from any. Curiosity, more likely. She was new and she was to be their queen soon. Of course they would want to catch a glimpse of her. She smiled at the women and all smiled back, nodding their heads in her direction.

For the first time in a day, Noele breathed a sigh of relief. She had wondered whether she would be welcome here in Winterland. While they ate, no one cast her hateful glances. Perhaps living here would not be as terrible as she had imagined.

As they ate, the men discussed preparations for a possible invasion by the wizards. Noele shuddered, having heard stories for as long as she could remember about the evil, mystical lords of the dark realm. Though she had never seen them herself, many of her people had been whisked away in the night when they dared venture too far from the protected forests of D'Naath. And they had never returned.

"Tomorrow we will double the guards at the gates and towers. We can't risk having the wizard attack then," Garick said to Roarke.

Tomorrow. The day of their wedding. Noele could only imagine how Garick must feel about the ritualistic nature of their marriage ceremony. Especially considering the possibility of attack by the wizards.

"You worry for your people," she said, not realizing until he turned toward her that she had said the words aloud.

"Aye. It is my duty as king."

"Not all kings concern themselves with the welfare of their people. You are an honorable man to take your duties so seriously."

"I do what is necessary. What I have been destined for."

"My apologies to you, Garick," she said, feeling somehow responsible for taking his focus from his duties.

He turned to her and frowned. "For what?"

"Our marriage. It is quite clear that an attack of the wizards is imminent, and yet you must leave your duties to attend to our marriage. If it were not because of faerie custom that I must marry on the day of the Winter Solstice, our union could have been delayed to a much safer time."

His gaze held hers, and Noele lost herself in his wintry eyes. She wished she could read him telepathically. After tomorrow, they would be linked mentally as well as physically. Maybe then she would have some insight into his thoughts and feelings.

"You are no more responsible for the timing of our marriage than I, Noele. Elvin custom also requires it, so do not take this responsibility upon yourself."

"Nevertheless, I will alert the faerie in attendance to gird up their magic and be alert in case of attack. We are a small group, but have some powers of our own. We, too, have fought the wizards for centuries. It is my duty as your intended to assist you in any way I can."

His lips curled in a smile that sent her pulse skittering. "And would you take up a sword and defend me to the death, my princess?"

The low and husky whisper of his statement, meant only for her ears, sent her body into full awareness of exactly what she'd be willing to do for him. "Aye, if need be, Garick. I am as sworn to protect you as you are to protect me. It is my duty, and my pleasure, to do so."

Although she'd probably fall over onto her backside trying to wield one of his swords.

Garick's eyes widened and he threw his head back, laughing so loud it captured the attention of everyone in the hall.

"Now, that might be worth seeing, my faerie," he whispered, still chuckling. He swept the back of his hand over her cheek, his fiery gaze burning through her. "I'd like to catch another glimpse of that delectable backside of yours. Very soon, I will."

Stardust! He'd crept into her mind and read her thoughts. How easily she let her guard down around him, despite her intent to keep a wall between her mind and his. She must work harder to do so, lest he find out more about her thoughts than she wanted him to know.

"Would you like that, princess?"

"What is that, my king?"

"Would you like me to view your body, naked, your legs spread apart so that I can glimpse your beauty?"

Visuals assaulted her mind. Lying down, her legs spread, her pussy open to Garick's view. She wriggled uncomfortably on the hard bench, wishing she were anywhere else right now except under his probing gaze. "It is always my pleasure to serve you, Garick."

She felt the heat shoot from his body to hers, and had to grip the table to keep from sliding into a puddle on the floor. By the gods, how had he done that to her? Glancing down at his lap, she saw his erection outlined against his breeches. He slipped his hand in hers and gently pulled her arm under the table, pressing her palm over his rigid cock.

"Feel what you do to me, Noele. I am hot and hard and ready for you."

Panting at the meal table would be unseemly, but by the stars she struggled to maintain even breathing. Garick's wicked smile unnerved her, and when he moved his hips and thrust his cock upwards against her hand, she nearly whimpered out loud.

"Are you ready to feel my shaft inside you, my faerie? Do you think about how it will feel?"

She was certain her face flamed red from embarrassment. How could he discuss something so intimate with all these people around? And yet, she felt compelled to answer. "Yes."

"I, too, think about it. Your pussy will be hot, a tight sheath surrounding me. I look forward to consummation eve."

Instinctively, she began to rub his shaft, wishing they were alone, wishing she could open his breeches and take his hard cock in her hands, stroke him until he spilled his seed over her fingers or in her mouth. She wanted to offer him the same release as she had enjoyed earlier, but didn't dare do anything in a public place such as this.

"I want your mouth on my cock."

She stilled, her entire body shifting from this public arena to a time when the two of them would have privacy. "I'd…I'd like that."

"I'll dismiss the room. We can be alone. After our marriage tomorrow, we won't—"

"My king, a word with you in private, if I may?"

Noele quickly moved her hand from Garick's lap and turned her attention to the guard standing before them.

"Now?" he asked, his voice gruff.

Noele allowed a small smile, knowing why he sounded so irritated.

"It is urgent, my king."

With a sigh, Garick adjusted his breeches and stood, turning to Noele. "I trust you can find you way back to your chambers?"

"Aye, that I can."

"I will see you in the morn, then." He turned and walked off with the guard.

What had he been about to say? After tomorrow he wouldn't what? He wouldn't be her lover, her husband? Would he turn her over to Roarke?

It was clear where his duty lay…with his people. It seemed to occupy his mind completely. Perhaps he did not have time for a wife and did not want to be burdened with her.

Then again, there were times when he looked at her or said something that led her to believe he wanted her, not simply for the required consummation, but for always.

She was reading too much into his body language, his eyes. He felt nothing for her and had already hinted at not wanting to keep her.

It shouldn't matter which man she ended up with. She didn't know Garick any more than she knew Roarke. Both were well pleasing to the eye, and while Roarke had not yet pleasured her, she imagined he would not leave her wanting.

Why couldn't *she* make the choice? Why was it that her entire future lay in Garick's hands?

Suddenly realizing she was alone in the great hall, she stood and flew up the stairs to her room. She looked out the window, across the barren fields to the rich green forest of D'Naath.

Never before had she stopped to think how unfair this situation was. Not until the full impact hit her. Her very future was at the mercy of someone else's whims.

And that someone else had made it quite clear he had no use for her, other than sexually.

Tomorrow she would marry. By the next day, she would know her future. A future she would have no part in deciding.

With a wistful sigh she stared at the forests, for the first time in her life feeling utterly alone.

Chapter Five

සා

Garick paced his chambers, grumbling orders at his assembled warriors, wanting to ensure all steps were taken to insure the wizards would not appear during the mating ceremony today.

After he'd cursed them all and ordered them out, Roarke approached him.

"You have a burr up your ass this morning?"

He would only allow Roarke, his life protector, to speak to him that way. "I slept very little last eve."

"Difficult to sleep when your cock's hard?"

Garick glared at his friend, who only smirked. Unfortunately, Roarke was right. He'd not slept at all, his shaft pulsing with need for the faerie who was to become his bride today. Many times throughout the wakeful hours he'd wanted to stroke himself to release. Instead, he forced himself to wait, knowing what pleasures he would have today with Noele.

It had taken great will to pull himself away from her and walk out of the room yesterday. What he had wanted to do was sink his shaft deep inside her and make her his own. Possess her, mark her in some way, so that no one could ever claim her.

He shook his head at his wayward thoughts. Those were emotions unlike anything Garick had experienced before. Other than fucking for release, he'd never truly wanted a woman before.

To desire the faerie who was to be his mate, whom he'd sworn to protect…by all that was magical in the heavens, it was too much for him. He had to focus on his duty, not on his emotions. This mating between he and Noele had been ordained to unite their kingdoms, to strengthen their hold on the northern territories.

It was not for love or emotion or passion. Those ideals were beyond him...he was incapable.

Roarke's snort brought him out of his reverie.

"What?"

"You keep trying to convince yourself you're not falling in love with the faerie princess. It isn't working. You'll be drooling at her feet by nightfall."

His protector's smirk only heightened his irritation. "Don't you have some duties to attend to, Roarke?"

"Yes. I must stand by my king for the entire day and evening."

It was times like these that Garick wished for one moment alone both in thought and in presence. With a sigh, he allowed himself to be readied for the ceremony.

* * * * *

Noele conjured a magical calming chant to drown out the constant chattering of her sisters and Isolde as they prepared her. Her mind wandered to grey eyes and dark hair, firm muscles and a cock that would...

"Noele! You are *not* paying attention!"

She looked up at the sound of Solara's voice. "Did you say something?"

Solara fluttered her wings rapidly and stamped her foot. "Your mind wanders, Noele. We must finish if we are to arrive at the meadow on time."

The meadow. Shortly she'd be married there, and still have no idea what her future held. Insecurity surrounded her, making her wish for her old life where she knew what each day held. Now, a mystery unfolded with every passing second.

Would Garick accept her? Would he cast her aside in favor of another? And why was it only his choice to make? Why did she have no voice?

"Because it is the way of faerie," Trista responded to her thoughts.

"I know the customs and rituals, Tris. Which does not mean I have to like them."

"He will not cast you aside," Mina said, her copper eyes warm as the sun. "How could he not love you as we do?"

Tears welled in Noele's eyes as Mina gently caressed her hair. She pushed aside the aching sense of loss. Soon her sisters would be leaving her. "You are right. It is time to prepare."

Focusing on her duty instead of her emotions, she allowed herself to be dressed in the stark white colors of her bridal gown. The buttery soft garment fit her snugly at the breasts and waist, flowing to the floor and behind her in a narrow train. Long sleeves curved out into a bell shape at her fingertips. Small slits had been created in the back to fit her wings, allowing them to spread out wide.

A wreath of sterling silver roses was placed on her head, her hair curling in streams down to her waist.

"A man would have to be a fool not to be enraptured by your magical beauty, my queen." Isolde bowed, her eyes glistening with tears.

Noele reached for the young girl and smiled. "Thank you, Isolde."

"'Tis true," Solara said, her own eyes welling with moisture. "You are so beautiful, my adored sister. I wish you happiness on this your marriage day."

Her sisters surrounded her, gifting her with spells of love, fertility, passion and happiness. If only those spells would work on Garick, then perhaps she would not be cast aside.

Oh, what did it matter? She had no more feelings for him than he had for her. She wanted only to get past this ceremony, past tonight, and then live the life she would be given.

The life she could not choose for herself.

Sighing deeply, she affected a smile for her sisters. "Please, accompany me to the meadow."

Choking back the fear and longing for her former freedom, Noele trailed behind her sisters as they left the hall and headed outside.

The gods smiled on her today, gifting her with a warm, sunny morning. A large crowd assembled before them. Fluttering her wings nervously, she smiled tentatively, hoping they would welcome her into their community.

She breathed a sigh of relief when wide grins and applause greeted her entrance.

The meadow was huge and overlooked the northern sea. The view was breathtaking, and lifted her spirits for the first time today.

The crowds parted to reveal a long, white carpet leading to an elaborately carved arch. Roses, jonquils, tuliberries and dolaflowers weaved their colors through the lattice over the arch. Silver and lavender streamers blew lazily in the slight wind. The sun glinted off the waters, lending the whitecaps a silvery shimmer.

It was the most beautiful sight she had ever seen. Had this been a love match, she would be giddy with happiness at the breathtaking surroundings. This was a perfect place, a perfect day, to marry one she loved.

And one who loved her.

But this marriage was not a love match. She feared Garick did not have the slightest idea what love was.

She slowed her wings to keep from flying away. Her fear, at least momentarily, had dissipated. How could she not love the freedom of the outdoors? The beauty of Castle

Winterland's meadow was nearly as lovely as the forest glen of D'Naath.

More importantly, how could she not be awestruck at her soon-to-be husband waiting underneath the arches? Dressed in black breeches and a longcoat of a matching color, his dark hair blew away from his face in the slight wind, revealing his handsome features.

His eyes darkened at her approach. Despite Noele's determination to feel nothing today, trepidation filled her mind at his straight-faced visage. She swallowed past the dryness in her throat and wished for a cooling drink of D'Naathian spring water.

The high priest, tall and reed-thin in flowing black robes, motioned her forward. He inclined his head, smiled at her, then directed Garick to take her hands in his.

Garick turned to her. Noele fought for control as his gaze burned hotly into hers. What thoughts lay behind his scowling face, she did not know. Fearing the worst, she refused to speculate what her fate might be.

The high priest started, the ceremony steeped in elvin ritual. "Yea, let it be known in all the forests and castles of the northern kingdoms, that today, the first day of the Winter Solstice, Garick, King of Winterland, marries Noele, Princess of D'Naath."

A huge round of applause went up, the cacophony of cheers roaring through Noele's ears. The priest raised his hand and when all was once again silent, he continued.

"Garick, thou must pledge to honor thy wife, protect her against all enemies, and bring forth children to seal thy union and further the continuation of the two kingdoms. Thou will retain right of castoff if the faerie princess fails to please thee at the consummation this eve. If thou so choose, Noele of D'Naath will be given to thy Protector, Roarke. Their children will be thy children and fall under thy protecting hand for the remainder of their lives. If thou so agree to this, reply with 'aye'."

"Aye."

Noele let her eyes close for the briefest of seconds at the thought she could so thoughtlessly be given away. She felt no better than one of the horses the elvin warriors rode.

Before the high priest's words could sink in, he turned to her.

"Princess Noele of D'Naath, thou must pledge eternal loyalty to King Garick of Winterland. Thou agree to abide by the wishes of thy husband, and willingly accept the elvin customs described here today. If thou so agrees to this, reply with 'aye'."

It occurred to her for the briefest of moments to refuse to put her future in the hands of one man, without her thoughts, her desires, even considered. Yet duty pulled at her and she gave the only response she was honor bound to give.

"Aye."

"Let it be known throughout the kingdoms of Winterland and D'Naath, that King Garick has wed the Princess, Noele. By all the powers that are holy and revered, I bestow a marriage upon thee both. May blessings of magic, prosperity and children grace the rest of thy days."

Garick lifted her hand and slid a heavy silver band on her index finger, then brought it to his lips, sealing the settling of the ring with a kiss that flamed her skin.

The ring weighed heavily on her hand, a reminder that she was now bound to Garick. Her very future lay in his hands.

Before she could ponder any further, he pulled her against him, his eyes searching her face, then gently brushed his lips against hers. She held her breath, struck by the tenderness in his kiss.

Without thinking, she reached up and caressed his cheek with her trembling hand. Tears came, unbidden, and pooled in her eyes.

Garick frowned, taking her wrist in his hand and pulling it down to her side. Then he gathered her hard against his chest and seared her mouth in a kiss that stole the breath from her lungs. Hard and punishing, his tongue plunged inside and wrestled with hers. 'Twas not a kiss of emotion or tenderness…but annoyance, irritation, anger.

Noele reached up and placed her palms on Garick's chest, pushing gently to break the kiss. He pulled away and gazed down at her, his dark eyes pinning her.

What had changed? When he first kissed her it had been gentle, dare she say emotional. She'd felt his tenderness. Then when she touched him, his face had changed to one of irritation.

But why? Was he unhappy? Had she done something wrong? His expression gave her no clarity.

What could she possibly have done to anger him?

The question plagued her throughout the day's festivities. After the joining ceremony, they'd moved into the courtyard. Food, drink and merriment of all sorts ensued.

She and Garick walked arm in arm through the crowds, accepting well wishes and talking to the people. Noele enjoyed meeting so many of the Winterland people, and bade her sisters to accompany her so that they, too, could be introduced.

Solara spent most of her time near Roarke. Noele noticed on many occasions the two of them exchanging glances.

Worry for her sister occupied her mind. Noele felt the attraction between Solara and Roarke, and knew no good could come from it. She decided she would have to speak with her later, before the consummation.

Their celebration meal was held at a large table decorated with wildflowers and garland. Ale and bread were given in the age-old toast to prosperity and joy. Noele wondered if she'd ever feel joy again, wishing upon every star in the night sky that this marriage had been a more happy and love-filled event.

While they ate, minstrels played bawdy songs and serenaded the crowds. Dancing broke out in various forms, from the quick-stepping rodanda to the seductive talar. When it came time for Garick to dance with his bride, the music slowed and a sultry j'nada filled her ears.

Faerie waltz. Her favorite dance. Memories of her father sailing around the forest floor with her in his arms flew through her mind, making her ache for the simple days of her childhood.

But now, it wouldn't be her father's arms around her. Now it was her husband's. Her husband, and yet a stranger. A stranger who made her feel things she'd never felt before, a stranger who'd claim her virginity tonight and then decide whether or not to keep her.

Garick stood and held out his hand for her. Warily, she slipped her fingers into his palm and he led her to the dancing circle. Which man would dance with her now? The one who had kissed her tenderly after their union had been officiated, or the one who'd ravaged her mouth in a kiss meant to punish for some unknown transgression?

She was certain Garick could feel her tension when he wound his arms around her and pulled her against him. She tried to relax, but couldn't, her mind awhirl with uncertainties. When her back stiffened at his touch and her wings arched away from his hand, he raised a brow. Aware he scanned her thoughts, she held tight to her strength, forbidding him admittance.

"Do not hide your feelings and thoughts from me, my queen," he said, his voice tight.

Irritation from his earlier treatment of her remained. "I will give you what I am duty bound to, and nothing more, my king." Her jaw ached from clenching her teeth. Her annoyance at his attitude grew with every turn around the makeshift dancing arena.

"You will give me all of you, Noele." His brows knit together, his glare fierce. His fingers bit into her hand hard enough to draw her attention.

She should have been afraid, but she wasn't. Anger at her so-called duty and Garick's ambivalence forced her normally independent spirit to surface. "I will do what is required of me. That is all you can expect, that is all I will give you."

"What if I want more?"

What did he mean, more? Despite her bravado, she wanted nothing more than to be accepted by Garick and his people. Living out the rest of her life unhappily would crush her. Was it too much to ask for a little kindness?

"Answer me, my beautiful faerie."

She looked up and met his eyes. His face had changed. Gone was the angry Elvin King, replaced instead by a man with a handsome face and warm eyes that seemed to touch her soul. "You confuse me, Garick."

He sighed. "Aye, I realize that. I cannot help who I am or the way I am. I will take some getting used to. But I will never harm you, Noele. You have my pledge that you will be well taken care of in Winterland."

She already knew that. He was duty bound to protect her. What she didn't know was whether he would keep her.

And what of love? Would she ever find it, or was she doomed by her obligations to the faerie to live out her life miserably unhappy?

"It is time."

Roarke's voice over her shoulder made her shiver with an equal amount of dread and anticipation. Garick nodded and stepped away from her, leaving her to her sisters and Isolde to prepare her for the consummation.

In a few short hours, she would no longer be a virgin. By morning, she would know her future.

She and her sisters were led to Garick's chambers by one of the guard. A huge room filled with a heavy oak bed took up an ample amount of space. The hearth was twice the size of the one in her room, and there was a balcony through glass doors that overlooked D'Naath.

The room was lovely, and yet Noele was cold, her very bones turned to ice.

Oh, why couldn't she enjoy this special night, forget thoughts of what would happen after?

She vaguely listened to her sisters as they giggled about tonight's activities. Her body trembled in anticipation. No fear coursed through her, mainly curiosity and dread.

Isolde removed her wedding gown and carefully folded it. Noele spread her wings to the sides to stretch. Considering the activities of the evening, she'd need to retract her wings.

She was naked, as was custom. They brushed her body with soft cloths to bring out the silver flecks nestled just under her skin. With the firelight shimmering off the hearth, her skin appeared like pinpoints of moonlight shot out from her body.

"You are most beautiful, my queen," Isolde said in a hushed whisper.

"I wish you much happiness, Noele. We will see you at the morning meal," Solara said, pain evident in her golden green eyes.

As her sisters made to leave, Noele said, "Solara, wait. I wish to speak with you alone for a brief moment."

She nodded and waited while the rest of her sisters kissed and hugged Noele, then left. "What is it?"

"Roarke."

"What of him?"

"You feel something for him."

Solara lifted her chin. "I do not."

Noele laid her hand over her sister's heart. "As you told me before, you lie. I can feel it. You mustn't, Solara. You know you are betrothed to another."

"I feel nothing for Roarke, I assure you."

In her heart, Noele knew Solara was not telling her the truth. And what would happen this eve between her and Roarke was bound to cause Solara pain.

"What happens at the consummation, Solara, I want you to know that I—"

Solara raised her hand. "I do not wish to discuss it, Noele. You do your duty, as we all do. I realize where your heart lies, and it is not with Roarke. Nor is mine. Please, enjoy your wedding night and do not worry of me."

Solara kissed her quickly and fluttered from the room before Noele could say anything more.

Noele ran to the closed door, wanting to go after Solara and offer comfort.

Her sister could deny her feelings all she wanted, but Noele knew how she felt about Roarke.

At least Solara knew who she wanted, even if she couldn't have him.

Did Noele know what she wanted?

If Garick accepted her, kept her, then what? Did it mean he loved her? How did she even feel about him? Was it love she wanted from him, or merely acceptance?

Desperately wishing for her sisters' counsel, she stared at the door for a few minutes, then moved back to the hearth to warm the chill that had settled over her body.

Chapter Six

so

Nearly an hour passed and Noele was still alone in Garick's chambers.

Alone, and thinking entirely too much about things she should not think about.

Solara's predicament was one thing. She trusted her sister to know that some things could not be changed, and to accept her fate.

But acceptance was not easy. Noele knew that to be a fact. For twenty-five years she had done as she pleased, knowing her boundaries but having plenty of freedom to enjoy life as she chose.

Now, she had no choices. Garick held all the answers.

And yet, try as she might to blame him, she could not. He, too, was saddled with his fate as much as she was.

If he would but give her one inkling of where his thoughts lay, she would be content. But he kept his emotions, his heart and desires, a mystery from her.

That rankled more than anything. Did he not know how difficult it was for her to accept that someone else would choose her fate?

She fluttered nervously about the room, waiting. The heavy drapes had been pulled aside and moonlight streamed in through the windows, casting a soft glow throughout the darkened chambers. Dancing flames from the sweetly-scented candles flickered against the walls. The fire burned hot and bright in the hearth.

But she was cold. She lifted her arms and cast warmth from her fingertips. Silvery waves of heated air surrounded her, erasing the outer chill from her body. Still, she shivered within.

She let the waves roll over her, the magic calming her, the ethereal dust settling inside her soul to soothe her nerves. Was she more anxious about Garick's decision, or about the consummation? That she could not answer.

Garick walked in before she had a chance to dissipate the waves. His gaze focused immediately on her and he stopped. His eyes widened, his pupils dilated, and she sensed his arousal from across the room.

Tugging at her lower lip with her teeth, she waited. Roarke followed Garick and she swallowed, anticipating a quick tumble. Watching other couples have sex in the forest glen had always fascinated her and her sisters. It had always been heated—fast and very passionate. Now she would be the first of her sisters to experience it in kind. Would it be quick and fierce like so many episodes she'd witnessed?

Garick's eyes widened appreciatively as he scanned her from head to toe. She felt his growing arousal, her body in tune to his in some strange way that went beyond their magic.

"Release your spell, my bride," Garick commanded. His voice was neither gentle nor gruff, but was clearly an order. It rankled, but she wriggled her wings and the waves of heat disappeared.

"Wine?" he asked, his emotions now masked behind a visage of indifference.

She shook her head.

"Do you hunger?"

Her gaze met his, and she wondered what his question meant. Or even what her answer would be. "No."

"Come here, Noele."

She flew forward, then hid her wings within her body so they would not be injured or crushed during the consummation.

"You are beautiful."

She had not expected to hear him praise her, and warmed without benefit of magic. "Thank you."

"Do you fear me?"

"No, of course not," she lied.

"You're trembling."

"This is new. I...I do not know what to expect."

One corner of his mouth curved into a smile. Her heart leaped and a sudden urge to lick that slight curve of lips overwhelmed her.

"We will not harm you tonight. You are aware of Roarke's role in the consummation?"

She nodded. "I am well aware of elvin marriage custom. I have been prepared to accept both of you this eve." And possibly, she'd be leaving with Roarke on the morrow, if Garick so decreed. Why did that thought cause such misery? She did not really know either man, and yet some invisible thread drew her to Garick.

"Roarke will swear allegiance to you as he does to me, bonded through elvin magic. This must occur on consummation eve. He will penetrate you, merge with you, become one with you, as will I. Afterward, the three of us will be connected telepathically in the same way that Roarke and I have since our blood was spilled and merged during our childhood rite."

Noele nodded, barely listening to Garick recite the official elvin custom. Her mind raced ahead to the sexual activities she would experience tonight. Despite wanting to object, despite the fact she had no choice, her pussy dampened at the thought of taking both men at the same time, to merge with them physically, mentally, spiritually.

Garick poured goblets filled with wiloa, handing one to both her and Roarke. He lifted his in the air. "To magic, to marriage and to both the elvin and faerie. May this consummation join our people, our lands, and our future, so that we may be united as one."

She drank, barely tasting the sweet wine. Yet it filled her with warmth, with relaxation, with anticipation.

Thrusting aside her worries, she mentally prepared for what was to come, bound and determined to at least enjoy this one night with Garick and Roarke. Tomorrow was out of her hands. Tonight she would become initiated into sex with a man. With two men.

She resolved to enjoy every moment.

It was strange to be standing naked in the room with two fully-clothed men. And yet she felt no embarrassment. Soon, they would all be naked and enjoying pleasures that until now she had only dreamed of.

"We will take things slowly, Noele. Neither of us wish to frighten you. In this regard and as we begin, we wish for you to take the lead. You will tell us how quickly or slowly to proceed."

Noele shuddered. At least in this, their beginning together, he gave her some control. For that she was grateful.

Where to start? What did she want? Them, naked, as a beginning. "I want to undress both of you."

Garick nodded and motioned Roarke to stand at his side. "Then undress us."

She began with Roarke, unbuttoning his shirt, her gaze focused on his face. His gaze caught and held hers, his dark eyes melting her. Heat singed her shaking fingers as she fought to release the buttons on his shirt, but finally she managed and slipped her fingers through the down of dark hair on his chest.

Built solid, his muscles rippled under her touch. She moved her hands over his shoulders and pushed the shirt off, marveling at his muscular chest. His waist was lean, his stomach flat, the dark hairs curling softly into his breeches.

Then she kneeled, her face in line with the button of his breeches. She gazed up and watched his face as she slipped the button from its cover, opening his breeches and sliding them over his hips. She removed his boots and pants, moving her hands over his calves and steely thighs.

Truly, Roarke had a magnificent body. His cock sprung forth from the thatch of hair between his legs, powerful and strong like the rest of him. Hard like the rest of him too. She smiled at him and his lips curled upward.

A woman would be very lucky to have Roarke as her mate. He was a delicious male, and yet as she regarded his body, she knew he was not the one she wanted.

The one she wanted stared at her, his gaze darkening like a threatening storm in the winter skies.

"Undress, me, Noele," Garick said, his voice rough with passion.

"Gladly, my husband." She sent the word home, emphasizing it, wanting him to realize that, like it or not, she was his now, and he would have to start thinking of her that way.

She stood and undid the laces of his shirt, then opened her wings, fluttering to raise high enough to tug the shirt over his head. Unable to resist, she slid her palms over his skin as she lowered to the ground, her body reacting to even the slightest touch between them. Arousal poured through her, enticing her, making her legs weak, her heart pound and her throat run dry.

As quickly as she could, she bent down and undid the button on his breeches, sighing with delight as his thick cock sprung free. She removed his breeches and boots, then stepped back to admire the two men standing naked before her.

There were similarities between the two of them, but differences too. And not simply in their sexual organs, although one was thick and the other long. She smiled, imagining the many cocks she'd seen in her lifetime while she and her sisters had watched couples fucking in the woodland. Sexuality was open and embraced in D'Naath, not enshrouded behind private walls.

And yet, this privacy stimulated her, enticed her, emboldened her.

"I wish to touch both of you," she said, her gaze on Garick. He nodded and she stepped forward, nestling her body between the two of them, nearly touching them both but not quite.

Magical vibrations hummed between the three bodies. She reached out and trailed her fingers over two strong jaws, then slid her thumbs over their lips, loving the texture of their soft mouths. Her mind filled with delicious things their mouths could do to her body.

Roarke's mind was filled with the faerie queen, her body so perfect, so small and yet so powerfully sexual it was all he could do to remain composed as she touched him. He knew Garick felt the same way, except his emotions were tied into this consummation, where Roarke's were not.

He would perform his duty for his king and his queen, but he would not meld emotionally with this woman who clearly belonged with Garick. Their magic together was strong, stronger than anything he'd ever felt, with the exception of his moments with Solara.

Now that...that he would not dwell on tonight. Tonight he would join with the Queen of Winterland and offer his protection for the rest of her life. And in so doing, would pleasure her, and himself, too.

When she snaked her fingertips down his ribs and over his belly, he sucked in a shuddering breath. He longed to grab her wrist and wrap her small hand around his aching shaft. Stroking himself while watching her the other night had pleasured him greatly, but he wanted more, much more. He wanted to bury himself deep inside her dark cavern until she screamed with delight.

This night, he would make her come. He would make this a night she would remember always, and know that some of the pleasure she felt came from her protector.

And he would pray to all that was magical that Garick would realize the treasure standing before him, and never let her go.

"Does my touch please you, Roarke?" she asked, bending slightly to tease the hairs around his inner thighs.

"You know it does, my queen. I wish to feel your hand on my cock." And hope that he didn't explode at the first touch of her hand on him.

Garick listened silently to the mental and verbal interchange between his bride and his friend, trying to stem the jealous urges that seethed within him.

This night was preordained, he'd known for many years what would happen. It had never mattered. Consummate their union, fuck his woman and share her with Roarke, and then it would be over. His duty would be done.

How could he know of the emotion coiling through him? How could he have planned for these feelings that were so foreign to him?

Now, watching Noele reach for Roarke's shaft, knowing how much pleasure she gave his friend, caused him to grit his teeth to keep from wrenching the two of them apart.

He wanted this faerie for himself. Not just tonight, but always. By the stars in heaven, what he thought was not in his destiny now faced him squarely, and he recognized the truth.

He was in love with his wife.

Chapter Seven

ဆ

By the stars, he could not love her. Garick willed the thoughts away, the awareness that he had foolishly allowed his heart to be given to his bride.

Yet, they would not dissipate. With every stroke of her hand on his body, Garick was more certain than ever that his life mate was his destiny.

Watching her touch Roarke only confirmed the fact that he could not, would not, ever share this woman with another after tonight.

"Noele," he said, his tone more harsh than he wanted it to be. But by the gods, he needed her attention on him.

"Yes, my husband?" She turned beguiling crystal blue eyes on him. Even her lashes were tinged with silver tips, her body glowing like a starlit sky.

Her essence bathed him in magical stardust, her rose-like scent nearly driving him mad.

"Touch my cock."

"Aye, Garick," she purred. "With great pleasure."

He looked down at her small hand encircling his shaft and groaned as she began to caress him slowly. She moved her fingers over Roarke's cock in the same way, stroking them with a deliberate rhythm that nearly drove him insane.

The visual of her standing between them, both their shafts thrusting against her hands, had him nearing completion much sooner than he would like. How easy it would be to shoot his come into her waiting hands.

But he would not allow it. His seed was meant for her channel, her inner core, the virgin pussy that he would claim very soon.

He refused to think about what would happen afterward. Now, his balls tightened against his shaft, and all he could think of was driving his cock hard and deep inside her cunt until she screamed his name.

The feel of two cocks in her hand dampened her, a rush of arousal that moistened her thighs, readying her for her husband's penetration.

Oh please make it soon. I have waited a lifetime for this.

Roarke reached down and removed her hand from his penis, then moved behind her. He was so close his breath brushed her shoulders. Garick stepped forward and traced her collarbone with his knuckles. She shivered. Roarke circled her waist with his hands. They were warm, strong, and gentle.

Garick brushed his mouth across her parted lips, his tongue tenderly slipping inside to caress hers. Roarke pressed a warm kiss against the side of her neck and she shivered at the dual sensations. Their scent wafted over her; wine, the outdoor air and aroused male. She shuddered, her body pulsing and preparing itself for them.

She was ready. Tensed, eagerly anticipating what was to come. She wanted them to hurry, and yet this relaxed, slow pace was as enjoyable as an intoxicating wine.

"Relax," Roarke whispered in her ear. He squeezed her hips, his erection brushing against her buttocks. He rocked against her, his cock nestling in the cleft between her cheeks. By the heavens! He was huge and hard and burning her skin where he touched.

Her nipples brushed against Garick's chest and puckered, hardening to aching peaks. As if in answer to their need, he reached up and circled her nipples with his fingers, lightly tugging at the crests until they were swollen, tender and desperate for his mouth. He complied, bending to lick one and then the other, moving his head from side to side to lave her breasts. His beard scratched gently against her skin and she whimpered with the painful pleasure.

Oh, how could she bear this? Both men lavishing their hands, their mouths, all over her body. She could barely remain standing and wished for the hovering powers of her wings to keep her from falling to the ground.

Garick moved away, toward the long chaise near the hearth. She shivered at the loss of his body heat, until Roarke swept his arms around her and turned her to face him. He bent down and pressed his lips softly against hers. She shuddered at the invasion of his tongue, so gentle, so warm, coaxing the juices from her pussy with his erotic play.

His kiss was long and powerful, evoking a magical joining that she had just now begun to feel. Like a blissful invasion of her mind, she opened up to Roarke, allowing him to penetrate her telepathically. The doorway was open, he need only complete the consummation to enter fully.

His thoughts entered her mind. *Relax, faerie. I will cherish you tonight, and thereafter protect you with my life. But Garick will give you his heart. He is your one, true destiny. Give him time to realize this.*

She could only wish that Roarke's words were true.

When he released her mouth, he turned her to face Garick, who leaned casually against the back of the chaise. She walked toward his outstretched arms and stepped into them gladly. He took her mouth in a searingly possessive kiss, his hands wandering over her back, her buttocks. When he dipped his finger into the cleft between her buttocks, she pressed against him, her mound rocking against his erection. He groaned into her mouth and thrust his tongue rapidly against hers.

This torment was too much to bear! She must have completion, soon. Roarke let out a low chuckle behind her, and Garick's smile let her know they had both touched her mind.

"Soon, my little faerie," Garick said, licking at her lips. "Soon we will have you screaming with your climax."

Roarke crossed in front of her and slid his thumbs over her nipples. She whimpered at the sensation of his hot fingers rubbing the aching buds.

A desperate need burned within her, the heated desire to be possessed by them. The connection swirled through the room, waiting, hovering, nearly visible in the mist of both faerie and elvin magic. Particles of silver flew from her skin, her longing floating above them like stars on a clear, moonless night.

"You are so beautiful, my bride. Your body is the celestial heavens and the very stars themselves caress your skin. You are magic and light, the wonder of the faeries. I thank you for this gift."

Her eyes welled with tears at his words and hope began to grow within her. Silly, she thought. He spoke only the elvin expressions required by the rite of consummation. He did not speak from his heart, but from duty. And yet, the wish within her would not die, the hope that come morn he would want her by his side always.

Both men moved their hands over her naked skin, inciting her to heights of pleasure she'd never known by her own hand or that of the tubara stick. Her breath caught when each took a nipple into their mouths.

They were so different in their touch and ways of pleasuring her. Roarke licked her nipple lightly, swirling his tongue as if he licked at the fruit that hung from the forest trees of D'Naath. Garick suckled her breast, drawing the peak in his mouth deeply until she arched her back to give him more.

Whimpers of pleasure escaped her lips. Her inner thighs were soaked with her juices and she instinctively lifted her hips to beg for completion.

"Not yet, " Roarke said with a chuckle. "There is more."

The frustration of sexual desire burned within her. She reached for both of them, gasping when Garick pulled her forward, bending her at the waist. His cock brushed against her lips and she opened her mouth to receive him, her tongue lapping at the drops of fluid seeping from the head of his shaft.

She sucked him greedily, devouring his rod like a woman starving. Roarke stepped behind her again, his fingers trailing lightly over her hips and thighs. He bent and spread her legs, his warm breath caressing her throbbing flesh. When his tongue licked at the folds of her pussy, she moaned against Garick's swollen member, rewarded with a deeper thrust of his cock inside her mouth.

"Yes, my wife," he said, his voice as dark as the night. "Do you enjoy Roarke's tongue pleasuring you? Does his mouth on your cunt make you wet?"

She could do nothing but mumble her reply, so filled were her lips with his engorged shaft.

Oh, Roarke's mouth was magical, his tongue lapping her outer lips until he parted the folds and suckled her hidden clit, then slipped his fingers inside her core to fuck her.

She could not take much more. Release loomed near. So close she felt the contractions against Roarke's fingers. She sucked harder at Garick's cock, wanting him to come with her, to spiral into oblivion at the same time she screamed her completion.

"Not yet," Garick said, sliding his cock slowly out of her mouth and moving off her.

By the heavens, she had nearly made him explode into her hot little mouth. Watching her lips cover his rigid cock, listening to the sounds of Roarke's suckling at her cunt as well as her cries of delight had nearly sent him over the edge.

He had to pull away, had to gather his composure. The little minx was in her sexual prime and ready to fuck. Such pleasure he had never known with a woman, a connection that nearly dropped him where he stood.

And he did not want her to come yet. Not under Roarke's tongue, not when he wanted to be the first to make her scream.

"Roarke, it is time," he commanded.

When Roarke stood, Noele whimpered, her frustration evident.

"You will not come until I am sheathed inside you, Noele. Your orgasm must happen as does ours...during the consummation."

"No!" she cried. "Please, Garick, I need release!"

He smiled indulgently, caressing her cheek with his knuckles. "Your enjoyment of sex excites me beyond measure. It is time for us all to have release."

He gathered her in his arms and carried her to the bed, laying her upon the sheets. Roarke followed, climbing in beside her, caressing her body from her shoulders, to her breasts, to her pussy. Her body flushed with desire, so openly aroused that Garick fought hard to keep from immediately plunging inside her.

"Come, wife. Straddle me."

He rolled her over on top of him so she straddled his hips. His cock nestled against her mound and she rocked closer as Roarke settled behind her. Her clit brushed against Garick's shaft. Splinters of desire wracked her body and she knew she'd come in an instant if he continued.

But Garick was right. Despite her physical needs, there was a greater ceremony at play here. The consummation. And with the consummation came release.

"Raise up and take my cock inside you, Noele."

This was the moment she'd waited her entire life for—to feel a man inside her. She lifted and Garick positioned his shaft at her entrance. His heat sizzled against her sensitized skin and she slowly lowered herself on him.

Oh, so this was heaven! By the stars, a man's cock was nothing like the tubara stick. The tubara did not retain the heat, the life force that a man's cock had. Garick's shaft pulsed with a life of its own, a magic unlike anything she'd expected. Her pussy surrounded him, squeezed him, and in so doing sent shocks of pleasure surging through her.

Roarke leaned against her back, reminding her there was a third party to this event. His panting breaths against her ear let her know of his need for her. She leaned forward, nearly on her knees. Garick pulled her face toward his and kissed her deeply while Roarke probed her moisture, sliding his fingers to the spot where she and Garick were joined.

He swept up her juices and coated her rear entrance, his fingers teasingly playing at the puckered hole. She tensed, liquid heat pouring over her core.

"Relax," Roarke said, sliding his fingers near the entrance to her core and swiping more of her juices to lubricate her nether region. Then he moved against her, his cockhead pressing in slowly.

Garick's tongue plunged inside her mouth, his shaft thrusting upward hard and deep. She was lost in the sensations of his touch, his cock, his mouth.

And still, Roarke probed, pressing harder, more insistently. She was too tight back there. It wasn't going to work.

"Shhh, faerie, I will not hurt you." Roarke's soothing voice and caressing hands calmed her fears. "Relax your muscles. Let me pleasure you."

Noele closed her eyes, conjuring up the magic that relaxed her muscles. She was so tight with arousal, the tension building with her, that she had to calm down. Otherwise this would be painful. When she felt her muscles loosen, Roarke eased his cock inside, pushing past her tightened defenses until he was fully sheathed inside her.

Magic burst all around them and she let out a cry of delight. She was filled completely, their bond evident when she actually *felt* Garick's and Roarke's pleasure, tripling her own.

Her pussy flooded as Garick lifted his hips up and down slowly, caressing her core, rubbing against that magical spot in her pussy that made her tighten around him. She desperately craved release, could feel it like a vortex, swirling around inside her.

Roarke retreated and thrust again, with each stroke feeling more and more of Noele's mind, knowing she was now a part of him, body, mind and soul.

She was so tight, her nether hole squeezing him, pulling him deeper and deeper into her heated core. He could not hold much longer, and grit his teeth. Her cries and whimpers, the way she moved her ass back against him, begging for more, nearly sent him reeling.

What a gift she gave him, her entire being, open for his taking. Never had it been like this, never such a soul-shattering experience. And yet, he held a part of himself back, knowing this faerie was not the one for him. Visions of golden green eyes danced in his mind, red hair flowing in the winter breeze, her skin flecked with red, like the passionate creature she was.

He may be sheathed within Noele, but his heart cried out for another.

Noele was near the breaking point, all coherence lost as she cried out, desperate for the release that was so close. Yet her new husband held back, refusing that final thrust that would seal their union.

Garick pushed her hair away from her face. "Look at me, Noele."

Her gaze met his, his eyes stormy as the rolling sea.

She focused on his face, the way his jaw darkened with the stubble of his beard.

"You are mine."

He'd claimed her! As if a heavy burden had been lifted, she realized at that moment that her heart was lost to Garick. Despite the pleasure of being fucked by both men, it was Garick she wanted.

She'd never felt more completed, more a part of her destiny than she did at this moment. How could she have feared this? It was heaven and a hellish delight that sent her catapulting into the unknown with each movement.

Both men increased their movements. Sweat beaded on Garick's brow and she leaned forward to lick it away. Roarke pressed against her back, his cock plunging deep in her ass. She reached down and stroked her clit, knowing she was one with both of them.

The mystical magic faded away, replaced only with a heated lust. Now she relaxed, and enjoyed the experience of being well-pleasured by these two men.

"Fuck me harder," she commanded both of them, her pants and cries echoing in the chamber.

They complied, both of them driving furiously against her until it seemed as if they'd split her open. But she felt no pain, only the aching pleasure of impending release.

"Come for me, Noele," Garick urged, brushing her hand away from her clit. He slid his fingers between them and stroked her distended bud. "Come on my cock, drench me with your juices."

Roarke tightened against her, pummeling her harder and faster with each stroke. She gasped, rising up to give Garick better access to her swollen clit, then rocked against his cock until she could not hold back her orgasm.

"Yes! Harder! Fuck me harder, I'm coming!"

Roarke tightened and spilled his seed in her nether channel, clasping onto her hips and digging his fingers into her flesh. Her climax continued as Garick shot his come deep inside her, the magic of his essence pouring over her.

And yet still she climaxed, the contractions pulsing within until she could not breathe, could not think.

They were one. Wholly and completely one.

When finally it subsided, she collapsed on top of Garick's chest, barely noticing Roarke's withdrawal.

Her breaths came in gasps as she struggled to work through the haze of completion. Roarke bent over and pressed a tender kiss to her temple. "I will protect you with every fiber of my being, my queen."

She thought she heard the door to the chamber open and close, but could hardly lift her head from Garick's chest. Listening to his heartbeat, so rapid at first, then slowing gradually, relaxed her completely.

He rubbed her back, whispering words of tenderness against her ear.

Her eyes drifted shut and she smiled.

Chapter Eight

ജ

He had claimed her. Garick hadn't meant to do so, intending to turn her over to Roarke. He had no time or inclination for a mate. He was duty bound to protect his people, and by virtue of their joining, hers.

But when the time came and he'd slid inside her cavern, he knew then that no other man would possess Noele. She was his and always would be.

How strange for him to want things he'd never wanted before. A mate, children, someone to wrap his arms around at evening sleep. Someone to make love to from today until the day he died.

Why had she captured him so? She was faerie, and true she was magical. All faerie were beautiful, alluring, sexual beings. And yet one had never caught his fancy before.

But from his first look upon Noele he'd felt the bond between them. One he could not break.

He turned in bed, intent on pulling her into his arms, but she was not there. He reached out and touched the pillow where she'd slept. None of her warmth remained, so she must have left a while ago.

Dressing quickly, he looked first for her in the great hall, thinking perhaps she may have hungered and sought breakfast. It was late morn and other than a few servants, the hall was empty. She was not in the kitchens or in the gardens.

His heart pounding, he raced up the stairs and threw open her former chamber door. She was not in there, either. Panic raced through his veins, a cold dread that smacked of truth even though he fought to deny it.

Noele no longer occupied the castle grounds.

Roarke caught up with him as he raced down the stairs.

"She's gone," he said, nearly out of breath.

Roarke nodded. "Aye, I felt it too. Just within the hour."

"Where is she? She couldn't have passed through the gates without someone seeing her." Thoughts of what he could have done to displease her filled his mind. Had he said or done anything last eve to make her hate him so much she would flee the bonds of their marriage?

Why had she left him? He had claimed her, and this was her response? He had made his choice, and it had been to keep Noele. How dare she walk out on him!

"You are an idiot, Garick."

Garick stopped and focused on Roarke's angered face. "What do you mean?"

"She has not left you. She loves you."

Loves him? How would Roarke know of this? "Did she tell you this?"

"No, and she did not need to. If you but open your heart you could feel it. It fills Winterland, her love for you is so powerful."

Open his heart? He had never opened his heart. His well-meaning parents had filled his heart with duty and responsibility. They had been steeped in elvin tradition and roles, and had not thought to teach him of things such as love.

Love was for others, not for an elvin king.

And yet, he had fallen in love with Noele. Had chosen her despite his determination to turn her over to Roarke. She was his woman, his wife, and no other would touch her. He closed his eyes and opened the gates to his heart. Her love for him sailed inside, crashing against the protective armor he'd built there as a child. A warmth such as he'd never felt filled his body, his mind, his soul.

"She loves me."

"If we were not in public in the presence of your people, I would knock you on your ass as I did when we were children. You are stupid, Garick. Noele is a prize and you have lost her. You claimed her last night, but you did not open your heart, your mind, all that you are. She was whisked away right under your nose while you were sleeping because you refused to connect with her."

Despite the heated morning, Garick chilled. "Wizard."

Roarke nodded. "Aye. She has been taken."

* * * * *

Noele woke, but kept her eyes tightly closed, frowning at the chill seeping in her bones. She tried to move to snuggle closer to Garick's warmth, but all she felt was cold stone underneath her naked body.

Her eyes flew open, but she could barely make out her surroundings in the darkness. A dank, musty smell assailed her nostrils, and the scent of death permeated the air.

As did the smell of evil. Of hatred. Jealousy. All those things that told her quite clearly where she was.

The wizards had taken her.

Fear seized her, making her shiver uncontrollably. She fought for strength, summoning up her faerie magic to cast a warming spell around her body. Her teeth chattered as the heat surrounded her, gradually taking the chill away. And yet the fear remained.

Where was Garick? Why had he not come for her? How could she have been spirited away while lying next to him in bed?

Unless…no, he would not have done that. He had claimed her last night, not cast her aside. And even if he had changed his mind, he would simply have given her to Roarke. He would not be so cruel as to let the wizards take her.

No, she refused to believe it. But her mind was filled with thoughts of Garick and Roarke plotting to have her taken by the wizards. In that way, neither would have to be responsible for her. Winterland would still have access to D'Naath and all their holdings, but neither Garick nor Roarke would have to be bothered with a queen and wife neither of them wanted.

A horrid laugh emanated from the darkness, curling up her spine and invading her thoughts. She pulled her knees to her chest and shut her eyes, willing whatever voice she heard to go away.

"Oh, my faerie queen, it will not be so easy to rid yourself of my thoughts in your head."

The voice was old. Ancient. The evil ones. The wizards who had tried to take their minds, their bodies, to control every person in D'Naath and Winterland for ages. The faerie and elvin lands had been their goal for centuries. So far both had fought them off, but the wizards were cunning, evil, using subterfuge and magic to coerce, to gain control.

Mind control.

Her mind.

No! The thoughts of Garick and Roarke were wizard thoughts, not hers! Her mind fought for clarity, for reason.

Despite the risk, she had to do it, had to know the truth. She knew the thoughts planted in her head were lies concocted by the wizard to sway her to turn over her magical essence.

Taking in a deep breath, she quickly opened her mind and her heart, searching for reality, for truth.

The old wizard tried to invade her, tried to take the opening to steal her magic, but suddenly she wasn't alone. In her heart, her very soul, stood Garick. Behind him and also within her, stood Roarke. Her husband and her protector. The magic of the three was more powerful than any wizard. The evil one fled her mind.

Garick, I need you. Come for me. She prayed fervently that he would hear her plea.

A dim voice began, growing stronger every second. She rejoiced when she recognized it as Garick's.

I hear you, my wife. We are coming for you. Be strong. Do not let them take you, my faerie queen. Let my love give you strength.

His love. He loved her! Tears rolled freely as she left her mind and heart open to Garick, willing him to find her, sending her magic out to the four corners so he would know where she was.

"Try all you might to thwart me, faerie. I will win eventually. He will never find you."

The wizard's evil laugh grew closer.

"You and I will talk, exchange minds. You will give me your power, your strength, and you will become one of us."

Never. She would never give up all that she was. Noele ignored the cold, bony fingers threading through her hair, ignored the burning pain of the wizard's touch within her mind.

She was confident the man she loved would rescue her. As long as she felt the ties to Garick, she would not be alone.

She no longer feared.

* * * * *

Garick, Roarke and the Winterland warriors sped quickly through the forests of D'Naath, past the cottages in the woodglen and up into the mountains behind Noele's homeland. The mountains contained caves, and Noele was in one of those caves.

Opening her mind to him had pinpointed her location. The wizards were everywhere, hiding under ground and in the caves within the mountains. Rarely could one of their locations be uncovered. Thankfully, opening his heart to Noele had let her thoughts flood his mind. With her thoughts came her location.

He fought back the guilt that assailed him. How could he have failed to protect her? Married but for a few hours and he had nearly lost her because he'd been too afraid to open his heart.

Recriminations would come later. Now he had to focus on rescuing Noele.

"There!"

He turned at Roarke's shout, following his gaze to a small opening at the top of a steep cliff. They halted and dismounted, preparing to set off on foot.

The climb was treacherous, the incline nearly straight up. Yet craggy rocks and slight footholds gave them aid. He prayed by the time they reached the cavern it would not be too late.

"She is strong," Roarke reassured. "Her mind is even stronger. She will not let them take her."

Garick fought hard to believe him. "Let us hurry, then."

They raced along the narrow path until they reached the cavern's entrance. Garick drew his sword and called forth his magic. The cavern lighted as if the sun itself had shined inside the dank hole of darkness.

Opening his mind, he searched for Noele's essence. His heart stopped when he realized it was faint, barely present, and yet still enough that he could follow her signals. "This way," he pointed to a pathway on the left side of the cave.

Garick stayed alert, knowing wizard trickery could befall them at any moment. The pathway was narrow, hardly enough room for men his size, and yet they persevered, hugging the back wall of the path and inching their way forward.

They'd no more pushed through the narrow opening into some kind of empty anteroom when a dozen wizards rushed them. Skeletal creatures, more bone than skin, they seemed incapable of even moving, let alone the strength they were known for.

Raising his sword, he fought their magic fireballs, the electric arcs of pain that both froze and burned.

Roarke pressed against his back and fought a wizard on the other side of him. Their guards engaged the rest.

Elvin magic was strong, but so was wizard cunning. When Garick raised his sword to slice through the skeletal figure, it disappeared, only to reappear to the side of him and slide through his tunic with a bolt of magic.

Searing pain arced through his body, but he called up his own strength, wielded the sword to the right and beheaded the wizard. The bony creature fell in a heap on the cave floor.

His guards fought valiantly, beating back the wizards until several had disappeared or turned to run through one of the many narrow tunnels.

Yet when some left, others came in and took over, their refreshed strength more powerful than Garick and his wearying warriors.

Garick turned to take on another of the creatures, this one taller, stronger, his eyes blazing red in his hideous, sunken face. A cackle of pure evil rose up as the wizard raised his arms. Rocks rained down over Garick, which he fought away with his sword and his own magical spell. When his sword connected with the creature's bony flesh, a wailing scream echoed through the room. The wizard turned and slipped through an opening in the wall.

"That one has Noele," Garick said quickly to Roarke. "I can feel his connection to her."

Roarke nodded and Garick followed the wizard through the opening, confident Roarke and his men could take care of the rest of them.

His side burned as if a torch touched him, but he fought back the pain, convinced this wizard would lead him to Noele.

Her cries echoed in his mind, her pain piercing him, stabbing at his heart. Her agony injured him more than the gaping hole in his side. He must find her.

There! Ahead in the darkness, the wizard stepped through steel bars, its body so thin it did not need to open the doors. Garick reached the bars only to find the wizard holding an unconscious Noele in his arms.

"Kill me and your precious queen dies." His cackling voice and death grip around Noele's throat turned Garick's blood to ice.

He halted, his thoughts merging with Noele. He effectively blocked out the wizard's mental probing and spoke to her.

Noele, wake up!

She did not answer. By all that was magic, was he too late to save her?

Noele! My love, I need you to awaken.

He felt her stirring.

Do not move, he warned. *A wizard holds you by the throat. Do not let him into your mind, do not let him know you are awake.*

Aye, Garick.

Relief washed through him. Her voice was weak, and yet he felt her strength, wishing with all his soul he could somehow transfer some of his to her.

My love, are you well?

Aye, Garick. I am weak, but my mind is intact. He has not breached my magic.

He allowed a grateful sigh. His bride was indeed a strong faerie. *Can you conjure?*

I believe I can.. What do you wish me to do?

He gave her his instructions, hoping she was strong enough to withstand what was to come.

Noele opened her eyes, hatred shooting out from their crystal blue depths onto the wizards face.

"Ah, the faerie awakens, Garick. Now you can both watch what I do to her."

Noele reached for the skeletal arms of her captor, and pushed him backwards. Surprised, the wizard fell to his knees and Noele stood. "Be gone from here, evil one. My faerie magic compels you to be still."

Garick closed his eyes, feeling Noele's strength diminish.

"You are weak, faerie," the wizard said, fighting against the invisible bonds holding him.

"I will die rather than give up my magic to you," she sneered.

The wizard laughed, breaking through her holding spell and grabbing her against him.

Garick wanted to shout his frustration to the corners of the world. If only he could get to her!

"Now, Garick, King of Winterland. Watch your faerie die at my hands."

The wizard's black eyes bored into Noele's. She gasped and covered her face, shaking her head and pummeling the evil one's chest. The wizard only laughed, a maniacal sound that reverberated off the cold, stone walls.

Hang on, my love. Soon. I'll be there soon. You know what you must do. Garick prayed she would have the strength to see it through.

Suddenly, Noele slumped against the wizard.

Garick let out a mourning howl that spoke of loss, of grief. Echoes of his agony sailed through the cave walls and into the outside air.

"Rail all you want at the four winds, Garick. She is gone!" The wizard turned his gaze away from Noele's lifeless form to Garick and grinned, his face a twisted mask of evil.

"She has given up her soul to me. Her life force exists no longer. In moments, I will extract her essence and become even more powerful than you."

Garick railed against the bars. "You bastard! You will die for killing the one I love!"

The wizard threw his head back and laughed, then dropped Noele's limp body on the cold floor.

"Oh, the great king has found the love of his life, only to have her taken away on the night of their marriage. How sad for you Garick. How pathetic that you could not open your heart and protect her."

Garick refused to heed the wizard's words. "No! She is mine. She lives."

The wizard's laugh drove him mad. "She would have lived, had you the capacity to love her. We knew it was only a matter of time until you gave her to us."

"Noooooo!" Garick railed.

"Too late, elvin king. Watch as I take her magic and her soul." The wizard raised his hands in the air.

Now, my love, Garick pleaded. *Please show me you are still with me. I need you, Noele.*

Instantly, Noele's eyes opened. She transferred her magic into Garick's mind and he sliced through the bars as if they were wood instead of steel. They crumpled before him like stale bread.

With a cry of surprise, the wizard tried to run past, but Garick grabbed him and with one arcing slice, beheaded the evil one.

He ran to Noele and gathered her against him, transferring her essence back into her body. Closing his eyes, he prayed to the magical gods to restore Noele's magic, feeling it leave him and enter her body.

He only hoped it would be enough to restore her.

"Come back to me, faerie," he pleaded.

Her silvery tipped eyes partly opened. She lifted a small hand to his cheek and smiled.

"You came for me."

Garick fought back the emotions threatening to make him weak in the knees. So grateful for Noele's life, he sent up a silent prayer to all the gods in the heavens. "Aye."

"I love you, Garick."

Her eyes fluttered closed and he gently picked her up, carrying her back the way they came. By the time he reached the opening in the wall, Roarke and the guards had dispatched the wizards.

Roarke frowned and raced to his side. "Is she well?"

He nodded. "Weak, but she will recover. She has much strength."

Roarke grinned and nodded. "Your new bride is quite a warrior."

They left the cavern and made haste back to Winterland.

Garick's wounds were tended to, despite wanting only to remain at Noele's side. But the physician told him she only needed rest to build up her strength, and he was to leave her be.

By the time nightfall came, Noele's sisters had been to the chambers to impart some of their magical strength to her. Garick waited patiently by her side as her sisters fluttered about, asking her questions about her ordeal.

He wanted them to leave. He needed to be alone with his wife.

When he was ready to scream at them, they kissed Noele and bade her goodnight.

After they left, Noele slumbered deeply. Not wanting to wake her when she needed rest to restore her body, he undressed quickly and slipped into bed with her, cradling her close against him. His mind and heart remained fully open, not wanting a repeat of the previous night. He slept fitfully through the night, waking several times to be sure she still lay protected in his arms.

By the time morning came, Noele still slumbered peacefully. A fierce need to protect her coursed through him. He had failed her before. If she so allowed, he would never do so again.

She would have been safer if he had given her to Roarke. And yet he could not cast her aside any more than he could cut off one of his own limbs. She was his, and would forever be.

She murmured low in her throat, a husky sound that stirred his cock into full awakening.

No, he should not touch her. She needed rest.

But her voice entered his mind. *I am fully awake, my husband. And what I need has nothing to do with rest.*

He needed no further urging. Desperate to join with her again, he rose above her, his cock probing for her entrance.

She was damp. Her nipples hardened when he rubbed his cockhead against her clit. Her soft moans told him that even in partial sleep she desired him.

A pride unlike anything he'd ever known overcame him. This was his woman, his mate, and she possessed an inner strength he would have never thought possible in a female.

Gently, he slipped his shaft into her channel. She pulsed and contracted around him. Her eyes fluttered open, blue as the clear winter skies outside. He placed a kiss on her parted lips. "Good morning, my queen."

Her tentative smile stabbed at his heart. "Good morning, my king."

Noele could think of no better way to awaken from the nightmare of the past couple of days. Completely rested and her heart welling with joy and love for her husband.

His heat melted her insides, his hard shaft buried so deeply he touched her very soul. Joining with him was a sweet pleasure she wanted to wake up to the rest of her life.

When she lifted her hips and wrapped her legs around his back, he grinned. "Are you certain you are ready for this?"

Noele smiled and nodded, threading her hands through his hair. Arousal coursed through her body, the need for release tensing her eager muscles. "Aye. Fuck me, Garick."

Her tongue caressed his bottom lip, then she sucked it gently inside her mouth. He pulled back and plunged his cock inside her, deep and hard until he was buried to the hilt. She gasped and bit at his lower lip. He wound her hair around his fist and pulled hard, rewarded when her pussy flooded with her desire.

"Yes, like that," she cried, digging her heels into his back.

He devoured her lips and thrust his tongue inside her mouth, offering it for her to suckle. He drew his cock out and then stabbed it inside her again, drawing shrieks of delight from her.

Withdrawing quickly, he pulled her up and turned her over, slipping one of the feather pillows under her stomach.

He leaned over her and drove into her cunt again, pinning her arms to her sides. Relentlessly he pounded inside her. She lifted her ass and met every thrust with equal fervor. "Harder, Garick. Fuck me hard and fast. Make me come all over you."

Garick could not believe his fortune. A beautiful, strong faerie, with as lusty an appetite for sex as he. He was truly a lucky man.

Her pounding passion drew him ever higher. He let go of her hands and lay fully on top of her, reaching underneath to thrum her clit with his fingers. She gasped, her face buried in the mattress, her fists wound tightly into the sheets. She pressed her rear against him when he thrust hard, his balls slapping against her pussy.

"You want my come inside you, Noele?" he said, barely able to hold off his orgasm.

"Yes! Fuck me, Garick, fuck me hard and come inside me. Now!"

Her demands sent him over the edge and he took her along with him. He fucked her fast and furious, sending his seed shooting deep into her cavern. She screamed and pulsed around him, flooding him with her juices.

Afterward, they lay panting and stroking each other's skin. It seemed strange that despite the intimacies they'd shared, he did not know how to simply speak to her now.

"Garick?" she asked, her voice a near whisper.

"Aye."

"Did you mean what you said on our wedding night?"

"What did I say?"

She turned and leaned up on her elbows, her clear eyes mesmerizing him. "That I was yours?"

He arched a brow and smiled at her. Despite all that they had been through, she still doubted him. For that he was ashamed. "Aye. You are mine. I do not wish to cast you out nor hand you over to Roarke."

He read the relief in her eyes, and it pleased him. "I am glad."

His heart swelled and he knew then he'd found love. He'd never looked for it, never wanted it, and yet here it was and he would not turn it away. He trailed a finger over her silken cheek. "And what is your choice, my queen?"

Her eyes widened. "My choice?"

He nodded. "Aye. Do you wish to stay with me?"

Her frown amused him. "I do not have a choice, Garick. You know the customs of our people. This is our destiny."

"That may be, but if you had not wished to be with me or with Roarke I would have allowed you to make your own choices. You were never a prisoner here, Noele. I am sorry I did not give you the option of release before our marriage. I neglected to offer you a choice in the matter, and for that I am truly sorry."

Noele was certain she'd misheard Garick's words. "You would give me choice over my own life?"

"Aye. I would not wish to hold you here if it is not your desire."

He gave her a choice. What she'd always wanted…the freedom to make her own decisions. She fought to hold back the tears welling in her eyes. "If I wanted to leave, you would allow it?"

He nodded, but no happiness sparked his handsome features.

Her heart swelled with joy. He truly loved her. She'd worried that perhaps he had said it because of her capture. But in her heart, she knew it to be true. It was clear in his face, and yet he would let her go if that was her wish.

A few days ago she would have taken the freedom he had offered, and returned to D'Naath.

Or would she? Perhaps in her mind it was having the choice that mattered, not whether or not she wanted to be with Garick.

She searched within and realized that she'd fallen in love with the elvin king the moment she met him. If he'd given her the choice to leave or stay with him, she knew now what she would have said. "I wish only to remain by your side the rest of my days," she answered.

Garick grinned and pulled her against him, taking her mouth in a kiss that seared her senses and renewed her desire for him.

"That you shall be, my queen. By my side, in my bed, and always in my heart. From now until forever."

As Garick took her in his arms and made love to her again, Noele knew that her destiny had, indeed, been fulfilled. She may have been bound by honor and duty, but had freely chosen love.

Epilogue
Three Days Later

ଛଠ

Noele stood and looked out over the cliffs at the northern sea. Rolling dark clouds headed in Winterland's direction.

A storm was coming, and from the looks of it, a wicked one. She was glad that her sisters and the rest of the faerie had departed for D'naath this morning. Although she would miss her sisters greatly, Garick had surprised her when he said they would visit D'naath in the spring, and her sisters could visit Winterland any time she wished.

Thinking back on all that happened in the past week, Noele's heart soared. When she'd first arrived at Winterland, she thought she would merely be fulfilling her destiny, that her life would no longer contain the magic it once had.

She had been wrong. The magic of Garick's love filled her heart, her soul, her very being. Contentment surrounded her like a warm cloak.

Strong, warm hands enveloped her waist and pulled her against a hard, masculine chest. "You watch the weather, my queen?"

She leaned back and lifted her hand to caress Garick's stubbled cheek. "Aye. We are in for some wintry weather, I fear."

He turned her in his arms and pressed a gentle kiss on her lips. "Winter is coming. We will soon be shut inside with nothing to do."

She arched a brow. "Nothing to do? Are you sure of that, my king?"

Garick looked thoughtful, then said, "True. There will be many sword playing lessons with the guard."

She pushed at his chest. "Not quite what I had in mind."

Refusing to release her, Garick tightened his hold. "What did you have in mind, faerie?"

"I think I won't tell you now."

Garick kissed the affected pout of her lips, his heart soaring with love for his wife. "I think you will reveal all your secrets to me, Noele."

Her blue eyes sparkled with a teasing glint. "Is that a command, my king?"

He shrugged, offering a feigned indifference that he no longer felt. "Your choice, as always, my queen."

She arched a brow. "Ah, it is to be my choice, then. Let me tell you what I choose, then, Garick."

Noele whispered to him as they strolled back to the castle courtyard, her choices very compelling indeed. As they neared the archway of the gates, he stopped and turned to the sea, watching the approaching clouds.

His gaze gravitated to the cliffs and caves beyond Winterland, knowing that the wizards were merely lying in wait.

Until the next time.

Indeed, a terrible storm was brewing.

But he wouldn't think of that cold fact right now. Time would come for war with the wizards later.

Right now, warmth could be found in the arms of the woman he loved.

FIERY FATE

∾

Dedication

⁊

To my friend, Mel, aka Melani Blazer. Thank you for helping me add beautiful color to Roarke and Solara's story. Your friendship means the world to me, and I can't thank you enough for taking the time to read my stories. I wish you much success and happiness in your writing career.

To Patti and Missy. Thank you for all you do to help me. Truly, I'd be lost without you.

To my editor, Briana St. James. Yes, you can have all my "R" heroes (grin). And thank you for loving my 'men' as much as I do.

To my wonderful Paradise group – thank you for giving me a refuge and a place to laugh. Thank you for your friendship and warm acceptance of me.

And, as always, to Charlie. When you walk into a room, I feel the magic of your love. Truly, we were fated. My soul is forever yours. I love you.

Chapter One

ഇ

Solara, faerie princess of D'Naath, shifted her position on the stairs and peered through the slats, figuring her vantage point would leave her unnoticed by the two men. Or at least the one man she didn't want to notice her. She watched intently as Roarke, captain of the elvin guard, did sword battle with one of his soldiers.

Training, they called it. To her it looked like a fight to the death, both elvin warriors straining with the efforts of their exercise.

Moisture beaded on Roarke's brow as he lifted the heavy broadsword and struck a downward blow on his opponent. The clang of metal against metal rang out in the empty courtyard and echoed in the surrounding trees.

Roarke's well-muscled back strained and flexed, yet he wielded the sword as if it were no heavier than a dinner knife. But she knew it weighed half as much as herself. His powerful muscles gleamed with sweat in the already heated morning sun.

What compelled her to venture forth at daybreak? Was she purposely seeking him out? It did her no good to mull over that which was not meant to be. Soon she'd be leaving for Greenbriar, the land of the southern king, Braedon.

Her betrothed.

'Twas her fate to marry Braedon in less than a month. A man she'd never seen, a man known as cold and emotionless, the complete opposite in nature of his warm, sun-filled lands.

The complete opposite of her.

They had arrived only yesterday. Determined to spend

some time with her sister, Noele, Solara had brought along her three younger sisters, Trista, Elise and Mina. After all, this could be the last time they were all together, since Solara would be ensconced in the southern king's lands before long.

She was here to see Noele and Garick.

Not Roarke.

She hadn't seen Roarke until this morning. As yet, they hadn't spoken. She wanted these few moments to watch him. To gauge her own reactions to seeing him again. Would her feelings for him be as strong as they were when they'd first met? Had that been nothing more than a chemical reaction, or was there something more?

Now, looking at him again, she knew whatever reaction she'd felt when she'd met him the first time had not dwindled in the least. Her heart still fluttered against her breast. Her blood still pounded through her veins, her breathing labored.

All from merely looking at Roarke.

Oh, why did she have to meet Roarke all those months ago? Why had she made a connection with him that fired her blood and refused to leave her be? It had been six long months since Noele's wedding. Six months since she'd first laid eyes on Roarke. Surely enough time had passed that she would be over any feelings she'd had for him.

And yet from that first moment, that first time he had touched her in the official elvin greeting, she had known they shared a destiny. A destiny which could never be.

She'd tried to dismiss it as some kind of physical reaction to an attractive male. Not that Roarke was the first good-looking male to cross her path, but she'd certainly reacted to him as if he had been.

They'd been separated since she and her sisters had returned to D'Naath. Now, returning to Winterland, she realized nothing had changed. One glimpse of him and the same wild reactions occurred within her.

Solara sighed and once again fixed her gaze on Roarke's

naked back, imagining how his muscles would ripple under her touch, how he would bring her body to life with his strong, powerful hands. The same visions that had haunted every sleepless night since the last time she had seen him. No matter how she tried to fight the demon desire that lived inside her, one look at him and she was reminded of everything she had tried to forget.

How was she to marry one man when she clearly felt something for another?

But she had not come to Winterland to moon over a man she desired and could not have. She was here to visit her sister, Noele, before she made the long journey to Greenbriar.

She pondered the combatants, with every passing second more and more convinced that she would be unable to go through with a marriage to a man she did not love.

Noele had been lucky. She had been destined as Garick of Winterland's bride, and their match had ended up one of love. The passion between her sister and Garick was palpable to anyone who stood near them.

'Twas what she wished for herself. If that was selfish, so be it. Her heart ached for another. She could never be the bride of a man as cold and unfeeling as Braedon of Greenbriar was said to be.

Picking at a speck on her blue shift, she concentrated on her hands, willing the melancholy that had settled over her to vanish like a butterfly on a gusty wind. Yet it had remained for days now and she could not force it away.

Her fate was sealed, her destiny not of her own choosing. What could she do but see it through?

No. There had to be another way. She could not do this!

"What ails the beautiful faerie today?"

Glancing up, she squinted in the blinding sunlight. It did not matter that her sight was restricted. Roarke's voice entered her very soul.

"Nothing ails me." How had he snuck up on her when

she'd only averted her eyes for the briefest of moments? Had she known the men had ended their skirmish, she would have disappeared before Roarke had the chance to look up at the stairs and see her sitting there.

Now that he stood so close, her body reacted by flaming to life. 'Twas like an illness making her feverish. He kneeled on the stairs, blocking the light from her eyes with his body. His skin was bathed in a fine sheen of sweat and she balled her fingers into fists to keep from swiping her hand over the corded muscles of his shoulders and down his bare chest.

Truly, he took her breath away. Hair as dark as the bark of the trees in D'Naath hung long to his shoulders. A short, clipped beard and moustache graced his angular jaw. Would that beard tickle her lips and her cheeks when he rubbed against her? And what of his mouth? Could he perform magic on her body with that mouth?

How would his beard and lips feel lower on her body, rubbing against her swollen sex?

"Is there something wrong, Solara?"

She shook her head, forcing her thoughts away from pondering his full lips. "No. I was just catching the morning sun and breathing in the beautiful air of summer."

"You appear unhappy." He reached out and traced her forehead.

Shock registered deep within her at the power of his touch. Her sex moistened and began to thrum with a now familiar ache, and her nipples thrust hard and needy against her thin shift. She backed away from his hand, unable to bear the sweet torment.

"What is wrong, sweet Solara?"

Oh please go away. I cannot bear the pain of your touch, the fiery promise in your deep voice. She shut her eyes and willed him to disappear. When she opened them, she found his dark eyes studying her, a frown on his deeply handsome face. "There is nothing wrong. I must go find Noele now."

But when she stood and turned to leave, he reached out and laced his fingers around her arm.

"Don't go."

"I have to. I cannot stay here."

"What if I ask you to stay?"

His voice held a teasing edge, and yet the undertone carried a serious question. Were they still talking of her leaving to see Noele? Or had their conversation shifted to something deeper, more permanent?

Something she'd thought constantly of, but refused to lend voice to.

"You know I cannot. I am destined elsewhere."

He dropped his hand. "Aye, I know. It's foolish."

"Aye, it is."

She should walk away. Or he should. Neither of them had the right to be alone together. Solara knew that, and she was certain Roarke did, too. But he didn't leave. And she found her feet to be immobile.

But standing here next to him, inhaling his musky scent, forcing her hands to remain at her sides so she didn't reach out and touch him—'twas all too much to bear.

"I should go."

He still watched her, tilted his head to the side. "Aye. You should."

"There is no reason for me to stay."

"No, there is not." He reached for a scarlet curl, threading it through his fingers. "And yet you remain."

"You could leave," she offered, wondering why he expected her to be the one to walk away.

"I could. But for some strange reason I don't wish to."

She closed her eyes for a brief second. His words should mean nothing. He played a game with her, and nothing more. But when she opened them again, she realized he was as torn as she was, and unable to take a step either forward or backward.

"This is wrong, Roarke. We should not even be talking."

He released the curl he'd been holding and moved his hand over her bare shoulder, letting it rest there. She fought her body's reaction to his touch, to no avail. She was on fire.

"I think there is much unsettled between us," he whispered. "I would speak with you alone this eve, if you can manage."

Her breath caught and held as his eyes flamed, mirroring the desire she found so often in her own reflection. So, he had felt it too. That all-consuming passion for someone who was nearly a stranger. Knowing he had feelings for her only made their situation worse. And yet she was too curious to resist that which she knew she should.

"When? Where?"

"After all have retired. Meet me in the rear gardens at the end of the courtyard."

Against her better judgment, she nodded. With a seemingly reluctant slide of his fingers, he let go and turned away, moving down the stairs to greet the other guards who had entered the courtyard for morning training.

Garick entered the courtyard too, his booming voice resounding in the bailey, Solara sighed and walked away, climbing the wide steps toward the hall. She pushed open the heavy door, waiting for her eyes to adjust to the darkness of the room. Voices emanated from the corner of the hall, and she followed the sound. Noele should be somewhere about, likely in the kitchens.

She found Noele fluttering around the tables in the great hall, making sure that all the settings were in place before the men came in to break fast. She smiled when she saw Solara, and motioned her over.

"Did you sleep well?"

Solara lied. "Aye. Just fine. And you?"

A half smile lit up Noele's pale face, her silver sparkles shimmering in the rays of light streaming through the windows. "I did not sleep much at all."

Warmth spread within Solara, and she knew what she saw on Noele's face was the deep love she felt for her husband. Oh, why couldn't she have found a mate that matched her in heart and soul? She laid her fingers over Noele's arm. "I am very happy that you have found your love mate."

"As am I. Now let us hope the next of us to marry will do the same."

Noele meant her, of course. Not wanting to burden her sister with her foolish thoughts, she attempted a smile. "Let us hope."

Setting a goblet aside, Noele reached for Solara's hand, a questioning look in her clear blue eyes. "It was not too long ago that you asked me this question. Do you fear the coming joining?"

Solara well remembered asking Noele of her fears. Noele had been honest with her sister. Could Solara do the same?

"In many ways, I do. I have heard terrible things about this Braedon of Greenbriar."

Lips so like her own curved in a gentle smile. "Do not believe everything you hear, my sister. Stories like that are typically lore and have no basis in fact."

Then again, they could very well be true. But what she did not reveal to Noele was that it wouldn't matter if Braedon was the kindest man in all the kingdoms. She could never be happy marrying one while loving another.

Forcing that unpleasant thought aside, she worked with Noele, helping her serve the plentiful food and drink. The warriors kept close to the castle these days because of all the wizard attacks in the past. With so many of them present, the multiple tables took extra hands to serve them. Solara gladly assisted, thankful for something to do to keep her mind busy.

"When I first came here, they would not let me help,"

Noele mused with a chuckle. "It was only after I insisted repeatedly that Garick allowed me to do more than sit upon the throne and look like a simpering idiot."

"Faerie must stay busy or die of boredom."

"Aye. Which is what I had to convince Garick of. And then Isolde, and finally the servants. They were shocked I would wish to perform labors around the castle, but truly I gain pleasure from doing so." She swept her arm in a wide arc across the room. "This is my husband's home. It is my duty to see it is well-cared for."

Solara couldn't imagine having nothing to do to while away the days. The faerie people of D'Naath were known for frivolity, yes, but also worked hard to make sure that food was set upon the table and all their people were well fed, clothed and looked after. To sit and watch others toil was not in their nature.

As soon as they had finished setting the meals upon the table, the clatter of boots striking the floor signaled the approach of the guards. Solara took her place at Noele's side. Trista, Elise and Mina entered the room and took their places at the table next to Solara.

Solara was glad she had brought her sisters along. After all, it had been a half-year since they had last visited Noele. In that time, Solara had grown to rely upon Trista as her confidant and friend. Trista was the only one of her sisters who knew of her current turmoil, and was bound and determined to come up with a solution to Solara's "problem", as she called it. Trista patted Solara's hand, offering an encouraging smile.

Garick walked in, Roarke following. She watched Roarke's every movement, her breath catching and releasing on a sigh, as it did every time she gazed upon him. His powerful physique showed well in tight breeches and a dark shirt. The laces were half undone, revealing the fine chest that she'd glimpsed earlier this morning. She licked her lips and received a nudge in the ribs from Trista.

"What?"

"You are staring," Trista whispered, then winked. Her golden eyes sparkled with mischief. Solara cast her sister a glaring look, hoping she wasn't planning anything foolish.

"I am not. And say nothing. This is not the time for your schemes."

Trista let out a hmph and turned to Elise and Mina. The twins broke out in laughter.

Roarke turned at the sound of her sisters' giggles, and his gaze met hers. She wanted to look away, but she couldn't. He mesmerized her with his darkly golden eyes, communicating without words as something elemental passed between them. She closed her eyes and felt him enter her being, his thoughts surrounding hers. She fought hard to keep his probing magic at bay, not wanting him to know what was in her heart.

Heat settled between her legs and she clamped her thighs together to ward off the sensations of long, masculine fingers brushing against her sex. She shuddered, lost in images of Roarke's hands on her, his fingers parting the curls of her mound and petting her damp pussy. She let out a low whimper.

"Is there something wrong, Solara?"

Her eyes flew open at Noele's question. Her gaze flitted to Roarke, who smiled knowingly.

Damn him for invading her with such sensations.

"Nothing is wrong. I am enjoying the meal."

"You have not eaten a bite of it." Noele reached up and touched Solara's forehead. "Your skin is heated and flushed. I believe you have a fever."

Roarke snorted and took a long swallow of his drink. Solara wanted to fly away and hide in her room. "I am fine, really. Do not be concerned for me."

Fever, indeed. Foolish fever for a man who teased her in front of the entire castle population. She hurriedly finished her meal, then made herself as scarce as possible for the rest of the day, intending to stay far away from Roarke.

By nightfall, she'd grown weary of pacing her bedchambers. She'd bathed, dressed, undressed, then redressed again, deciding not to meet Roarke this evening as she had previously agreed.

What good would it do to see him? What would she say to him? That her heart, her very soul, burned for him, but she could not have him?

Ridiculous waste of time. They had nothing to say to each other. She did not even know how he felt about her. Aye, 'twas obvious they shared a connection of sorts. But that meant nothing.

Still, as the time grew near she could not stay away. She dressed to please him, brushing her hair until the red locks curled and shimmered over her bare shoulders and down her back, spreading over her wings like a cloak. A pale yellow shift that glistened in the light hugged her body's curves and made her red wings appear like a fiery sunset. She'd scrubbed her skin until the scarlet sparkles glimmered in the full moon's light.

Solara entered the courtyard, searching for anyone who might be about. It was late, and most of the castle inhabitants were long ago abed. By the time she reached the gardens near the end of the courtyard, she felt silly.

Roarke had probably been teasing her about meeting. She would come out here only to find herself alone and embarrassed at her girlish stupidity.

Nevertheless, she was here so she might as well see if he would even appear. She spread her wings and fluttered above the tall hedges. The moon cast a silver glow over the greenery, lighting the path like a map. 'Twas easy to wind her way through the maze of bushes toward the cliffs. Not too far down the path she spotted a bench and stopped there, in awe of the view of the ocean. She inhaled deeply and marveled at the quiet calm of late night. The only sounds were the breakers crashing against the massive sea wall protecting Winterland.

Which was why she screamed when warm hands grabbed her from behind. Whirling around, she saw Roarke lift a finger to his lips.

"Let us not wake the entire castle with your screaming."

'Twas hardly her fault since he surprised her. "I did not hear you."

He winked and grinned. "I know. I wouldn't be much of a warrior if I crashed through the hedges like a charging bear, now would I?"

The thought of him thrashing through the brambles like a lumbering animal made her giggle.

"Ah, now that is what I wanted to see." He caressed her cheek with the back of his hand.

Her heart fluttered as rapidly as her beating wings. "What is that?"

"My faerie's smile. You have gone much too long without one."

His faerie. The words should mean nothing, and yet were what she had dreamed of for a very long time. But dreams and reality were neither close nor attainable.

Nearly invisible in the darkness wearing his black breeches and tunic, she nevertheless could easily make out every curve and angle of Roarke's body. His nearness unnerved her, sparked desires she should not be having for a man who was not her betrothed. Yet she knew no way to stop her feelings other than to stay away from him.

Something she had failed miserably at doing.

"Why did you ask me here, Roarke?"

He reached for a scarlet curl that lay just over her breast. Her nipple rose to greet the brush of his hand. She gasped at the tightening pleasure spiraling through her.

"I don't know what I want. I just know that I wanted to

see you. Alone."

"Being alone is not such a good idea."

"Yet you came when I asked you."

"Aye." That she did, but she shouldn't have. Not when she belonged to another. Yet he pulled her like an invisible force that she could not deny.

"What do *you* want, Solara?"

She turned away from him and fluttered to the edge of the cliff, trying to immerse herself in the sounds of the ocean instead of answering Roarke's question. "It does not matter what I want."

"To me it does."

Heat emanated from his body as he stepped behind her. She steeled herself from turning around and leaping into his arms. "This was a mistake. I should go back to my room."

But when his hands caressed her bare shoulders, his breath ruffling the hair on top of her head, she couldn't move. Memorizing his touch, his scent, she vowed that despite her fate, she'd never forget the way her body came alive when his hands touched her. The dark promise in his eyes, the way he smiled, would always be a part of her mind.

"Look at me, Solara."

She dare not. Admittedly weak where he was concerned, one glance and she'd be lost. Too much was at stake to take that step. She held firm to her resolve, refusing to waver.

Her mouth fell open in a gasp as he whirled her around, pulling her tight against him. She wriggled away, afraid of him. No, that was not true. Fear was her own making, fear of her own reactions to him. "Let me go, Roarke."

Concern etched his face in a frown and he loosened his hold on her. "Am I hurting you?"

He'd taken tender care with her wings, sliding his hands below them to pull her close. His fingers burned through her shift and set fire to her skin. "No."

"Then tell me why my touch revolts you?"

She paused, stricken that he would think such a thing. "Oh, no. Your touch does not revolt me at all."

"Then what is the problem? Why do you seem as if you want to be close, but when I touch you, you pull away?"

The words hovered on her lips, but she feared lending them voice. Telling him how she felt put her feelings in the open. She dared not. "Because you shouldn't touch me."

He looked away. "You are right, of course. You belong to another, and I have no right."

But when he stepped away, doing exactly as she asked, her soul cried out for him. A chill crossed her body at the loss of his warmth. She wanted to ask him to come back. She wanted to tell him that it didn't matter that she belonged to another man.

But it did matter. To both of them.

"Why don't I feel guilty when I look at you and think things I shouldn't?" he asked, his voice so faint 'twas almost as if he asked the question of himself.

Solara flew over to where he stood and laid her hand on his shoulder. "Because we want something we can't have."

When he turned to face her, she knew his pain mirrored her own. "I know. The problem is, I *want* to touch you, Solara. It's almost a burning need that I cannot resist."

She wanted that more than her next breath. Yet a part of her still held on to her duty, more for his sake than her own. "You can't."

"Why?"

"Because your touch awakens something in me." As soon as the words left her lips, she knew she had made a mistake. Now he knew exactly how she felt. Already weak where he was concerned, she wasn't certain she'd be able to tell him no again.

Moon glow shone on his face, lighting up his features. His

eyes held a melting warmth, their color toasty brown with flecks of dark gold, like sunshine peeking through a thick canopy of trees.

He bent his head and brushed his lips against hers.

Her internal battle was lost. She gave herself up to the magic of Roarke's mouth.

Chapter Two

ଈ

Roarke should have never touched Solara. Never pressed his lips to hers.

What was he thinking?

He wasn't. Not with his head anyway. His cock propelled him to make stupid choices. This woman in his arms was betrothed to another. His honor forbade him to touch her.

But touch her he did. Her lips tasted as sweet as fresh dolaberries, her tongue tantalizing as it brushed up against his. When she whimpered into his mouth, he knew he was lost.

Damn her fate, and his. He was no king, could not claim a faerie princess as his bride. He was nothing more than an elvin warrior, a commoner among the royal elves and faeries.

What he did now tarnished his honor and that of his king, his friend, a man who was as close to a brother as he would ever have. They shared a telepathic link forged since childhood, their lives bound together forever.

And yet he could not stop. Solara gave with all her being, moving closer to him. She retracted her wings so he could fit his arms fully around her, her acquiescing movements an invitation he could not resist.

His faerie craved their joining as much as he did. Aye, it was wrong, but let him be damned for eternity, for he'd not let her out of his arms.

With a burgeoning ache, his cock hardened. He pulled Solara toward that sweet pain and rocked against her. A moan escaped her lips and he drank in her desire, sipping at the delectable nectar of her mouth.

Passion overcame common sense and he lifted her into his

arms. Finding a secluded spot within the hedges, he laid her down on the soft mound of grass and marveled at the moon's glow shining over her. Her skin twinkled in the night like red stars. Kneeling down beside her, he tentatively brushed his fingers over her shoulder, then down her arm, eliciting small shudders of delight.

Her nipples hardened to tight peaks against her transparent shift. Unable to resist, he swept the gown over her shoulders, baring her breasts. He sucked in a breath at the perfect beauty of the small globes. Anxious to taste her, he bent down and fit his mouth over one hard nub. She gasped and threaded her hands in his hair, whispering his name.

Her pheromones invaded his senses. The sweet smell of flowers in the summertime wafted over him, covering him with the desire to lick her skin and discover if her taste was as arousing as her scent. The urge to tear her shift away and bury himself deep within her was nearly overpowering. He fought the desire, knowing it would be a dangerous road from which neither of them could return.

Already he had breached that which he should not. But he was a man possessed, unable to halt his actions.

And, stars, she did not wish it either. Her body writhed against the soft earth and she held out her arms to him, beckoning him to take her. A small part of him knew this was wrong, knew they should stop before they went too far.

"Solara, we should not—"

"Roarke, please," she begged. With an urgency he clearly understood, she grasped his shoulder and pulled him down against her. Eagerly, she reached for his shaft and palmed it over his breeches.

He sucked in a tight breath, panting like an animal. Heated to near boiling, he was delirious with the fever she gave him.

She would never be his, he would never take her virginity, but by all that was magic he would have a small part of her tonight.

With a low growl he covered her body with his hands, clearing his mind of guilt and hesitancy. For many long months, since they had first met, he had wanted her, dreamed of her, desired her.

The long separation had done nothing to quell his need for her. Every night he lay unable to sleep, feeling a connection to the scarlet faerie who resided so far away in D'Naath. Many times he had wondered if she felt the same way, if she burned for him despite being apart.

Her response now told him that she had.

Like a blind man relying on touch, he memorized her skin. The hollow in her throat, the way her neck arched as she swallowed, the way her breasts rose and pressed against his hands. The small buds nestled perfectly in his palms, her nipples teasing him with their tightened tips.

Her waist was so small he could circle it with his hands. Her hips were slender, yet with enough substance she could accommodate his form between them. That thought brought about another painful tightening of his balls.

No, tonight he would not have her in the way that would make her his forever, but he would hear cries of ecstasy pour from her lips and know that he'd given her pleasure.

"Raise your knees, Solara."

Her shift parted and slid down her silken thighs, revealing the treasure between them. Scarlet curls covered the mound of her sex. Her pussy glistened with moisture, an invitation he was unable to resist. He swiped at her nectar, watching her shiver, hearing her moan of pleasure as he brushed against her clit.

With deliberate slowness, he brought his finger to his mouth, licking her essence from his fingers. Solara watched him with rapt attention, her tongue darting out to sweep over her own lips. The urge to give her his cock was overwhelming.

"Aye, Roarke, let me taste you."

A smile graced her lips. She'd made telepathic contact with him. He laughed, realizing that he'd let his guard down and allowed her insight into his thoughts.

"So you'd like to suck my cock, faerie?"

"Yes, you know I would."

He thrilled at the promise in her words, the enticing way she eagerly licked her lips as if she were starved for him. Moving quickly, he unclasped his breeches and took out his penis, stroking it slowly.

Greedy hands took over for his and she enveloped him, emitting a sigh of pleasure as she stroked his throbbing shaft. He bit back a groan and watched the movements of her small hands over his length.

She seemed a master at touch, knowing just how hard to stroke him. Pleasure unlike anything he'd ever known surged inside him. Suddenly eager to feel her mouth on him, he straddled her shoulders and bent forward, letting her take the lead.

Her tongue snaked out and licked the tip of his cock. Goosebumps rose on his skin at the contact of her warm, heated tongue on his sensitive flesh. He moved closer until her lips enveloped him.

Then she hummed, low and throaty, making him mad with the desire to thrust his shaft, hard, into her mouth. She teased him with her tongue, swirling it over the tip.

"That's so good, Roarke," she whispered, her gaze locked on his face as she took one long swipe of the head of his cock before engulfing him completely. His body shook with the force of his desire.

Cradling his balls in her hand, she tugged lightly. The sight of her mouth surrounding him was erotic, sinful, more arousing than anything he'd ever seen. She whimpered against his heated flesh.

Pleasing him excited her—what an astounding woman his faerie was. And she brought him to such heights he found it difficult to hold back.

"You had better stop, my faerie, or I will be filling that sweet mouth of yours with my come."

She smiled, then urged him to do just that by squeezing his shaft harder, sucking furiously on his cock. His balls drew up tight against his body, preparing for release. Bracing himself, he leaned over her, forcing more of his shaft into her hot, wet mouth, then exploded.

Swallowing greedily, she milked him until he had no more to give. Roarke panted, his body soaked with sweat. Despite the fact she'd emptied him, he was still hard, a fact that apparently wasn't lost on her as her eyes widened when he pulled his erect cock from her lips.

She was a magical woman, the very sight of her driving him to extremes of desire. She'd given him more pleasure than he thought possible, but they were not finished yet. He moved off and lay on the grass, pulling her against him. Her heart beat frantically against his ribs. Her sweet mouth called to him and he bent down to kiss her lip, his taste lingering on her mouth. That she would do such a thing for him, to him, without hesitation, proved that her potent sexuality more than matched his.

And now it was his turn to bring her the same release.

Solara's lips still tingled, her body burning with the need to come after taking Roarke over the edge. His cock was magnificent — more than she could have ever imagined. Taking him into her mouth had brought her to such a state of frenzy she wasn't certain she could stop from touching herself and obtaining release with him. Only his position over her chest had kept her from caressing her aching clit.

The throbbing between her legs had grown more insistent as she waited for Roarke to make the next move. Would he leave her, now that he was satiated?

Of course not. She'd no more thought it than his hands moved over her body, his skin as hot as hers. When his palm grazed her nipple, she gasped. His hand stilled and she looked up at him.

"Your body is so sensitive to my touch, Solara." To prove his point, he once again moved his fingers over her breast, lightly pulling the already distended nipple. Her core flooded with juices and she arched her hips.

Her body was much more than sensitive to his touch. She had been made just for him.

Only for him.

Fighting back tears, she refused to think about what would happen beyond this night. Tonight, she belonged to Roarke. What may come after that, she would not dwell upon.

"You brought me great pleasure, my faerie. And now I will try to please you in the same way."

It would not take much trying on his part. Already she was near orgasm. He had but only to brush his hand over her aching sex and she would cry out release.

Instead, he slowly trailed his fingers over her ribs, her belly, her hips, moving his body down until he was nestled between her spread legs. Her inclined position on the little hill afforded her a view of his dark brown locks. She reached for him, gently winding her fingers into his hair. With his gaze locked on hers, he took a long, slow swipe of her sex.

Surely the cries of ecstasy could not be hers. She was aware they were in a public place, knew that should someone be walking nearby, they would have heard her wails of pleasure. Yet she could not hold them back. Roarke's lips and tongue performed a magical dance along the folds of her pussy, lapping up the juices that had gathered there and lightly teasing the knot of pleasure aching for a suckling.

No man had ever pleasured her before. Truth, no man had ever touched her, as it was not allowed for a faerie princess who was betrothed to a king. Yes, she had pleasured herself many times, both with her hands and with the faerie tubara stick. But for her first actual lovemaking experience to be with Roarke was everything she had hoped for.

She felt no guilt at giving something that belonged to another. In her mind, her very heart, she knew she was Roarke's.

The sensations soaring through her body, however, were nothing like she could have imagined. Tension knotted her muscles. She drew up her legs, giving Roarke access to all of her.

"Such a beautiful cunt you have, my faerie," he murmured against her thigh, lightly nipping her tender flesh. He swept his fingers over her folds.

"Roarke." She breathed his name on a blissful sigh, her gaze transfixed on his mouth and his hands.

He pressed his palm against her, petting the area below her pussy, then dipping his finger against her moisture and wetting her nether region.

"I may not be able to take you with my cock. I may not be able to slip deep inside your hot pussy, but I will enter you tonight, my princess."

Unable to speak, her body cried out the words she could not say. Roarke added more moisture to his finger and then lightly breached her anus. She stiffened, expecting pain, but he covered her clit with his lips and lightly licked until all she knew was pleasure.

He continued to suckle her bud, at the same time probing deeper and deeper into her anus until he breached the barrier and slid his entire finger inside. She cried out at the pleasure. Relentlessly he lapped at her, swirling his tongue over her sex and fucking her lightly until she contracted hard around him.

"Roarke, please, I cannot hold back."

"Then come for me, my faerie. Let me drink your sweet honey."

When he pulled his finger nearly out of her body, then thrust hard inside her nether hole, she let out a keening wail of climax as she poured her essence onto his awaiting tongue.

Her hips bucked off the grass as she fed him her sex, the swirling sensations taking over her thoughts, her voice and her actions.

Roarke held onto her as she rode out her orgasm, then gently removed his finger and cradled her body against his, taking her mouth in a heated kiss. She tasted her sex on him as he devoured her with his lips and tongue.

Clutching him as if she was never going to let him go, she pressed a kiss against his neck, noting the throbbing of his pulse. His rigid cock brushed her thigh, only inches away from her sex.

Oh, why could he not make love to her? They were fated to be together, the fire they brought forth consuming them both. Could he not see that?

Roarke sat up and helped adjust her clothing, then tucked his still hard shaft in his breeches. "It will be dawn soon. We must go before someone finds us."

"Go? And then what? After what we have just shared, has nothing changed between us?"

With a wistful smile he pressed a light kiss to her lips. "What could possibly change, my faerie? You are still betrothed to Braedon of Greenbriar. As it is, we should never have done what we just did. My apologies to you, princess, for taking advantage."

He was sorry for their love play, as if he'd just made a terrible mistake. Her joy of a few minutes ago evaporated, replaced by utter defeat. Her heart wrenched into a knot of pain. "I see. Being with me was only to release your lust?"

His tight-lipped visage told her the answer. "It meant much more than that, my faerie. But you are bound to another. I must honor your betrothal to King Braedon."

Just like that, he would let her go, into the arms of another man. He cared nothing for her. Fighting back the pool of tears welling in her eyes, she nodded. "I thought I mattered more to you than that. I thought…"

From the resigned look on his face she knew it was pointless to tell him how she felt.

"We cannot fight fate, Solara."

If he wanted to, he could try. By all that was magic, she was certainly trying to rail against the cruel destiny bestowed upon her.

Clearly, Roarke did not want to. She wasn't enough for him to fight for. "I understand. Goodbye, Roarke."

Before he had a chance to speak again, she opened her wings and flew above him, racing to the stairs leading to her quarters. Once safely inside her room, she shut and bolted the door, then threw herself face down on the bed.

Being with Roarke had only made things worse. Now she knew her feelings for him were genuine, and yet he would do nothing to change her fate.

His honor was admirable, even if she hated it right now. He would not betray his king or the southern king. Yet, Solara knew now that she could not honor her vow to marry. Something had to be done. Something had to change. What or how, she did not know.

Wiping away the moisture on her cheeks, she went in search of Trista.

Chapter Three

ʂↄ

"Solara is gone! I cannot find her!"

Roarke's head shot up at the sound of Trista's voice, dread turning his blood cold.

She entered the hall in a rush and threw herself into Noele's arms.

"What? What do you mean she is gone?" Noele's frantic look mirrored Roarke's feelings.

Trista's golden-flecked face was streaked with tears. "I went to find her this morning because she usually awakens before the rest of us. Her room was empty, her bedcovers undisturbed. I looked everywhere for her, Noele. I cannot find her!"

"Are you certain?" Garick asked as he stepped beside his wife. A concerned frown etched lines on his brow.

"Yes. I can feel it. She no longer resides at Winterland."

Garick turned to Noele, who closed her eyes and became very still. When she opened them a few seconds later, she nodded. "Trista speaks truth. Solara is not within the castle grounds."

Roarke remained silent and waited for instructions from Garick, despite his immediate desire to strip the castle walls bare and find Solara. Which was ridiculous since Noele had just stated she was nowhere on the grounds. And yet, he wanted to search for her, as if he could find her when no one else was able to. He could not reveal his feelings for the faerie, as she was not his to worry over.

But worry he did. After Garick called the guards into the search, they tore apart every inch of Winterland. By nightfall, it was confirmed—Solara was not there.

Noele sat in the hall with her chin drooping miserably on her chest, unchecked tears dropping onto her shift. Her sisters surrounded her, holding her hand and trying to console her. But they, too, were miserable, judging from their saddened faces.

Garick and Roarke sat across from the women, discussing their next plan of action and trying to determine whether Solara had left on her own or was taken.

"She could not have simply walked through the gates. Our guards posted there would have seen her. They would have stopped her."

Roarke nodded at Garick's statement, knowing it to be true. "Then she did not leave on her own."

Which meant she'd been taken, but by whom?

The thought of wizards capturing her was something he refused to consider. And yet they were the only likely source, having been known to spirit away the inhabitants of Winterland on a whim, without anyone noticing them. It had happened to Noele shortly after she'd married Garick.

But the people of Winterland had kept their psychic thoughts open, and not once had a resident of Winterland been abducted since that episode.

"I want to search the forests. Let me take a guard to patrol the area."

Garick nodded, then leaned over to whisper so that only Roarke could hear. "Be on the lookout for wizards. I would wager they have her. The who is a given. The where is another matter."

"Aye." Garick had been fortunate when Noele had disappeared that he'd been psychically connected to her. Garick had felt her, and that was how they'd managed to find her. But with Solara—

Wait. She had connected with him telepathically last night. Surely if she were captured she would know to open herself up so that he could find her. He closed his eyes and concentrated on her being. After several moments of no contact, he opened his eyes and cursed.

Garick was staring at him. "What is it?"

"Nothing."

A frown creased Garick's forehead. "You were trying to connect with Solara, weren't you?"

If he admitted to that, then Garick would know something intimate had transpired between him and Solara. "No. I am simply frustrated."

Guilt assailed him at having to keep his true thoughts from Garick, yet he would not compromise Solara by revealing what had happened between them.

Garick eyed him as if he suspected Roarke was lying, yet he simply shook his head and nodded. "Take some of the guard and search outside the castle."

Relieved at being allowed to do something productive instead of standing around, Roarke assembled a contingent of guards and rode out of the castle, determined that he would not return without Solara.

They rode in silence, Roarke leading the way into the western forests. The density of the forest created a wall of trees and sharp branches—no hope of finding a trail or to even know if someone had passed through there.

Beneficial as a protection around the castle, the thick forest prevented their enemies from using this venue to launch an attack. While one or two people could make their way through here, it was unlikely an entire army could. The trees grew thick here, almost too thick to guide the horses through. After awhile they stepped off and tethered the horses, then wove their way through the dense forest on foot.

Thick roots lined the forest floor, rising up from the ground and making travel precarious. Thin birch trees with low-hanging branches swiped at his face. He muttered a curse at having to look both down and up to ward off either a root or a tree branch.

At least Solara's red wings would stand out against the light-colored trunks of the trees. If she were even in there.

His mind strayed often to what had happened between him and Solara last night. Guilt mixed with a heady pleasure constantly interrupted his thoughts. The way he had left things with her — letting her believe she didn't matter, that she had to marry the southern king — was wrong. He could have taken time and care with his words, instead of letting his frustration answer her questions.

No, he could not ask for her. He had no right, he was not a king. The stricken look on her face when he'd dismissed her was painful, and yet he could not help but hurt her. What he said was truth. She would not, could not, ever be his. There was no point in telling her how he really felt about her. It would only have made her departure today more difficult, for her as well as for him. Better that she leave hating him. At least then he would know her heart would be clear when she reached Greenbriar.

Thoughts of Solara lying in the arms of Braedon of Greenbriar sent his blood boiling. He forced the visions aside so he could concentrate on finding her.

And when he found her, he would take her to another man.

No! Stop this. She does not belong to you, and she never will. Your fate lies down a different path, not with Solara.

His mind told him this, yet his heart refused to believe.

By early the next morning, they had scoured acres of forests and miles of steep, rugged cliffside. No sign of Solara. Roarke was loath to return to Winterland and have to tell Noele that her sister could not be found, but there was no recourse. He turned the troops around and headed back to the castle.

Where could she be? If the wizards had her, surely she would have opened herself telepathically, if not to him then definitely to her sisters. And yet not one of them felt the connection.

Unless she was already —

No. He refused to believe that. Even if they had kidnapped her, they would not have killed her. Taken her magic, yes, but the wizards typically left their captives alive. Without a magical soul, but alive nonetheless.

And in the transfer of magic he'd have felt her. He was sure of it. One thing he knew about Solara was her strength of will. She'd have fought to the death rather than give up her magic or any part of herself.

Despite the early hour, Winterland was a bustle of activity. Roarke dismounted and immediately set off for the hall to find Garick and Noele.

A half-dozen sets of hopeful eyes settled on him as he pushed open the door. He walked toward them as if in slow motion, wanting to delay the inevitable.

It didn't matter. Noele's lashes draped over her cheek and a single tear fell. She knew.

"You didn't find her."

Garick's statement was more of an answer than a question. Roarke had never felt more inept, had never felt like such a failure. "No, I did not."

"This makes no sense," Noele said, swiping at the tear. "She wouldn't have left on her own. If the wizards took her she'd have opened herself up so one of us could sense her. Unless she's — "

Noele stopped herself from saying the word Roarke had refused to think about. But the stricken look on her face told him she'd considered it.

"No. It can't be. I will not even think she could have come to fatal harm." Her eyes wide and filled with tears, Noele swept from the hall, Elise and Mina following.

"What next?" he asked Garick.

"Braedon will have to be told. He is expecting his bride-to-be, and custom dictates that she either arrive on time, or an emissary arrive explaining why she has not come forth."

Roarke sighed. Not only did they have Solara's safety to consider, but also the potential of a breach of custom, putting the relationship between the southern king and the faerie of D'Naath in jeopardy. Uniting all the lands north and south with D'Naath was paramount to developing a stronghold against the wizards.

"Aye. What would you have me do?"

"I will take half the guard and travel to Greenbriar. You must remain here and guard Winterland, and keep searching for Solara."

"And when she is found?" Roarke refused to consider "if".

Garick shook his head. "Hold her here until I return. You cannot escort her to Greenbriar with a contingent of guard. If I am to travel there, it would leave Winterland vulnerable to attack."

"Who from the faerie will you ask to take with you?"

"I will go."

Roarke turned at the sound of a small voice. Trista stood behind him, slowly fluttering her green and gold wings. A spot of color darkened her cheeks.

"You are volunteering to act as emissary for the faerie?" Garick asked.

Trista nodded and moved forward. "Aye. "

"Why?"

Something was wrong. Trista refused to meet Garick's eyes. Roarke had never known her to be shy. In fact, she was the boldest of the sisters. "I merely wish to assist you, Garick. And my sister, of course. Plus, as we will pass through D'Naath, I will alert our parents to Solara's disappearance. They will want to know so they can search for her there."

"So be it." Garick stood and whispered to one of the guard, then faced Trista. "Prepare yourself to leave by tomorrow morning."

Garick left the hall and Trista made to do so, but something in her manner made him curious. "Trista, before you go I wish to have a word with you."

She halted and turned. "Yes, Roarke?"

"Do you know something of Solara's disappearance?"

Her golden eyes widened and she shook her head, her wings flapping so furiously they created a draft around him. "Oh, no! Nothing at all, I swear it! I wish merely to help you."

Her denial broke too quickly from her lips, making Roarke suspicious of her intent. Trista was the trickster, the devious one, according to stories Noele had told them. Always one to play games, she never took anything too seriously. Surely she wouldn't think of doing anything to upset the delicate balance of the kingdoms.

"Make sure your intent is honorable, Trista. There is much at stake here."

She nodded soberly and fluttered up the stairs to the chambers.

Perhaps he'd misread her. She seemed genuinely concerned for her sister, and yet something in her manner led him to believe she was holding back. Had Solara told her what happened between them? Did Trista harbor some ill will towards him because of what he had done with Solara?

Ridiculous. He was merely worried for Solara's safety, much the same as he would be for any inhabitant of Winterland. Delving into Trista's every action was unwarranted. She knew nothing.

Roarke sat and contemplated additional areas he could search for Solara. This mystery of her disappearance became more vexing by the minute. She could not have been kidnapped by the wizards. Even if they had rendered her unconscious, her powers of telepathy would have reached her sisters. Or perhaps, he hoped, to him.

Something was not right. He felt responsible for her disappearance. A vague uneasiness had settled within him and refused to let go.

He had to find her.

* * * * *

Noele worried her bottom lip and fluttered about her bedchamber, assisting Garick with preparations for his departure to the southern lands. Her worry was insurmountable. She worried for Solara, and for her husband's and sister's safety on the long journey to Greenbriar.

That, and she had a secret that she now could not tell her husband, for fear he would not make the journey and jeopardize the faerie treaty with Greenbriar. A joyful secret that would have to wait.

"I will miss you, my husband."

Garick turned warm gray eyes on her. "And I will miss you, my wife. Who will warm my bed at night?"

She heated under his penetrating gaze. "And who will warm mine? 'Twill be many a cold night until you return."

He gathered her into his arms and pulled her close. She laid her head on his broad chest, comforted by the steady beat of his heart. Garick tipped her chin up so she could look at his face. "My love will warm you in my absence. My heart always remains by your side."

She never knew she could experience love such as this. All her trepidation about marrying a man she had not chosen had flown away in a winter breeze when she realized her destiny. She loved Garick like she never thought she would be able to love. And now that love had borne fruit, and she was anxious to tell him her news.

But the news would wait. It would have to wait. She had to remain behind while he made the journey. His queen could not act as emissary for the faerie people. "How long will you be gone?"

"A fortnight at least, maybe more. Since we will pass through D'Naath, Trista and I will break the news to your parents. Travel itself will be seven days there and seven days back. Delivering the news to Braedon will not take but a day."

"What will you tell him?"

"That Solara has been delayed. That she is missing and we fear she has been kidnapped. I will tell him the truth."

Noele prayed the truth would be enough to satisfy him, that he would be willing to wait until Solara was found.

"You are a wonderful diplomat, Garick. You will find a way to convince him to wait."

Garick pulled her closer and touched his lips gently to hers, then enveloped her in a kiss that curled her toes and made her wings flutter madly.

"Make love to me, my faerie queen. Give me a memory to last a fortnight."

Her heart soared, her body awakening with a passion that could never be quenched as long as Garick held her in his arms. "With pleasure, my king."

Chapter Four

ဢ

"Roarke! Roarke, where are you?"

Noele's cries echoed in the courtyard where he stood with the guards. Roarke sheathed his sword and raced up the stairs to the hall. The doors were open and he hurried in, running to her side. "What is wrong?"

She waved a crumpled paper in front of him. "I cannot believe this was not discovered when we searched the castle, but Isolde found it when she was sweeping under my bed. It must have fallen from the bedcovers."

He took the paper and opened the note, scanning the words written in faerie script.

My dearest sister, Noele,

I will not abide by this decision which has been made for me. Forgive me. I realize what is at stake but I simply cannot be led blindly where I do not wish to go. I must be able to make my own choice. My mind is a mix of confusing thoughts, and I depart now to be alone. I need time to think. Do not fear for me, as I will be safe and will return soon.

With my love, Solara.

The worry that had held a tight grip on him for two days was washed away by a cold anger at the havoc Solara had created. "Is she insane? On a childish whim she decided to run off and pout instead of facing her fate like a woman grown?" He thrust the paper back into Noele's hands and turned away. Frustration ate at him and he wanted to crush something with his hands. Anything to take away the anger over Solara's idiotic act of selfishness.

Noele touched Roarke's arm. "This is so unlike Solara. She knows her duty, has always known it. No, she was not fond of the idea of marrying a man she never met, but she knew it was her fate and she was determined to see it through."

Roarke snorted and pointed at the note. "Apparently she changed her mind."

"Something must have happened. It had to have been monumental for her to run off like this. 'Tis not like her at all."

Her words gave him pause, forcing his anger aside. Had the "something" that happened been him? Had he pushed her beyond her ability to face her fate? Did her feelings for him run so strong that she would give up her destiny rather than marry a man she did not love?

More importantly, how did he feel about her decision, if that was the case? Before now he refused to face his desire for Solara. From the moment he met her he'd felt their connection. No woman had ever touched his emotions as she had.

His feelings didn't matter. Despite what his heart told him, she still was not his. She belonged to Braedon. She knew that as well as he and it was ridiculous for her to play such a game. "Do you have any idea where she might have gone?"

Noele shook her head. "No. And she clearly has blocked all of us out of her thoughts. You searched the forests well?"

"Aye."

"Might I suggest you search again? I am convinced that is where she is hidden, as the forests would give her the comfort of home. She would wish to be near D'Naath, but would not travel so far by herself."

"I have already thoroughly searched the forests. She was not there."

Noele's lips crooked into a smile. "Did you look up?"

"Up?"

"Up, as in the tree branches."

Bloody hell. Solara *was* a faerie, after all. Had he not been so wrapped up in thoughts of why she had disappeared, he would have remembered to search the branches of the trees.

"I'm an idiot. I'll go search for her there."

Noele laughed. "You are no such thing. And Roarke?"

"Yes?"

"Please find my sister and bring her back."

He gave her a solemn nod. "I swear to you I will find her."

Whether he brought her back in one piece or not was another matter. She might just have a bruised backside when he was through with her.

As he waited for the guards to assemble, his mind strayed to punishing Solara for running off. His cock twitched to life at the thought of spanking her bare ass, then turning her over and fucking her until she was his forever.

With a disgusted sigh at his wayward thoughts, he rode through the gates of Winterland and headed for the forests.

* * * * *

Solara pulled her knees to her chest and wrapped her arms around her legs, easily balancing on the top branch of a willow tree. Wistfully, she put her chin on her knees and stared at Winterland castle.

For three days she'd remained in the forest and thought about the alternatives to marrying Braedon of Greenbriar. Three days of watching Winterland from the tops of the tree branches, eating berries and nuts and drinking from the small streams. Three days of not sleeping much at all. And after all this thinking she had come to no other conclusion than she would have to go through with the marriage.

"What does it matter?" she said out loud, hoping the forest and the wide-open sky above her would provide the answers her own mind and heart could not. "Roarke has no feelings for me. To him, I was merely a female who released his desires, no more, no less than any other woman he has known. Better to meet my fate head-on than to suffer the rest of my life pining away for a man who would not give me his heart."

She closed her eyes, knowing she would have much explaining to do when she returned to the castle. No doubt, Roarke had already left for Greenbriar to explain her delay to the southern king.

"Good. I hope he chokes on his apology for my absence. I hope that Braedon is already so full of desire for me that he punishes Roarke for my tardiness. I hope —"

She hoped that Roarke would admit that he loved her, and tell the southern king she would never arrive for their marriage, that he intended to defy law and marry her.

Laughing at her own ludicrous thoughts, she fluttered from the trees and landed softly on the earth. A knot formed in her stomach as she started toward the castle.

'Twas hunger that caused her belly to tighten, and nothing more. Certainly not guilt at sending Roarke and his guard on an unnecessary trip to Greenbriar. Definitely not remorse at worrying her sisters. Surviving on berries for three days had increased her hunger. That explained the pain in her stomach.

Hopefully Trista had explained to them that she needed time away for a day or so. She had entrusted the note into Trista's hands and gave her sister instructions to present it to Noele the morning after she'd snuck out of the castle.

Creating a momentary diversion for the guards at the gate had been simple. She'd summoned her magic to create a disturbance in the rear courtyard. By the time the guards had returned to their posts, she had flown over the tall, stone gates unnoticed.

But now it was time to return and face her fate. She froze

at the vibration of footsteps on the forest floor, hesitant to fly to the branches for fear she'd be seen.

She ducked beneath the drooping limbs of a thick willow, sheathing her red wings so they would not cast a glow beyond the greenery. Holding her breath, she shut her eyes tight and willed the intruders away.

Muttering a silent prayer that it was not the wizards crashing through the forest, she chanced a peek through a thick curtain of leaves, then smothered a gasp as she spotted the back of a man.

Whoever stood there heard her, and whipped around with sword over his head, ready to strike.

Recognizing the clothing as that of one of the guards of Winterland, she shouted, "Nay, do not strike! 'Tis Solara, faerie princess of D'Naath!"

Before she could inhale another breath, she was dragged roughly through the branches and brought up against a chest as solid as an oak tree. Warm hands dug into the tender flesh of her upper arms.

Solara tilted her head back and stared into the angry face of Roarke.

"Roarke! 'Tis you!" Without thinking, she stepped closer, relieved when he wrapped his arms around her.

"You are safe, faerie." His heart pounded against her cheek, his arms crushing her to him. She'd never felt safer in her life, even if she was in no danger to begin with.

"Of course I am safe," she whispered.

He pulled back and looked her over. "Where have you been?"

"Right here, atop one of the willow branches." She inhaled him, her body awakening to his earthy scent. Her nipples hardened against her shift at the contact of his chest against hers.

But he pushed her away so hard that she struggled to

maintain her balance.

What was wrong with him? Why was he so angry with her?

"Stupid faerie," he muttered, then grabbed her wrist and turned, dragging her along behind him.

"Wait!" She dug in her heels until he stopped and regarded her with an impatient stare. "Is that all you have to say to me?"

"No. There is much I would like to say to you, but honor forces me to bite my tongue so as not to speak harshly to a princess."

Curiosity spurred her on. That, and a decided irritation at his annoyance. "You have my permission to speak freely. And why are you not leading the contingent to Greenbriar?"

"I do not need your permission to speak, but I doubt you wish to hear what I would like to say to you. Garick has gone to Greenbriar to explain why his sister-in-law is a fool."

Her eyes widened at his insult. "I most certainly am not a fool."

Roarke grabbed her arms and hauled her against him, his eyes as dark as the earth floor. "Do you realize the wizards could have captured you? There is a reason we do not allow our people to wander alone outside the gates of Winterland."

She wrenched her arms away from his grasp. "I was in no danger. I can take care of myself."

His arched brow told her he believed otherwise. "You are one small woman, and no match for an army."

Glaring back at him, she said, "You think so? Then explain why you brought an army yesterday and could not find me."

"You saw us searching for you, and yet you did not hail us?"

Perhaps she should have, and yet she had not been aware it was Roarke who looked for her. Would it have made any difference? "I was not ready to come back yesterday."

"And I suppose you are ready today."

"Aye. I was making my way back to Winterland when I heard your approach, and hid to be certain there was no danger."

"Danger? No. But you imperil yourself in another way with your childish actions."

"I feel no threat."

"You should."

"From where?"

"More likely from whom." He picked up her wrist again and began to pull her along. She fought as long as she could, but finally gave up. It was either follow along or be dragged.

Why he was so angered was beyond her. Yes, perhaps this delay was foolish. She had not expected Garick to leave the castle and venture to Greenbriar. But she thought Roarke would be happy to see her. Instead, he was furious. Why? Was he disappointed that she had not already left? Was her constant presence at Winterland a burden to him? She had so many questions, yet she refused to ask him again to explain himself.

"We could meet up with the guard much faster if you'd cooperate."

He'd been mumbling as they walked, but she at least heard that part. Digging in her heels, she pulled at him. "Roarke, stop. Your stride is much longer than mine and I am having a difficult time keeping up."

Truth, she was trying her best to delay returning to the castle, knowing she would have to depart for Greenbriar as soon as they went back.

He stopped finally, glaring at her. "You should have thought of that before you ran off to hide in the forest."

"I did not run off and hide. I came out here to think."

"About what?"

"About...things."

Rolling his eyes heavenward, he took off for the clearing without her. She scrambled to keep up, no longer wishing to be left alone. "I saw that look you gave me. Did you not see the note I left?"

He whirled around and pointed a finger at her. "Aye, we found your hidden note. The day after Garick and half of Winterland's guards left for Greenbriar."

"What? I left the note with..." Oh no. Trista. She closed her eyes and knew that she was in serious trouble. Trista had not given the note to Noele after she'd left.

"You left the note under the bed, hoping no one would discover it until they were well away."

"That is not true!"

"You are a coward, Solara. I had thought you a brave woman until you acted like a spoiled child and ran off."

He was not even willing to listen to her explanations. Irritation made her blood run hot. "I am not a child, and I am certainly not spoiled."

"You deserve a spanking for the way you've behaved. Do you know how worried everyone was when they could not find you? They thought you had been captured by the wizards. Your sisters cried for two days. Garick has had to leave his castle, accompanied by Trista, to explain your absence to your betrothed."

This was not going at all the way she had envisioned. She had told Trista she needed some time alone before leaving to Greenbriar. Trista had changed everything. No doubt, some scheme had formulated in her little sister's devious mind. The stars only knew what Trista had planned once she reached Greenbriar.

"Believe me when I say that is not what I intended. I only meant to—"

"You only meant to hide from your fate. You can't escape it, and now others must face it for you because of your cowardice."

He thought so little of her. "I am no coward. Let me explain."

"You owe me no explanations. Save them for Noele. Explain to her why she has to be without her husband for a fortnight, and then another contingent will have to take you to Greenbriar after they return."

"After? I thought I would be escorted as soon as I came back to the castle."

He towered over her, his long frame casting a dark shadow over her body. "Once again, you thought incorrectly. The journey to Greenbriar is fraught with danger. Garick has taken half the Winterland guard with him. You think we would leave Winterland vulnerable to guide you there now? Nay, you will remain at the castle until Garick's return. Then you will be taken to Greenbriar."

Roarke was right. She had created a disaster. Worse, he did not believe it was not what she had intended.

Blaming Trista was convenient, but wrong. In fact, she had only herself to blame. She lowered her lashes, embarrassed at what Roarke must think of her. "I will accompany you back to Winterland with no objection."

"'Twouldn't matter if you objected or not. I can easily sling you over my shoulder and carry you that way if you fight me."

She walked along beside him, scurrying to keep up with his quick stride. Everything she had tried to accomplish had failed miserably. Was it so wrong to want a day or two alone? How was she to know that Garick would set off immediately for Greenbriar without waiting for her return?

How could Trista have manipulated them so? What was her sister's intent? She shook her head, knowing she shouldn't have trusted the little minx. Trista had offered her help, had told her to go to the forests and think while she tried to come up with a plan to prevent Solara's marriage to Braedon.

How easily she had grasped the opportunity to escape her fate.

How foolish she had been to think that her destiny could be changed.

Or that Roarke would care enough to be glad she remained behind.

Chapter Five

℘

Solara's reunion with her sisters was bittersweet. Noele, Elise and Mina cried and hugged her, relief showing on their tear-streaked, smiling faces.

Guilt pounded away at her, the ache in her belly remaining long after she'd been fed. Having bathed and slipped on a warm gown, she paced the confining chamber, wishing she could have a single moment of peace.

But peace would not come. She remained unsettled despite her days spent in the forest thinking over her fate. Resigned to the fact that nothing would change, she would simply have to wait out the days until Garick returned so she could then be taken to Greenbriar.

The time for feeling sorry for herself was over. Marrying Braedon was her destiny, her duty, and she would follow through no matter where her heart lay.

What a terrible day this had been.

Once she and Roarke had met up with the guards, they had ridden silently back to Winterland. Solara had been forced to sit with him on his horse, her body painfully aware of his broad chest and muscular thighs as she rode in front of him. With every jolt, her buttocks had rocked against his groin.

Despite his obvious irritation, he had hardened, but she refused to turn around and look at him, fearing what she might see there.

Or not see.

After they had returned to the castle, Roarke had presented her to Noele, then turned on his heel and strode out of the hall without another word. She had not seen him at dinner that night, either.

Whatever attraction she felt for Roarke would have to be tamped down during the two weeks she awaited Garick's return. It was time to think of her new life as the Queen of Greenbriar. She would spend time with her sisters, knowing it would be a long while before she could see them again.

A soft knock sounded at her door. She called entrance, and Noele stepped in, closing the door gently behind her.

"Are you still hungry?"

Solara shook her head.

"Are you comfortable?"

"Aye." She and her sisters did not sit on formality. "What is on your mind, Noele?"

Noele sat on the couch near the hearth, patting a cushion next to her. Solara took her place at her sister's side and waited for the questions.

"Why, Solara?"

Now she felt like the foolish child that Roarke had called her. She laced her fingers together and contemplated her lap. "I wish I knew. The night before we were to leave...something happened."

"What happened?"

How much should she tell Noele? Could she confide in her sister about her feelings for Roarke? If she told Noele about what happened between her and Roarke, Noele would have to tell Garick. Or lie to him to protect Solara and Roarke. That, she would not ask her sister to do.

"I simply had a feeling that my betrothal to Braedon was not right, was not my destiny." She looked up and met Noele's blue eyes. "I wrote the note and gave it to Trista. She swore to me that she would deliver it to you that morning."

Noele pursed her lips. "Ah, I see our little sister is up to her old tricks."

"I had no idea she would hide the note from you. You

must believe I would never intentionally worry you so."

Noele took her hands and held them. "I believe you. I know how difficult this has been for you, betrothed to a man you have never met. Uncertainty fills your life right now, mixed with a bit of fear at the unknown."

"I know you of all people are aware of my feelings." Only Noele had not been in love with another man when she met Garick. There was the difference. A difference she could not begin to explain to her sister.

"I beg your forgiveness, Noele. I am sorry that Garick had to leave and explain my absence to Braedon. I know you hate to be apart from him."

"I do not blame you, sister. How could you know that Trista would hide the note?"

"I should know better than to trust the little minx. I worry about what kind of havoc she will create once in Greenbriar."

"Oh, Garick will make sure she maintains proper decorum. Have no fear on that count."

When Trista was involved, one never knew what could happen. Already she'd made a bigger mess of the situation here than Solara had made by herself. As if she had needed help causing chaos at Winterland.

"Nevertheless, I will still beg forgiveness from you, and from Garick upon his return. As far as Trista, I will be having a firm word with her when she arrives."

Noele laughed. "As will we both. Come now, let us get some sleep."

When Noele stood, she swayed and grabbed for Solara's hands. Alarmed, Solara gently sat her back down.

"What is wrong?"

Noele offered a gentle smile. "I felt a bit faint for a moment. I am fine now."

"You're pale. Something is wrong with you." She stood, intending to call for Isolde, but Noele grabbed her hand.

"There is nothing wrong with me, Solara. Sit down."

She shook her head. "No. You are dizzy and obviously something ails you. Let me get Isolde and she can fetch the physician."

"I have already seen the physician, and he pronounced me fit. And pregnant."

Solara sat abruptly. "Pregnant? You are having a child?"

The color began to return to Noele's face, the silver on her cheeks sparkling. "Aye. In seven months time."

Joy replaced her earlier anguish and she hugged Noele fiercely. "I am so happy for you. May all that is magic in the universe bestow the gifts of love and happiness on your child."

Noele nodded. "Thank you, Solara."

"I imagine Garick is beaming with pride."

"He will be, once I tell him."

"He does not know yet?"

"I only found out two days ago. I did not want to tell him before he left for Greenbriar, knowing how he would worry."

The guilty feeling returned. "Oh, Noele, I am so sorry that you had to delay telling Garick your good news. I truly have mucked things up, haven't I?"

Noele graced her with a beautiful smile, the magic of her happiness giving her a silver glow like a halo surrounding her body. "You have followed your heart, Solara. There is nothing wrong with that."

"I have been impulsive and stupid for no reason. There is plenty wrong with that."

Noele laughed and kissed her forehead. "Rest now. We will talk more tomorrow. There is much to plan now that the baby is coming."

After Noele left, Solara paced her chambers, with every passing moment convinced that Garick needed to return to Winterland immediately. She worried about the danger he might face traveling to and from Greenbriar.

What if something happened to him? Not only would his child not have a father, but he would never even know about the child he'd created with Noele. And it would be entirely her fault.

She had to do something, and now. Hurrying out of her room, she crept down the hallway, stopping in front of the massive door leading to Roarke's chambers.

It was late. Would he be abed? Images of him throwing open the door naked refused to leave her mind.

Now is not the time for fantasies of Roarke. He is the only one who can help you. You need his warrior's heart right now more than you need his man's body.

If only she could convince her own traitorous body of that fact. Before her courage failed, she rapped on the door.

Her heart leaped into her throat as Roarke threw open the door. She tried to keep her eyes focused on his face, except he wore only half-laced breeches and no shirt. His chest gleamed strong and smooth in the light of the hallway.

"What do you want?"

His gruff voice nearly scattered her flagging courage. "I need to speak with you."

"See me in the morning. I'm busy right now."

He made to close the door. "Roarke, please. It's urgent."

With a resigned sigh he motioned her inside and shut the door. "It's very late and you should not be here in my room."

She walked in, her gaze gravitating to the huge bed in the middle of the room. Fur coverlets looked warm and inviting. Shaking off thoughts of Roarke's bed and the endless possibilities of what they could do there, she stepped in front of the hearth and warmed her cold hands, preferring to stare into the flames rather than his half-naked body. "I have something important to tell you."

"I think we've said enough."

"This is not about you and me."

"Then what is it? And will you turn around? I find it difficult to converse with your backside."

She whipped around and looked at his face. He had stepped close to her, so close the golden flecks in his eyes glowed from the firelight. Shots of molten heat emanated from his gaze.

She swallowed past the dry lump in her throat and concentrated on his face, rather than his bronzed chest. Except his face was a work of art, too, his angular features accentuated by his closely trimmed beard. She remembered the softness of his beard against her thighs, and clamped her legs together to ward off the moisture gathering there.

Unfortunately, she could do nothing about her nipples beading against her thin gown.

Roarke must have noticed, because he dropped his gaze to her chest, then back up again at her face. "Make it quick, Solara."

"It's…it's about Noele. She is with child."

His eyes widened. "Are you certain of this?"

"Aye. She told me tonight."

"Does Garick know?"

She shook her head. "No. She did not tell him before he left for Greenbriar."

"Why not?"

"Because she was afraid he would not go if she told him. She feared for D'Naath if Braedon was not advised of the delay."

He did not have to say the words, because she felt them within herself. Because of her.

"And what problem does this present? She can simply tell him upon his return."

Obviously Roarke failed to see the urgency in getting Garick to return. "Garick should be alerted so that he can immediately return to Winterland. He belongs here, with his wife and child."

"That is not possible."

"Please, Roarke. Can't you ride out and bring him back?"

"Is everything so simple to you, Solara? I cannot leave Winterland. I am sworn to protect it during Garick's absence."

"Then send a few of the guards to catch up to him. He would be delayed in D'Naath for a day."

"No. We can spare no guards. Besides, it would do no good. Garick must go to Greenbriar with haste. He will not stay even a day in D'Naath, merely alert your parents to your disappearance and move on to the southern lands. Braedon must be told immediately."

"Oh, why must we have all this ritual and custom? If I was not expected on a certain day, this would have been much simpler."

"If you had stayed here and left for Greenbriar when you should have, there would be no problem."

"If you hadn't touched me, perhaps I would have."

His eyes widened. Her fingers brushed over her lips, unable to believe what she'd just uttered.

If she had but one wish right now, it would be to take back what she had just said.

* * * * *

Roarke stared speechless at Solara, unable to find a retort for her revelation.

Because of him she'd run off? Because of him she had not wanted to go to Greenbriar?

"If I hadn't touched you. Care to explain that?"

Her dark lashes fluttered against her cheeks as she looked down. "No. 'Twas not what I meant."

"Then what did you mean?" *No, do not ask her to explain. Do not spend any more time alone with this faerie than necessary.*

She is too dangerous.

"I meant…what I meant was…oh what does it matter? Can't you take me to Greenbriar yourself? If we cannot bring Garick back, then you can escort me there so he can hurry back. Maybe we would even catch up with him and he could turn around."

He grasped her shoulders and forced her to meet his gaze, hoping he could make her understand. "Have you listened to anything I've told you? I cannot leave Winterland, I cannot fetch Garick and I cannot take you to Greenbriar. You are simply going to have to wait until he returns, then you can go."

Perhaps she had decided to hurry on to Greenbriar because she'd found nothing in Winterland to stay for.

And now he was being ridiculous. He did not want her to stay. Her destiny lay with the southern king, not at Winterland.

"I have heard you; I just refuse to believe there is no other way."

Her skin was soft as cream, her scent permeating the air and making him mad with the urge to bury his lips against the pounding pulse in her neck. She stood with her back to the fire, the flames from the hearth appearing as if they burned through her scarlet wings. Her face was shadowed and her entire body glowed like a bonfire.

The same way she lit him up, setting him afire each time he was near her. She was the magical flame, he the tinder that longed for the spark.

Damn his desires, and damn her for tempting him this way. His only recourse was to make her so angry she would leave.

"You will get what you want soon enough, Solara. For now, you will simply have to be patient and wait until Garick and the guards return. Your childish actions have put both Garick and your sister in danger. Why don't you spend the time praying for their safety instead of concocting more ridiculous schemes?"

He heard the rush of air as she sucked in a breath. Unfortunately, it also forced her breasts against the thin gown she wore, outlining nipples that he remembered touching, tasting. His cock came to life and he realized that railing against her would never tamp down the need he had for her.

"Why do you act as if I've injured you?" she asked, folding her arms across those delectable breasts. "I have done nothing to you, Roarke. I have asked nothing of you."

Her skin burned against his hands, and he pulled away as if she'd just set him on fire. "You have injured my king with your foolishness. You have put Winterland at risk by diluting our guard strength. And you have taken Garick away from Noele when they should be celebrating together, not suffering apart."

She winced and turned away, swiping at a tear creeping down her cheek.

Remorse fought hard over the need to remain impervious to her beauty. Not one to hurt a woman, he wanted to take her into his arms, stroke her hair, and murmur apologies against her soft lips.

But that he could not, would not do.

Ever.

What he could do, what he had to do, was stay as far away from her as possible. Beginning with removing her from his room before he did something foolish like carry her to his bed and sink his shaft deep inside her sweet cunt.

"It's late and I have much to do tomorrow. You should leave."

She nodded, her eyes like moist, green pools. Blinking against the tears, she said, "Aye, that I should. My apologies for wasting your time, Roarke."

She fled his room quickly, shutting the door behind her. Roarke released the tension knotting his shoulders and turned to his bed, knowing that sleep would not come for him tonight.

He cared for Solara, that much he could admit to himself. But caring and wanting warred with honor and duty, and in the end, he would do what was expected of him.

He would leave Solara alone, no matter how much he wanted her.

Chapter Six

Solara busied herself tending to the tables, making sure the cloths were set so the dishes could be brought out.

"I saw you last night, Solara. What were you doing sneaking out of Roarke's bedroom in the middle hours?"

She turned at the sound of Noele's voice. Attempting a nonchalant shrug, she said, "I asked him to fetch Garick."

"You did what?"

She refused to look at her sister. "I asked him to bring Garick back and take me to Greenbriar."

"I assume he told you that notion was ridiculous."

Did no one take her side? "Yes, he made that quite clear."

"I'm surprised you would put yourself in a compromising position like that. You know better than to go to a man's room. You are a virgin Solara, and promised to another."

Solara didn't respond.

"Aren't you?"

"You know very well I am promised to Braedon. Your comment did not require a response."

"And are you still a virgin?"

Solara looked up and scanned the room, grateful that she and Noele were alone. "Aye, I am still a virgin."

"You play with fire, sister."

"I play with no such thing. I am resigned to my duties, Noele. Do not fear that I will do anything else to embarrass you or Garick."

"I do not worry for that. You have done nothing to

embarrass us. You are simply confused. I want to make sure your confusion does not lead you to make a mistake."

How easily it would have been to make a mistake with Roarke that night. If he'd told her he wanted to make love to her, she would have gladly given her virginity to him, only to discover later that he cared nothing for her.

As it was, he had made it clear that he couldn't wait for her to leave Winterland, that she was nothing but a hindrance.

"You do not need to worry. My head and my heart are clear and I will fulfill my destiny."

"I can only hope you find love at the end of the road, Solara."

She let out a small laugh. "The kind of love Garick gives to you is a miracle, Noele. I do not hold out hope that I will ever be loved like that."

At that moment Roarke walked into the hall. Solara felt the heat cross her face. Despite her resolve to do her duty, she could not stop her body's reaction to seeing him, nor could she keep from watching his progress. He nodded to them as he approached.

"Good morning, Roarke," Noele said, gracing him with a smile.

His face lit up and he stopped, took Noele's hand in his and pressed a light kiss against her knuckles. "Good morning, my queen. I trust you slept well?"

"Very, thank you. What are you about today?"

"Shoring up the main gate, training of the guard, sharpening of swords. Typical daily duties. And you?"

"Seeing to the cooking, making sure the linens are changed in all the bedchambers, and tending to my garden, as always. May you have a pleasing day, Roarke."

"You too, my queen." He turned, then as if in afterthought, inclined his head slightly in Solara's direction before leaving the hall.

She might as well have been invisible for all the attention he paid her. Turning away, she grabbed the dishes and began to slam them down on the tables.

"If you take your anger out on my dishes, I fear we will need to replace them."

Noele's teasing voice did not help her disposition at all. "I don't know what you're talking about. I am merely setting places at the table."

"I think you are jealous of the attention Roarke pays me."

"Jealous?" She whirled around to face her sister, only to find a teasing grin on Noele's face.

"Aye. Jealous. Roarke pays only the appropriate amount of attention to me. We are friends. He is my guardian and my protector."

He had also been her sister's lover for one night. Granted, it was elvin custom that the king share his bride with his protector, but Solara would not soon forget that Noele had shared a part of Roarke that she never would.

Noele bent her head to Solara's and whispered. "What happened with Roarke and I was required custom. One time, and nothing more. You know where my heart lies, sister."

Solara realized she hadn't shut off her thoughts from Noele. She took her sister's hands. "I meant nothing by my thoughts. I'm being foolish, 'tis all."

Noele motioned to a group of women just entering the hall, giving instructions for serving the food. "Come walk with me to the gardens. The meal will not be served for a bit and I wish to speak alone with you."

She followed Noele, nervous and anxious at what her sister had to say.

Noele had been right. She had no business going to Roarke's room last night. What if something had happened? Something…compromising.

Of course for that to occur, Roarke would have had to be

interested. Which, clearly, he was not. Since that night in the gardens he hadn't touched her, hadn't indicated he wanted her as he had then.

With a sigh she kneeled on the sun-warmed ground next to Noele, helping her tend to the flowers and herbs. And waited.

Noele contemplated what she would say to her sister about Roarke. She plucked at weeds while planning her words carefully.

She sighed, wondering if she should even broach the subject. If she delved deep, used her magic, and saw a destiny for Solara that she shouldn't see, then what would she do?

And yet the sense that Solara's fate lie down another path had wriggled its way into her mind since the day her sister had arrived at Winterland.

The feeling grew stronger when Solara and Roarke occupied the same room.

"The onions and cabbage are coming along nicely," she murmured absently, pulling away weeds threatening to choke the new vegetables. "The herbs will be ready soon. I must remember to pick them."

"What is on your mind, Noele?"

Placing the weeds on the warm grass next to her, Noele gazed into Solara's eyes. "I wonder about your fate."

"What of it?"

"Simply curious. Indulge me." She took Solara's hands into her own, closed her eyes and concentrated on the magic within her.

Pregnancy had seemed to provide a clarity she hadn't possessed before. She saw farther, felt more deeply, than she'd been able to previously.

A warmth enveloped her like a cloak, shielding her from the cold chill of being out of her body. She saw a land similar to Winterland, a castle as beautiful as the one she called home.

But it wasn't a castle deep in the southern lands. Snow surrounded it, and forests just like the ones where she lived, with cliffs overlooking the northern sea.

She saw Solara standing on the cliffs, and the shadow of a man behind her. His features weren't visible, but he had dark hair flowing in the breeze and from the back looked like —

Jerking her hands away from Solara, she opened her eyes to find her sister regarding her with a wide-eyed expression.

"What? What did you see?"

Noele stood and brushed the grass from her shift. "Nothing. It…it was unclear. I have things I must tend to. We will speak later, sister."

She nearly ran from the gardens, needing to put as much distance between her and Solara as possible. She closed her thoughts in case Solara became curious and decided to probe.

Once she reached her bedroom, she shut the door and sat on the bed, curling her feet underneath her. Her heart pounded madly against her ribs and she placed her palm over her breast as if to quiet the riotous beats.

What she'd suspected was true. Solara's fate did not lie with Braedon of Greenbriar.

Her destiny was with Roarke. 'Twas Roarke Noele had seen in her vision, standing at the cliffs with his arms around Solara. 'Twas Roarke's heart she saw entwined with her sister's for all eternity.

But how could that be? Solara was promised to another. Their customs demanded the faerie princesses marry a king to whom they were betrothed, unless that king refused the marriage or chose another.

Roarke was neither a king nor the one to whom Solara was betrothed.

Their match could not be.

And yet, she had seen it clearly, knew it to be the truth.

Roarke and Solara shared a destiny. All was unfolding as it should.

Or was it? She'd felt the tension since Roarke had brought Solara back to Winterland. They avoided each other completely.

Perhaps destiny would find its own way with those two.

And perhaps she would give it a little nudge in the right direction.

She smiled, a plan already formulating.

* * * * *

"I feel so weak. I can barely stand. I fear my pregnancy sickness has begun."

Solara worried over Noele, picking up her hand and cradling it in her own.

Lying in the middle of the huge bed, Noele looked like a small child, so frail and weak. Yesterday in the gardens she had seemed fine.

"I am sure once you have something to eat, you will feel better."

When Noele had not come down to oversee the breakfast preparations, Solara had gone in search of her, finding her still abed and pale as her white wings.

"I cannot eat. Please, Solara, help me if you will. Go downstairs and see to the morning's preparations."

Her? Oversee a meal for hundreds? "I do not know how. Surely Isolde—"

"Oh, I could not ask her to run to and fro. As it is she has been staying by my bedside tending to me. Please, dear sister, I have no one else to rely on."

Seeing her sister's pitiful countenance convinced Solara to do whatever was necessary to make sure Noele rested and didn't worry about the castle. If it were not for her running off, Garick would be at Noele's bedside right now, caring for his wife.

"Of course. I will see to things immediately." She scurried toward the door, then paused, turning back to Noele. "What things should I be seeing to?"

By the time the castle inhabitants had sat down to the morning meal, Solara had managed to get the cloths and dishes on the table and ensured the kitchens were preparing the food Noele had ordered. She mentally ticked off the items on the list Noele had given her, marveling at what it took to ensure a castle ran smoothly.

"Where is Noele?"

She jumped at the sound of Roarke's voice. He took a seat next to hers, much to her dismay. "She is ill."

He frowned. "Is it the child?"

Nodding, she added, "'Tis common in pregnancy for the woman to fall ill during the first few months. She did not look at all well this morning, and cannot hold down any food."

Roarke swallowed hard, and Solara focused on his neck where the line of his beard ended and his skin began.

"I will see to her after the meal," Roarke said, then stood and moved down the table to sit with his men.

She watched him with a hunger that no food or drink could satisfy. No matter that he didn't want her, despite the fact she knew she could never have him, she wanted him with all her being. In her mind's eye, whenever she thought of her future, she thought of it with Roarke. Foolish notions, indeed.

She ate her meal with Elise and Mina, who bombarded her with questions about Noele. She placated them as well as she could, having promised Noele that she would not breathe a word of her pregnancy to anyone. Only she and Roarke knew of the child Noele carried. Noele wanted to tell Garick before anyone else found out.

After the meal, she made sure the rooms were cleaned

and the temporary tables stored. Then she went to check on Noele.

Only Noele wasn't alone. Roarke sat on the edge of the bed, holding Noele's hand.

She stepped in the room and cleared her throat. Noele smiled weakly in her direction, but Roarke did not even turn to acknowledge her.

"Breakfast went well," Solara reported.

"Thank you."

"Are you better?"

She nodded. "Somewhat, although I am still weak. I fear I will have to find someone else to tend to my duties around here for a bit. I am so tired I can barely stay awake."

Solara slipped onto the edge of the bed, ignoring Roarke. Their knees touched and he moved his away.

Noele smiled, then put her hand over her mouth and yawned. "My apologies. I do not know why I am so tired."

"You carry a burden beyond your own body," Roarke said, then patted her hand. "You must rest. There are others here who can fill in."

His gaze gravitated to Solara. "Your sister, for example, has nothing to do to occupy her time until Garick returns."

Did he think her lazy? She had helped out whenever she could before now. Truly, the man was insufferable. "I have already offered my assistance."

"I'm afraid I will need more than just a little help, Solara. If this pregnancy is anything like Mother's, she was abed quite a bit in the beginning."

"I will do whatever you ask of me."

"Thank you. To begin with, I will need you to work with Roarke."

"I do not need her to work with me!" Roarke shot off the bed, backing away as if Noele had just set him on fire.

"Of course you do," Noele explained. "My sister knows nothing of running the keep. You know everything. In Garick's absence I need you to show her what needs to be done."

Show her? Solara swallowed past the lump in her throat. "Surely someone else can—"

"No, I think it would be best if you and Roarke worked together. With Garick and I both unable to fulfill our duties, there is much to be done beyond the daily running of the castle. Decisions must be made, and I trust no one else but the two of you. Solara, Elise and Mina can help with some of the daily chores. Roarke, put someone else in charge of training the guard so that your time is not consumed there."

Noele had changed from sister to Queen of Winterland. Solara had no choice but to do as she bid. "Aye. We will see it done."

Roarke nodded his assent, bowing his head. "You need but tell me what must be done, and I will make it so."

Noele's lips curled in a satisfied grin. "Perfect. Shall we get started, then? I have a very long list."

Chapter Seven

🎜

A very long list, indeed. Solara had no idea Noele was responsible for so much. Running the castle took up much of her day.

Apparently, her sister added on some of Garick's duties for Roarke to do, because the way the list read, Solara would be spending a considerable amount of time with Roarke, going over accounts and holding meetings with the townspeople.

The last thing she wanted was to spend time in close proximity to Roarke. He'd made it abundantly clear he had no interest in being with her, and in fact could not wait for her to leave Winterland.

Now that she knew how he felt, or how he didn't feel, she was anxious to move on to her new life. In the meantime, she would work alongside him in an effort to help Noele and Garick, and for no other reason.

They were to meet in Garick's offices this morning. Nervous flutterings in her stomach would not go away, and she blamed it on worries about doing a good job for Noele. After all, she had much to learn in a short period of time.

Shortly, she would be queen of her own lands. The sooner she became accustomed to her duties, the better she would handle the transition.

After checking on Noele, she headed to Garick's office. When she opened the door, she found Roarke sitting at the desk going over some papers. She admired the strength of his profile as he bent over two sets of ledgers sitting open on the desk.

He hadn't heard her enter, so she took a moment to watch him.

Stars, he was a beautiful man. Her breath caught and held as he ran his fingers through his long hair, and she recalled the exquisite sensation of touching him in the gardens.

That night had remained so fresh in her memories, and yet made her long to recapture a moment which seemed to have occurred a lifetime ago. She closed her eyes and recalled the way he touched her, his earthy scent fueling her desire for him. The way he had brought her to pleasure had been a dream fulfilled.

With a sigh, she opened her eyes and found Roarke staring at her.

"Daydreaming?" he asked, his sharp gaze sweeping from her head to her feet.

She shifted, not wanting to acknowledge the sensual darkening of his eyes.

You will not toy with me this way, Roarke. I will not stand by while you tell me you don't want me and then look at me like you wish to ravish me. "No, I was thinking of all the duties I have to fulfill. Not only here to assist Noele, but as Braedon's wife and Queen of Greenbriar."

His gaze lingered for a few seconds, then he turned away and looked down at the journal on the desk. "Come here, then. There are accounts that need settling. You will be managing accounts of your own soon enough."

He'd brushed her comment aside as if it meant nothing to him. Folly to think he would be bothered by thoughts of her marrying another man. She approached the desk and Roarke stood, pulling over a chair for her to sit. She retracted her wings and tried to position herself as far away from him as possible. His scent, so like the earthy smell of the forest she loved, permeated the room.

Attempting to concentrate on the books, her mind kept wandering. First, to the crisp, dark hairs on his forearm, then the way his shirt bunched up around his muscled biceps. She glanced down at her arm next to his, marveling at how much bigger he was than her.

"You must account for the number of sheep, geese, and chickens bought, marking them in the ledger in this column. Then, as they are butchered or sold, you track them here."

They spent the entire morning going over the accounts. By the time they had finished, Solara was miserable. She had watched every movement he made, breathed him in until his scent became a part of her, and wished with all her heart that once, just once, he would have touched her.

It did not matter how far away she was, or whom she was wed to. Her heart, her body, her very soul would belong to Roarke.

"You learn quickly," he said, turning in his chair until his knee brushed against her thigh.

Forcing the melancholy aside, she nodded. "I have had some experience in managing things. Our parents taught us much of what we would need to know."

"But there is more you have yet to learn."

She gazed up at the sound of his husky voice, his heated gaze causing her pulse to race. What did he mean? "What is it that I have yet to learn?"

"Running a keep, tending to the gardens, dealing with the various arguments and requests from the villagers."

"Oh." Of course he meant her duties as queen. How silly of her to think he would suggest she needed instruction in more passionate pursuits. Or that he would be the one to teach her. Although the thought of exactly what type of training he could provide had her body flushing with heat.

"And what did you think I meant?"

"Nothing." She stood and pushed back from the chair, circling around the desk to put some space between them. "Are we finished here?"

"In here, yes. Next we will have our meal, and after that meet with some of the villagers who have complaints and concerns."

She nodded, following him into the hall. During the meal, Roarke ignored her, sitting with some of the guards. She ate alone, since Elise and Mina were having their meal in Noele's room.

Which left her with nothing to do except watch him. With his men, Roarke laughed easily, smiled often, his booming voice echoing down the table and surrounding her, making her tremble with the desire to hear the husky tones whispered in her ear in the darkness.

After the meal, they took their seats at two large chairs normally reserved for Garick and Noele. It felt strange to be sitting with Roarke in chairs made for the king and queen of the castle. Almost comfortable, expected.

They spent the better part of the rest of the day solving disputes, granting requests and meting out disciplinary action to the villagers. Solara found Roarke to be diplomatic, stern, but also fair. She did not object to any of his edicts, and would have made the same recommendations had she been asked.

Which she hadn't. She laced her fingers together, contemplating strangling the man who did not once seek out her counsel on any of the affairs. By the time the hall emptied she was seething.

"Will that be all, my king?" she asked, not even trying to keep the sarcasm from her voice.

He turned and narrowed his eyes at her. "I am not your king."

Hands on hips, she faced him squarely. "You certainly acted as if I were nothing more than a servant at your feet. Not once did you ask my opinion of any dispute or request."

"Have you suddenly gone mute?"

"Obviously not."

"Did you disagree with anything I said or did?"

"Well, no."

"Then you have no reason to complain. If you had objections, you could have spoken up."

"'Tis not how it should work."

Mirth caused the gold flecks in his eyes to sparkle as if the sun shone directly on his face. "I see. And how should it work?"

"There should be discussion, compromise if necessary. But the king and the queen should discuss all matters relating to the inhabitants of their lands and come to a mutual agreement."

"Hmm, perhaps you are right. I shall keep that suggestion forefront in my mind for the next time we hold court together."

Which would hopefully be never. If she had to sit through another one of these episodes with him, she *would* strangle him. "Will that be all?"

"Here, yes. But now you will accompany me to the falconry."

It was already near dusk, and they had been working steadily since early morning. She could swear he was deliberately trying to exhaust her. "Why?"

"To tend to the birds there, of course. It is your job to oversee their care, make sure they receive the food and medicines necessary. While you will not perform these functions yourself, you will need to be aware what must be done so the birds are in prime hunting condition."

"Noele did not mention anything about the falconry."

"I am certain Noele was in no condition to explain every minute detail that goes into running a castle, especially in her condition. You will simply have to trust that I know what you need to learn."

She followed him out of the hall and across the courtyard, convinced that Roarke knew absolutely nothing about what she needed.

With a quick intake of breath she inhaled the fresh air, hoping it would clear her mind. Roarke's quick step was difficult to keep up with and she had to hurry along, not even able to take time to speak to Elise and Mina who waved at her from the entrance to the gardens.

They entered the falconry and observed the caretaker of the birds feeding one of Garick's most-prized gyrfalcons. A small chicken was brought into the open yard and the jesses on the gyr were released, allowing it to hunt and capture its prey.

Solara watched in fascination at the voracious appetite of the huge bird.

"They eat a lot, don't they?" she asked Roarke.

"Aye." He slipped on a leathered glove and held out his arm, letting loose a whistle that had the gyrfalcon instantly flying to him and settling upon the glove. He grabbed hold of the jesses. Solara followed him inside the mews, watching as he returned the falcon to its perch.

"Such beautiful creatures." Falconry was not practiced in D'Naath, and she had never ventured forth into the area where they were kept here in Winterland. This was her first opportunity to view the gyrfalcons and peregrines housed here.

"They are. Even more magnificent to watch them hunt out in the open fields and streams."

"I should like to see that some day," she murmured, her gaze transfixed on the gyrfalcon's actions.

"Perhaps you will have an opportunity to do so after you marry Braedon."

At the mention of Braedon's name, she looked up, surprised to find she and Roarke were alone. "Perhaps I will. I am certain he will be more than willing to teach me anything I'd like to know."

Dusky shadows fell over the dwelling, Roarke's face half-hidden in the murky light. He approached her, and she moved back a step.

"You are anxious for him to teach you?" he asked, his voice lowering to nearly a whisper.

"Aye, there is much I need to learn."

Roarke advanced another step and she retreated two, only to be halted by the rear wall of the falconry. Even the birds were quiet, lending a deafening silence to the ever-shrinking room.

"Tell me, Solara, what will you be asking Braedon to teach you?"

He was so close that if she inhaled strongly, the tips of her nipples would brush against the leather of his shirt.

"He will teach me things that I do not know."

"Such as?"

His nearness drove her mad. She could reach out and touch his broad chest, run her fingers through his long hair and capture the lips that had taunted her dreams for the past days. Trying to find her voice, she answered his question. "Such as how things are between a man and a woman."

Now his face was visible as he leaned over. She hid her arms behind her back, curling her fingers into her palms to keep from touching him.

"You are curious about sex, aren't you?"

"Aye. You should know that."

He laughed, a husky whisper that sent jolts of pleasure to her dampening pussy. Tension coiled deep in her belly. The air in the room seemed to thicken and she found it hard to breathe.

"Your curiosity is enticing. Any man would be more than happy to teach you the fine art of lovemaking, Solara."

Any man but him. She lifted her chin and said, "I look forward to it."

She teased him, she knew, but could not help herself. The language of his body spoke more of his feelings than any of his words to the contrary. He wanted her. She felt his desire everywhere as if he'd draped her in a blanket of his arousal. His breath came in short gasps, the same as hers. Did his heart race erratically as hers did?

Unable to hold back, she laid her palm on his chest, rewarded with his heartbeat thumping rapidly against her hand. A pulse pounded in his neck, calling to her. She wanted to lick that spot where his life's blood flowed, then nibble until he threw her down on the straw-laden floor and made love to her.

But he wouldn't. He would not touch her, and she knew that.

"Do not be so certain that you know what I will or will not do, my faerie," he responded.

He'd heard her thoughts. She'd let her guard down and he'd reached inside her mind. How easily he threw her off balance, made her forget to be wary. Had he not hurt her enough the other night? "You confuse me, Roarke. I do not know what you want."

"I know exactly what I want. Do you think it easy for me to see you every day, wanting you so much it takes my breath away, but knowing you are not mine to have?"

She closed her eyes, her heart soaring at his revelation. Was it possible to be so happy and yet so distraught at the same time?

"What are we to do, then?"

His hands encircled her waist, drawing her against him. "I know what we cannot do, but there are many things we can. You are a fire in my blood, Solara. I burn for you. Feel my flame."

He reached for her hand and placed it over his rigid cock. She gasped at the fierce heat emanating from his shaft.

Roarke tilted his head back and groaned. "Ah, yes. Your touch ignites me, faerie. I have a desire to feel your pussy under my hand, to dip my fingers in your sweet nectar and lick it from my fingers. Would you like that?"

She could not find the words to tell him, to beg him to do just that. She could only stare and nod, her throat too dry to voice a response.

His erection brushed against her thigh as he leaned in, licking the seam of her lips with his tongue. The dragon blew fire against her already heated mouth. "Open for me, Solara. Let me in."

Without hesitation she gave him her mouth. He slid his tongue inside, crushing her against his chest and winding his arms around her.

His tongue danced devilishly against hers, teasing, enticing, stealing what little breath she had left. She reached for his hair, tangling her fingers in the silken depths and tugging him closer. Her erect nipples brushed against worn leather and she whimpered, needing so much more than merely touching him.

"I know what you need, my princess." Roarke trailed kisses along her jaw and down her throat, licking along her collarbone and just below. She stood on her toes as if the very act of doing so would align her aching breasts with his mouth.

But he continued to tease her, swirling his tongue just above the swell of her breasts. His hands moved over her waist, then her hips, before traveling to her buttocks. He squeezed the twin globes there, then raised his head, crushed his mouth to hers and lifted her off the ground.

She wrapped her legs around his waist and he pushed her back against the wall of the falconry, rocking his erection against her pussy.

"Roarke, please," she cried, raining kisses along his throat, finally licking at that spot where his pulse pounded erratically against his neck.

"What do you seek, Solara? Tell me what you want."

Read my mind. You know my thoughts. You know my needs.

Aye, but I want to hear it. Talk to me, faerie. Tell me what you desire.

I need release. I want you to make love to me. I want your thick cock buried deep inside me. Please, Roarke.

In response, he muttered a curse and set her down until her feet touched the ground, then tore open her shift, baring her breasts. He covered them with his hands, finding her sensitive nipples and plucking them until they stood hard and needy. He bent over her, licking first one tip, then the other, until she could not think, could not breathe, could not do anything but experience the glorious sensations catapulting through her.

She reached for him, desperately needing to feel him in her hands.

"Not yet, faerie. Right now we will see to *your* needs."

Before she could utter a protest, he turned her around so her back rested against his chest. His fingers grazed her thighs as he raised her shift and gently slid his palm over the curls of her sex. He unlaced his breeches, his hot, hard cock pressing against her buttocks.

Despite his heavy breathing and the rigid length of his shaft thrusting between the globes of her rear, he was surprisingly gentle in his quest of her pussy. He lightly trailed his fingers over the swollen lips of her sex, slipping his fingers between the folds and finding the nub. With fingers moistened from the juices of her arousal, he circled her clit in relentless pursuit of her release.

Solara reached behind her to clutch Roarke's legs, barely able to stand. She cried out as he teased her entrance with his fingers, slipping just the tip inside her pussy.

"Please," she begged, so near release that tears of frustration trickled down her cheeks. "Please, Roarke, I need you inside me."

His whisper against her ear was harsh, tinged with the frustration they both felt. "I cannot fuck you, faerie, no matter how much we both want it."

She didn't understand. She no longer had the virginity

barrier, having long ago dispensed with it by using the tubara stick in seeking her own pleasure. It was common for faerie to have no hymen when they reached the marriage bed.

"Oh, but I would know, and so would you. On my honor, I cannot fuck you."

"Damn you, Roarke." She whimpered, the combination of her deep arousal and frustration taking its toll. The inability to become one with him when she so desperately needed it compounded the tension building inside her. And still, Roarke continued to stroke her sex, taking her ever higher to the edge of the cliff.

He licked the spot between her neck and shoulder, then grazed his teeth along her tender skin. When he bit down, she cried out, sparks of painful pleasure setting her afire.

"I cannot take this, Roarke. Please."

He bit again, harder this time, at the same time driving his finger between the folds of her pussy. Her legs would not hold up and he wrapped one arm around her waist to steady her.

"Come for me, princess. Come hard. Scream for me like you never will for another man."

No other man could ever make her feel what Roarke made her feel. No other man would ever be able to elicit the response she gave him.

The tension built inside her like rushing water beating against a weakened dam wall. She felt it push at her, felt his fingers at her core, his thumb circling her engorged clit, and she could not hold back the torrent.

The dam burst and she screamed her orgasm, grinding her buttocks against his swollen cock and flooding his fingers with her juices.

He held tight to her, murmuring into her ear as she rode out the tidal wave of pleasure. Roarke stroked her hair, kissed her neck, then turned her around to face him, regarding her with a heated expression that nearly set her on fire.

With a low growl he laid her on the ground, lifting the shift above her hips and roughly spreading her legs apart.

She held her breath, afraid to move or speak, knowing what he wanted, what he needed, because it was the same thing she'd wanted since the moment she laid eyes on him.

His cock was swollen, the veins pulsing. The head of his shaft was purple and engorged. He squeezed the tip between his thumb and forefinger, droplets of pre-come spilling over his hand.

"Is this what you want, faerie? My cock in your cunt?"

"Yes," she whispered, lifting her hips as if to guide him to her entrance.

"Then it's what you shall have. Because by all that is magical, I cannot hold back any longer."

He reached for her sex, dipping his finger against the entrance to her core and spreading her silken fluid on the tip of his shaft. "You feel like soft butter, princess. Hot, creamy, butter. Tell me, are you as hot on the inside?"

"Make love to me Roarke. Make love to me now, and you will see."

He surged forward, then suddenly stopped.

She waited expectantly for him to plunge his heated shaft inside her, her body on fire for him.

But he did not move. Instead he backed away, tucking his hard shaft into his breeches and lacing them back up. He pulled her roughly to her feet and picked the straw from her shift.

"I don't understand. What did I do wrong?"

He laughed, but it was bitter, not full of joy or the promise of pleasures to be shared. "You did nothing, Solara. It was my mistake entirely."

Not again. Oh please, do not do this to me again.

"I almost fucked you. And that I swore I would not do. You are a temptation I cannot resist, Solara, and yet I must. We must. You are betrothed to another. Braedon deserves a virgin on his wedding night, and a virgin he shall have."

He turned from her, opened the door and walked out, leaving her alone in the gathering darkness.

Chapter Eight

&

"He is so consumed with honor and duty, he cannot see past his chivalrous attitude to realize we are meant to be together."

Solara muttered out loud and paced her bedchambers. She had not slept at all last night, her body quaking with the need to be possessed by Roarke. A need that, once again, had gone unfulfilled. Last night's play had merely whetted her appetite for more.

More that had not been forthcoming.

"He thinks he can simply toy with me and use me, taking me to the brink of insanity over and over again, only to cast me aside as if I'm a trollop and he's the gallant knight of honor." She picked up a pillow and tossed it at the window. Sounds of the guards' activities echoed over the courtyard and into the half open window. She heard Roarke's voice bellowing out orders to the master guard taking over his training duties, but refused to look down upon the yard to watch him.

The morning sun sparkled bright and high in the sky, and yet Solara still had not gone downstairs. She'd been to see Noele already. Her sister remained abed, still apparently too ill to tend to her duties. After that, she returned to her chambers.

She couldn't very well hide up here all day, although the thought was tempting. If not for Noele, she wouldn't leave the room until Garick returned and she was on her way to Greenbriar.

Avoiding Roarke was not possible, unfortunately. She would simply have to endure him until it came time for her to leave.

After last night, it was a certainty he would not touch her

again. He'd taken her to such heights of ecstasy, to a place she had never dreamed existed.

But he had left himself unfulfilled, all because he refused to take her virginity.

She stretched her wings and raised her arms, hoping to diffuse some of the tension inside her.

Tension caused by sexual frustration, no doubt. If she weren't a virgin, she wouldn't be having these problems.

She stilled, her thoughts jumbling one on top of another as an idea surged forward.

If she were not a virgin, Braedon would not want to marry her.

If she were not a virgin, there would be hope for her and Roarke.

No, she couldn't. Dismissing the thought as a very bad idea, she started to leave her room, then stopped again, turning and walking to the window to peer down at Roarke.

How would her family react? Would she be disgraced? She wouldn't be the first faerie princess to forego marriage to a king in favor of physical pleasures with a commoner. It had been done before.

Her parents loved her, as did her sisters. They would forgive her. Another princess could marry Braedon. There were other kingdoms. Other potential brides for the southern king. Why did it have to be her?

In frustration she flopped onto the chaise and stared into the dark, cold hearth, realizing there was no way she could ever be with Roarke. As much as she wanted him, she would not disgrace her family. She had a duty to perform, and she was honor bound to do so.

Hopeless. Her wants, her needs, did not matter. To anyone.

Except her.

Could she not control one aspect of her life? Did she have

no power at all?

Then she smiled. Perhaps she did wield some power, small though it might be.

Roarke may have done the honorable thing by not making love to her, but he'd certainly taken her to the brink and beyond, before stopping abruptly and leaving her aching with want for him. Toying with her, teasing her, heating her, then tossing a cold bucket of water over her inflamed senses.

Perhaps it was time she showed him exactly what he *wasn't* going to have.

Soon, it would be time for her to leave. By now, Garick and Trista would have arrived at Greenbriar, delivering the message of her delay and heading back to Winterland.

She did not have many days left here.

But what time she did have, she would make of good use.

Before Garick and Trista returned, Solara would make certain Roarke knew exactly what he was letting go.

* * * * *

Trista inhaled sharply and pulled back on the reins of her horse. Looming ahead of them was the castle of Braedon, King of Greenbriar. The sun glinted off the moat like a shining beacon. For the first time in her life, she wondered if her impulsive nature had led her to make the wrong choice.

No, she was certain she was doing the right thing. Telling Braedon of Greenbriar that Solara did not want him would release her sister from having to marry. Braedon could simply choose another wife, and Solara would be free to marry whomever she chose.

For love, not for duty. The way it should be with all of them.

Temperatures soared once they'd reached the southern lands. She'd long ago pulled off her cloak, then discarded the heavy overdress until all she wore was her sleeveless shift. She opened and stretched her wings, thankful for the freedom the warmth allowed. Now if only she could fly instead of sitting on the horse Garick had provided her.

Reluctantly, she pulled forth her overdress and refastened it around her shift, feeling the heat press down on her.

"Are you tired?" Garick asked, sidling his horse beside hers.

She'd purposely evaded Garick for nearly a week, speaking minimally to him in order to avoid confessing her plot to keep Solara from having to marry Braedon.

"Aye. I am anxious to get back home."

"As am I. Hopefully Braedon will be understanding, and we can impart the news of Solara's delay, turn around and head back to Winterland."

And in the process, allow Solara the time she needed alone with Roarke. What would happen when they returned, she did not know. But she was hoping Braedon would give up on Solara and allow her to make her own choice of mate.

This custom of the faerie princesses having to marry a king was ridiculous. Too many faerie and elvin laws were antiquated and should be changed. Trista's own marriage to a king was coming up soon, although in her case one had not yet been chosen. The king she had been betrothed to since birth had died two years earlier, leaving no siblings and no other heirs. Had he lived, she would have been domiciled in lands adjacent to Noele. But since the king had no heirs, Garick had taken in the kingdom of Boreas as his own, so the people would be protected.

She glanced to her other side at her father, who had insisted upon accompanying them to Greenbriar. In truth, this made her deception more complex, as her father knew her better than anyone. When they'd arrived in D'Naath, the first thing he'd asked upon hearing of Solara's disappearance was whether she had any part in it.

Trista denied it, of course. Her father would be furious if

he knew what she had done.

The castle loomed before them, surrounded by lush green meadows littered with bright yellow wildflowers. The sun sat high in the sky, illuminating the gray stones until they glittered like silver.

As if they were expected, the gates opened as soon as the front hooves of the lead horses struck the wooden planks of the drawbridge. Trista's throat went dry at the thought of having to go through with this charade. Yet she loved Solara and would do anything to see her sister happy.

If only Garick and her father would let it happen.

But she knew protocol, knew if she spoke first, her words would be heard.

They rode through the gates into a courtyard littered with people, who suddenly stopped and stared in awe.

At her.

Heaven's stars! Hadn't any of these people ever seen a faerie before?

But as she looked at them, she realized they were different from her, from Garick, from any people she knew.

By all that was magic, these people were humans! She fought hard to think, wondering if her father had ever mentioned that the people of Greenbriar were neither elvin nor faerie, but human.

Surely she would have remembered a fact as important as that.

An entourage approached, several men holding swords flanking one in the middle.

The one in the center was extremely tall. As tall as Garick and Roarke, she would guess.

Garick dismounted, as did her father, who came over to help her down. She stayed behind her father, curious and yet still shocked at having her first glimpse of humans.

Not that different from elvin or faerie men, actually.

Although the faerie men tended to be shorter in stature than the others.

She squinted in the heated sunlight, trying to make out the features of the dark shapes approaching them. Her father reached for her hand and she grasped his fingers with gratitude, suddenly more nervous than she expected.

This plan had sounded much better in theory. Now that the time approached, she wondered if she would be brave enough to see it through.

Peering around the ample girth of her father, her eyes widened as the giant in the center of the crowd came into view.

"Stars," she whispered against her father's back. The man was beautiful. Dark brown hair bore golden-flecked streaks as if kissed by the very sun that shone down on them. Eyes as blue as the southern sea studied her.

What he could see of her, anyway.

His lips were full, his face clean shaven, rugged, his skin dark as if he spent his time outdoors. His ears were small and flat, nothing like the elvin men she was accustomed to meeting. Kind of funny-looking ears, actually. Where were the points?

But his body had surely been shaped by celestial beings. Broad-shouldered, muscles stretched taut against his leather jerkins, lean-waisted with strong legs.

For the first time in her life, Trista was incapable of speech. Not a very good thing, considering what she must do.

"Braedon of Greenbriar, we finally meet. I am Garick of Winterland."

This was Braedon, king of the southern lands? Perhaps she was remiss in keeping Solara from such a fine specimen of man. No, not true. No matter his beautiful appearance, this man was not destined for Solara.

"'Tis good to finally meet the king of the northern lands." He held out his hand and clasped Garick's.

"This is the father of my bride and king of D'Naath, Fraynor."

Her father nodded and also shook Braedon's hand.

"I welcome you to Greenbriar."

Once again, he stared at her. Surely he didn't think she was Solara. If so, she would have to correct that misconception immediately. She was not destined to marry this man.

If she had her way, she would marry no man that she did not choose for herself.

Open your mouth and say something, Trista, before your father or Garick does. It would have to be now or she would have made the trip for nothing.

Slipping her hand from her father's, she stepped boldly in front of him, trying to quell the shaking of her legs.

Braedon frowned as she stood before him and looked her up and down, assessing her from head to foot. Heat that had nothing to do with the sun had her flapping her wings to create a cooling breeze.

She tried a polite smile, but his facial expression did not change.

Did the man know how to smile? Maybe he was completely toothless. A grim line sealed his lips together.

Where was her voice? She swallowed and tried to speak, but no sound came out. If she did not say something soon, all would be lost.

"Braedon of Greenbriar, I am Trista, faerie princess of D'Naath and younger sister of your betrothed, Solara. I wish to speak." Her voice quaked and squeaked, but she pressed on. The last thing she wanted was for her father or Garick to stop her.

Braedon arched a brow, then nodded. "State your piece."

Breathing a sigh of relief that he had given her permission to continue, she nodded, wiping the sweat from her palms onto her shift.

"Trista," her father warned under his breath. She ignored him.

You can do this, Trista. Remember, it is for Solara.

"I am here to ask for release for Solara. It is my right as kin to request that you choose another bride, and that Solara be released from her betrothal to you."

"Trista!"

She winced at the sound of her father's booming voice, refusing to turn around and see what she knew would be his very angry face.

Braedon's lips curled upward. She supposed that was as much of a smile as he was capable of. Surely the stories of his grumbling personality were not true. No one could have as sour a disposition as he had been rumored to have.

He crossed his arms and regarded her. "So, your sister does not wish to marry me."

It was not a question, yet she answered anyway. "No, she does not."

Garick reached for her arm. "Trista, be silent!"

Braedon held up his hand. "Let her speak freely."

The hand gripping her arm loosened. For a moment she was afraid Garick was going to toss her onto the back of her horse and drag her out of the castle. She knew she was going to be in deep trouble with both her father and Garick when they left, but if this worked, her sister would be free to choose her own man.

"Trista, tell me. Did your sister send you here to inform me that she did not wish to marry me?"

If she told him the truth, he could still ask for Solara to hear the words from her directly. She hated lying, but it was the only way. "Yes."

"May I speak, Braedon?" her father interrupted.

"Yes."

"It is vital you marry a D'Naath princess. Our lands are

bound to be joined by custom and law, which can only be done with the marriage of a faerie princess and the king of Greenbriar. In joining, we have strength against the armies of wizards bound to take over our lands. I ask that you reconsider this foolishness spouted by my daughter and allow us to bring Solara to you."

"I am aware of the protocol, Fraynor. I am also aware that your daughter Solara has every right to beg release from our betrothal contract. And it appears that through Trista she has exercised that right." Braedon rubbed his thumb over his bottom lip. Trista wondered if he did that while thinking. His mouth was generous, and she had a fleeting image of tugging on his lip with her teeth.

Shocked at the direction of her mind, she inhaled sharply and forced her mind to stay clear of such thoughts.

"Are all your daughters betrothed, Fraynor?"

"Nay. Trista here was betrothed to the King of Boreo, who as I'm sure you know suffered an untimely death several years ago."

"Ah yes, I had heard that."

Trista frowned. Something was amiss here, something she hadn't considered when she'd concocted her plan.

"It is true I am to marry a princess of D'Naath. Since one princess has invoked the right of refusal, perhaps I will take this one."

Trista's heart dropped to her stomach when Braedon pointed at her.

"No!" she cried, then clamped her mouth shut and closed her eyes, mortified at her own outburst.

"Trista!" her father hissed in her ear. "Enough of your talk. I think you have spoken enough. It is my turn now."

Before she could turn and beseech her father not to take Braedon's suggestion seriously, he grasped her by the elbow and propelled her forward. She stumbled into the arms of the king.

He wrapped his arms around her to hold her upright, his body as solid as the trunk of the tall oaks in D'Naath's forest. Afraid to even look at his face, she gazed into his chest.

That is, until he tipped her chin upward with his finger. His blues eyes mesmerized her, made her forget things she should not forget, and made her all too aware of things she should not be thinking of.

"Aye, this one will do. After all, one bride is as good as another. Trista, princess of D'Naath, I claim you for my betrothed. We will marry in one month, allowing us time to get to know one another and for arrangements to be made."

She waited, holding her breath, for her father to deny the request.

Instead, he said, "You are most kind to accept my daughter Trista. I am honored to betroth her to you."

Despite the warmth of the morning, a cold dread filled her body.

This could not be happening.

In less than a day, she was left behind while her father and Garick returned to Winterland. Her father left her strict instructions to do nothing to upset Braedon, then reinforced his warning by telling her that because of what she had done, she had sealed her own fate. The kingdom of D'Naath depended on her marrying him. She could not refuse to marry Braedon as he had already asked for her and her father had accepted.

She was stuck, trapped in a web of her own weaving.

This had not gone at all the way she had planned.

Chapter Nine

ഇ

"Really, Noele, could you not have someone else perform these tasks?" Solara beseeched her sister, who rested on the mauve-colored chaise in her chambers. Elise and Mina sat with her, all of them gaping up at Solara.

Noele shook her head. "I trust no one to handle things but you. Is there some problem?"

Yes, but not one she could discuss with her sister. "No, no problem. It's just that..."

Just what? That she could not handle one more day of having Roarke underfoot? That he was like the devil's temptation, one that she could not resist?

Only this time the devil was doing the resisting. Not once in the past two days had he done anything to encourage her. Nor had they been alone. Roarke had made sure they either remained in public or that one of his guards accompanied them.

Really, she was much smaller than him. She could hardly pounce on and ravage him without his consent.

It was quite insulting, the more she thought about it.

"It's just that what?"

"It's Roarke."

She ignored the gawking stares of Elise and Mina and looked away from them, embarrassed that she had even brought up the subject.

"What is wrong with Roarke?"

"Nothing is wrong with him. Everything is wrong with him. I don't know. He treats me like a child, as if I couldn't make an intelligent decision if the very survival of the world depended upon it. Really, Noele, he is insufferable."

"Perhaps you care for him, and that is why it upsets you to be so close to him."

Solara whirled at Elise's statement, dumbfounded as to how to respond. Elise smiled innocently, her golden eyes sparkling with warmth.

Leave it to Elise to state the obvious. Even if it wasn't what she wanted to hear.

"I do not care for him. Perhaps you could take over my duties, Elise?"

"I need Elise to help me elsewhere," Noele interrupted. "Besides, neither she nor Mina are old enough or experienced enough to run a castle."

The twins were merely two years younger than her. And yet Noele was right. They hadn't yet been trained. She, at least, had received basic instructions on the daily goings on. And she had to admit that the past few days she had learned much under Roarke's tutelage.

What she wanted to learn from Roarke, he would not give her. Her training in the fine art of lovemaking would have to come from Braedon of Greenbriar, a thought which turned her stomach. She had never met the king, and the thought of anyone but Roarke touching her sent shudders of revulsion down her spine.

"Come, sit with us while I read to Noele," Mina said. "Really, Solara, you complain too much. Your time here is limited as it is. Surely you can bear up under whatever perceived torture Roarke bestows upon you."

And leave it to Mina to be insulting. "I am not tortured by him. I am merely perturbed at his attitude."

Mina fluttered her copper wings and stood, peering out the window at the guards training below. "Roarke is a male. They are annoying. One must learn to deal with that, I suppose."

Noele laughed, color rising to her cheeks. For the first

time in days Solara saw her sister smile. Perhaps the torture would not last much longer. Once Noele was past the sickly days of early pregnancy, she would want to take over her duties again, thereby freeing Solara from Roarke's scrutiny.

"And speaking of duties, shouldn't you be seeking out Roarke to see what he has planned for you today?" Noele asked, setting down the needlepoint she'd been working on.

She'd sooner conjure up some magic and turn him to stone. "Yes, I suppose I should."

Noele stood and reached for her hands, squeezing them gently. "You may think you handle your troubles alone, sister, but remember that we are linked. I feel what you feel, I know what you know. Destiny will find a way. Be patient."

Noele may think she knew everything, but Solara had kept her thoughts and actions where Roarke was concerned locked up inside herself.

After she left Noele's chambers, Solara thought about what her sister had said. Destiny, fate, it was all a ridiculous notion. Her life was set in stone and could not be changed. Even if it could, the elvin warrior she wanted would never suffer dishonor to follow his heart. He was too steeped in ritual, in how things had always been done, to even consider the notion that perhaps there was another way.

Well, he might not choose her, but by the stars she would make certain he knew exactly what he was giving up.

It was time to put her plan into action.

* * * * *

Roarke finished overseeing the repair and refitting of several of their battle weapons, confident that should a wizard attack occur, they would be prepared.

Next he had to find Solara.

A sigh of frustration escaped his lips as he searched the hall and courtyard for her. Clearly, she had been avoiding him since that night in the falconry.

Not that he blamed her. He had acted stupidly, nearly taking what was not his to take. No doubt she was confused by his abrupt change in attitude again.

If confusion reigned anywhere, it was deep within himself. He wanted Solara to the point of distraction, yet honor and duty forbade him from having her. The struggle he battled within himself was one he shared with her. And that was not fair. To her, or to himself. So he vowed to keep his distance, instruct her in her duties and go about his business instead of sniffing around her like a dog scenting a bitch in heat.

'Twas the most difficult thing he'd had to do. Every waking moment of his day was spent wanting her, aching for her. Walking around with throbbing cock and balls was more than a bit distracting, and yet such was his typical day.

Perhaps tonight in his chambers, he'd stroke his shaft and obtain release. Surely that would abate some of his pain. Already, thoughts of what he could do with Solara if she were his entered his mind. Yes, tonight, he would let his imagination run free, envision all the wicked things he wanted to do to the faerie princess, and release the tension threatening to explode.

But right now, he had to force back the hardening of his shaft and search out the elusive faerie. He found Isolde in the hall and she told him that she had last seen Solara heading toward the gardens.

The late afternoon sun beat down on his body, making him wish he could strip off his clothing. Instead, he wiped the sweat from his brow and weaved his way into the gardens.

She was not near the flowers, so he ventured further into the secluded recesses. Here, herbs and vegetables were grown, far away from where most of the castle inhabitants could be found. Tucked away here, they were safe from trampling along the well-used walkways. The seedlings were protected in the shrub-covered enclosure.

The sound of her voice emanated from the back row of plants. A lilting, faerie song escaped her lips, its notes melodic and haunting.

She had a beautiful voice, her song resonating with the poetry of unrequited love. Ignoring the stirrings of the music, he meant to call to her, then stopped dead when he spotted her.

On her knees in front of the herb seedlings, she bent over and reached outward for a weed. She had discarded her overdress. Her scarlet hair was unbound and willowing behind her in the slight breeze. Clad only in a flimsy shift, one strap spilled over her left shoulder, giving him a tantalizing glimpse of a creamy breast.

A rush of lust tightened his breeches as he hardened painfully. A haze of near madness filled his blood and he realized a desire to toss her onto her back and slake his arousal within her hot cunt.

He shuddered at the vision and fought for control. Wanting to catch her attention so he could state his business and make his exit, he was loath to do so for fear she would see his erection pressing tight against his breeches.

She must have heard him, because she looked up, capturing his gaze. She held the flowering weed in her hand, and lifted it to her nose, her eyes drifting partly closed as she inhaled its sweet fragrance. Then she had the audacity to smile at him! A wickedly sensual upward curving of her lips that made him think of hot nights and long, silken limbs wrapped around his back.

Solara sat back on her heels, as if waiting for him to speak. But he could not find his voice. She hadn't righted the strap of her shift, and in her sitting position the swell of her breast peeked above the top of the garment, her nipples straining against the silken fabric.

Could he die from such a painful erection?

Why didn't she speak? Clearly, he was unable to at the

moment. And he feared if he moved he might actually lose his control and ejaculate. His cock throbbed, the sensitive head rubbing against his breeches. Despite his attempts to the contrary, his mind conjured up images of Solara walking over to him, unlacing his breeches and taking his shaft in her heated mouth, then sucking him until he exploded down her throat.

And yet she continued to watch him, her green-eyed gaze focused on his face. She hadn't uttered a word, as if she expected him to make the first move.

"I...I..."

Brilliant. Now he sounded like a lovesick boy who'd just had his first glimpse of a tit and couldn't form a coherent word. The faerie exercised some kind of magic over him, making him unable to utter intelligent words.

"Is there something you're trying to say, Roarke?" She fixed him with an innocent batting of her eyelashes, but clearly the vixen had spellbound him somehow.

Had the mere sight of a half-naked breast caused a total loss of his ability to speak? "I...I have work for you."

"I see. And what is it that you would like me to do for you?"

Suck my cock. Ease this tormenting ache in my balls. Lie down upon the grass and spread your sweet thighs so that I might sheathe myself in you. "There are accounts we need to go over."

"Can it wait? I'm pruning the seedlings."

"Can't someone else do that?"

She huffed and crossed her arms. "You were the one who told me that I should see to the seedlings myself."

"Oh. I did, didn't I?" Now he sounded like an imbecile. "Very well, then. I shall go over the accounts myself."

He should turn and walk away. Their conversation was over. But she looked so delectable sitting there on the ground, her scarlet wings combating for wild color with the fierce green grass, he stood rooted to the spot.

Solara shrugged and turned her attention to the seedlings and dirt. "You do that. I still have much to do. First I must finish up here, see to the evening meal, check on Noele, and then I feel in need of a bath."

Truly he was about to turn away, but the mere mention of her bathing conjured up those blasted images in his head again. He coughed to clear the dry lump in his throat. "I see. Well, I will take my leave of you now."

"Very well."

She didn't even look up at him. He walked away, feeling for all the world like he'd just been spurned by a woman whose attentions he sought.

This entire charade grew more ridiculous by the second.

He had work to do. Yes, work would occupy his mind.

And he would *not* think about her bathing!

* * * * *

Solara smiled as she watched Roarke stomp away, supremely satisfied by his discomfort.

He'd left his emotions unguarded, and she felt every tantalizing moment of his frustration as he'd watched her. His desire matched her own, his need as fierce and uncontrollable as hers.

Touching his emotions was dangerous. She knew she should not pry into his mind, into his soul, and yet the opening he'd left surprised her. Like an irresistible temptation, she felt compelled to seek out the truth.

Yes, he'd hidden his desires quite well, at least internally. But the hard evidence of it could not be hidden from her. One look at his erection had her mouth going dry, her nipples beading against the thin material of her shift. Moisture gathered between her legs and she fought to keep her hand from straying there to massage the ever-growing ache.

An ache she would have to relieve herself, despite her

wish to take Roarke's hand, place it on the curls of her sex and beg him to release her from the torment.

With a sigh, she realized this game she played would have more than one victim. Yes, she would teach Roarke a lesson, but she would also painfully face the same realizations as he.

But she vowed to continue, a plan for tonight already forming in her mind. She had seen the way his eyes darkened when she mentioned bathing this eve, and she would make sure that he was in a position to watch her.

It may agonize them both in the process, but she'd show him that he had much to lose, the least of which was his damnable honor!

Chapter Ten

 හ

Roarke had endured quite enough from the faerie vixen today. First the episode in the garden, then at the evening meal. She had spent time with one of his guards, clearly amused at everything the man said.

His blood boiled, roaring in his ears every time her lilting laugh sailed across the hall. She tormented him on purpose, he knew it.

And the guard who dared openly flirt with a woman betrothed to a king would find himself demoted and shoveling horse shit tomorrow.

Tired of the ridiculous display, he had left immediately after eating, determined to spend the remainder of the night in his chambers. Once there, he was unable to relax, pacing back and forth within the confines of the small room until he drove himself mad.

If he wanted to, there were many women who would be more than happy to slake his lust. Not one to go long without female companionship, he had always been able to find a willing woman to spend a night with.

Or he used to. Since he met Solara, the thought of being with another woman did not appeal to him. He had not lain with a woman in months.

With a disgusted curse, he left the chambers, determined to forget all about Solara by visiting the pub and getting soundly drunk.

He sat with a few of the guards, listening to their ribald stories of the latest wench they had tumbled, refusing to think of a certain wench he could have had on multiple occasions and yet foolishly walked away.

Goblet after goblet of mead dulled the sharp ache inside him, yet his thoughts still focused on a scarlet-haired faerie with golden green eyes and creamy breasts that fit perfectly in the palm of his hand.

'Twas unfortunate the liquor did not quell the ache in his balls. Instead, it only served to fire up his libido, making him want to go in search of the woman who haunted his dreams.

And that he refused to do. He left the pub, determined to avoid the bathing area. Yet before he knew it, he found himself exactly where he swore he wouldn't go.

The room was quiet and dark. Perhaps Solara had already left.

He shouldn't be in there, he reminded himself as he entered the small chamber. Warm, humid air greeted his entrance, yet he heard no sounds. He should be happy she wasn't there. Running into Solara here could only lead to trouble. And with every day that passed, he found it more and more difficult to avoid his desires.

The bathing chamber was little more than a small room at the end of an enclosed wooden building. The walls had been put up to afford privacy, yet many times entire families bathed together.

This summer had been so intensely warm, most had taken to bathing in the outdoor chamber, but he did not figure Solara would want to be outside. Yet she wasn't in the enclosed room, so he took a chance and walked through the doorway leading to the open bath.

He blinked once, then twice, certain the vision before him was due to too much mead and not enough food at the evening meal. Solara sat in the round wooden tub, the full moon's rays shooting down and surrounding her in an ethereal, silvery light. She was alone, completely secluded by the tall, stone enclosure that kept the eyes of the villagers away, but allowed the bath to be open to the stars above. Her body appeared gossamer as she stood, her back turned to him.

Rivulets of water streamed down her back, her wings folded inside her, affording him a glimpse of her perfectly formed body.

Had he ever seen her completely nude? No, he'd been close to her, had touched her, yet he'd never had the opportunity to view her body from afar.

Roarke forgot to breathe. Slender shoulders led to a waist that dipped in nicely, reminding him of the feel of his hands spanning her slender form. Her full, lush hips and rounded buttocks were made for a man's hands. Shapely thighs led to very long legs. Legs he wanted wrapped tight around him.

His cock rose and strained against his breeches. How simple it would be to strip, slide into the tub with her and quench his lust within her hot pussy. He wanted it, she wanted it, yet his damned honor and allegiance to Garick prevented him from taking what was so willingly offered.

For the millionth time, he reminded himself that Solara belonged to another man. And that kind of vow he could not breach.

She bent over to retrieve a cloth from the water, and he sucked in a breath at the sight of her pussy so clearly outlined between her buttocks. An urge to bury his lips between her legs and lick the creamy juices from her cunt had his knees quaking. He let out a sigh borne of the frustration of the past week.

This was more than one man should have to bear.

Solara must have heard him, because she turned, holding the long cloth against her body. Her eyes widened as she caught sight of him leaning against the doorway.

Now would be a good time for him to leave. He'd gotten what he came for. He had seen her. And yet something compelled him to stay. Perhaps Solara's lack of protest, perhaps his own weakness where she was concerned.

Her lips curved into a sensual smile as she took the cloth and dipped it into the water. She raised it high and squeezed it over her breasts so that the water ran down over her belly and between her legs. Droplets fell from the thatch of hair on her sex.

Nipples that glowed a silvery rose in the moonlight hardened to sharp points. She rubbed the cloth over first one breast, then the other, caressing her body the way he wanted to. Her tongue snaked out and ran over her bottom lip before slipping back inside her mouth.

And still, her gaze remained fixed on him.

Like a seductive dance, she touched herself the way a lover would touch her, lightly tracing the swell of her breasts before teasing the upthrusting nipples with her fingers. She rolled the buds in between her thumb and forefinger, her mouth opening as a gasp of pleasure escaped.

Roarke opened his mouth too, licking his lips like a man thirsting for drink. The drink he was desperate for stood before him, drenched in bath water and weaving a torturous spell over him.

When her hands moved from her breasts to her sex, petting the curls at the juncture of her thighs, he let out a groan.

"Touch yourself, Roarke," she whispered, her voice husky and thick as the night surrounding them. She dipped her fingers alongside her inner thighs, hovering near her clit. "I will not ask you to come near me, nor to touch me, but I wish to see your release."

He should walk away, now, before he lost control completely. Yet her bold request compelled him, and he could not move his feet.

No, he would not touch her, would not have her in the way he wanted to, but he would obtain the release he so desperately needed. He moved his hand down and palmed his erection.

Solara arched a brow and fixed her gaze on his breeches. Knowing she watched made him harder, his balls tightening high against his body. He caressed his cock, loving the way she licked her lips, knowing by the flushing of her body that she was as aroused as he, and wishing to all the magical gods in the universe that their destinies were entwined.

But wishing would not make it so. This brief interlude with Solara would have to be enough to sustain him.

"Let me see your cock," she said, her voice shaky, her fingers disappearing into the nest of curls between her legs. He pushed away from the wall and approached her, wanting her to see, needing to see her, knowing he had to be closer as he watched her pleasure herself.

She let out a low whimper and spread her legs wider, affording him a glimpse of her distended clit. The lips of her pussy were swollen. Stopping at the edge of the tub, he squeezed his shaft, rewarded with her gasp. Mere inches separated them. Her panting breath sailed across his cheek. He had only to reach out and he would be able to caress her skin, take her mouth, brand her as his.

But he didn't.

Not taking his eyes off her questing fingers, he unlaced his breeches and took out his cock, slowly stroking it from base to tip. She watched the movements of his hand, her own keeping time to the rhythm he set.

When she dipped one slender finger into her swollen cunt, his breath caught and held. The sheer erotic pleasure of watching her touch herself nearly caused him to spill his seed. But he held back, wanting to let go at the exact moment she reached the pinnacle.

"Your cock is strong. Long, thick, pulsing with life. It was so big I could barely fit it into my mouth the first time. Do you remember that first time we touched, Roarke?"

How could he forget anything about this faerie? She was everything he had ever wanted in a mate. "Yes."

"Your tongue is soft and warm. I've never come as hard as I did when you licked me. Now, at night when I'm lying in my bed, I touch myself, visions of your tongue licking my pussy driving me to climax over and over again."

A groan escaped his lips before he could hold it back. His grip on his shaft tightened and he thrust it through his hand until just the tip appeared above his enclosed fist. A drop of pre-come spilled from the head, and he moved to swipe it off, reaching his hand out toward Solara.

As he knew she would, she leaned over and licked the fluid off his finger. His cock jerked and throbbed, his balls tight.

Foolish to get so close to her, yet Roarke could not stop himself. He inhaled and caught her sweet scent, a mixture of roses and the heady musk of aroused female.

"What do you dream of at night, Roarke? Do you think about me? In your mind, do you see me naked like this, touching myself like this?"

Yes, he dreamed this, and so much more. "I dream of taking you, making you mine, entering you and taking your virginity so that no other man can ever have you."

Her eyes blazed hot, her panting increased as she slipped two fingers inside her pussy. Clearly outlined in the well-lit night, her juices glistened on her fingers when she withdrew.

"Taste me, Roarke. Taste my need for you."

She held out her hand. Without hesitation, he took her fingers in his mouth, sucking the nectar from them. The taste of her desire flamed his senses. He licked at her fingers as if he had her pussy in his mouth, all the while thrusting his hips forward to propel his cock through his enclosed hand.

"Yes," she whispered. "Lick my fingers like you want to lick my cunt. Taste me, take me with you, Roarke. Make me come so hard I scream."

He wanted all that, and more. While arousing to the point of insanity, this play wasn't nearly enough to satisfy him. Yet with every passing second the head of his cock swelled, his balls trembled, and he knew it would not be long.

"Come for me, Solara. Imagine your fingers are my cock. Show me how you want me to fuck you."

He shifted back to allow himself a clear view of her driving fingers, this time setting his rhythm to hers. She tilted her head back and closed her eyes, with one hand teasing her clit and the other fucking herself faster and harder. Whimpers and soft mewls escaped her parted lips as she increased the tempo.

Finally, she opened her eyes and met his gaze, and he knew it was time. He let go a torrent of come that splashed across her belly at the same time she stiffened.. Her keening wail filled the night air as she trembled and held her fingers still inside her pussy.

Afterward, their gasps were the only sound that could be heard. Roarke slipped his softening cock into his breeches, then sat on the edge of the tub next to Solara. She removed her fingers and slipped into the water up to her breasts.

Roarke took the floating cloth and moistened it, wiping the fine sheen of sweat from Solara's face and neck. She smiled wistfully at him, and he knew her thoughts mirrored his own.

What they had together was amazing, miraculous, like nothing he'd ever experienced before.

They were fated, meant to be together, and yet were still held apart by his sense of duty and the requirement she honor her betrothal.

This time, he could not walk away from her. Nor could he tell her all that was in his heart. He had already revealed too much.

"I will be leaving soon," she murmured, staring off into the distance.

"Aye. In less than a week, Garick will return and then you will be escorted to Greenbriar."

"I should have gone before. I should not have run off."

She was right, and he knew that. Yet he could not tell her that he was glad she hadn't, that despite the fact he could never have her as he wanted to, he wouldn't trade the few days they'd had together for anything.

"All things happen for a reason, or so your sister tells me."

A soft smile graced her coral lips. "She tells me that, too."

So much was left unsaid between them, but Roarke could not utter the words he wanted to. Instead, he knew he had to continue to put distance between himself and Solara.

"Tomorrow I will ride off on patrol."

Her gaze met his. "I thought you were to stay within Winterland."

"I will be. I will patrol the outer boundaries. It is common for the guard to do so."

"Common for the guard to do so, but not common for you?"

"It is good for me to go with the men."

"How long will you be outside the gates?"

"Three days."

"I see. You do so to avoid me. It is unnecessary. You need only say the word and I would keep my distance."

He knew this would hurt her, yet also knew it was necessary. The more she hated him, the easier her new life would be.

"I do what I must. Not everything has to do with you, Solara."

Her eyes moistened and she turned away, refusing his offered hand as she climbed out of the tub and reached for her shift, tossing it over her head.

After she was dressed she stood in front of him, anger and pain blazing in her eyes. "Some day, Roarke, you will realize that your honor and your duty aren't enough to sustain you. When that day comes, remember what you could have had, because it will be long gone by then."

She turned and walked away, her long, scarlet hair streaming in wet strands down her back.

Roarke stayed seated, watching Solara's departure until she disappeared from sight. He stayed long after the door of the chamber closed with a resounding slam.

He didn't have to wait for someday to know what he could have had. Every moment of every day reminded him that he loved a woman who could never be his.

Chapter Eleven

೫

Roarke led the guards around the base of the castle, inspecting for any weaknesses in the structure. The gray stone wall was solid, and he already knew it.

The ride and guard duty were his way of escaping Solara.

After last night, and the episodes before, he knew he was weakening where she was concerned. That he could not allow. Better to keep his distance, put the wall of the castle between them, until she left.

With every day that passed he grew closer and closer to throwing away all that he believed in. He'd actually contemplated risking banishment or even death. His desire for Solara had become more important than his honor, his vows, his duty to his king.

Keeping his mind and body occupied with tasks such as assessing the castle's strengths and weaknesses was the best thing for both he and Solara.

After all, what would happen to her if he compromised her? She would be shamed, banished, would lose her right to become a queen.

Nay, he would not do that to her. His inner will was strong; he had always been able to rein in his baser impulses. He could do so now.

Today, he would concentrate on his duties.

Clearing his mind, his senses told him something was amiss. A sense of urgency had his muscles tensing, his hand reaching for the hilt of his sword.

Something was happening, and he needed to be on guard for any possibility. With their garrison half depleted due to

Garick's sojourn to Greenbriar, he and the remaining men would be the only defense should something occur.

He inhaled, scenting a foul, wicked wind shift. Gazing toward the thick forest, his spine tingled with a sense of foreboding that he could not quell.

That sense had been bombarding him for days, but he'd not recognized it because his mind, his magic, his entire being had been consumed with Solara.

"Keep your eyes open. We are not alone," he whispered to the guards behind him, who in turn passed the message along to the others. Gazing upward at the crenellations of the tower, he motioned to one of the guard. "Head back inside the castle and warn the rest to stand ready at the battlements for possible attack. Move all the people into the keep. Alert the interior guard to man their posts, weapons ready. Make sure no one wanders outside. Have the gate closed behind you as soon as you enter."

The guard nodded and turned his horse toward the drawbridge, quickly riding inside. The gate was pulled up soon after.

Turning his attention back to the trees, Roarke directed half the men to ride out to the edge of the forest with him. The other half were instructed to stay along the castle boundaries in case of attack from the cliffs.

The wizards had been quiet of late, which meant they must have been plotting an attack. Now that the elvin community had become wise to the wizards' magic, whisking away one of their own in the dead of night was no longer possible. If they were going to attack, they'd have to do it physically, head on, by storming the castle.

Knowing this, Winterland was well prepared for what may come. But Roarke would still feel more confident once Garick returned with the other half of the garrison. Having the castle weak in guards made them vulnerable, and that he did not like.

They patrolled the perimeter of the forest, Roarke keeping a keen eye out for anything that moved or made a sound.

The pounding hooves of horses turned his attention to a dust cloud in the distance ahead. He'd been prepared for an attack from the cliffs or the eastern forest, but not one from directly in front of them. Calling out to his guard, they raced to the front of the castle, forming a line with the rest of the garrison.

Orders were shouted to the battlements above them, and men could be seen within the crenellations, bows and arrows made ready.

Everything was in place. Roarke could only pray that everyone inside was as well. As the approaching horses drew near, he could tell they were badly outnumbered.

This attack could end up being a massacre. He feared nothing for his own life, but worried for the people of Winterland. If the garrison were killed, they would have minimal protection inside the walls.

Roarke called forth his magic, telepathically merging with Garick and urging him to hasten his return to Winterland.

Then, because this might be the last time he could do so, he searched and found Solara's thoughts.

Raising his sword in the air, he sent her a goodbye.

* * * * *

The needlepoint dropped from her lap and Solara let out a gasp. "Nay! Do not say goodbye to me!"

Noele looked up at her. "What is wrong?"

"It is Roarke. I must go."

She stood, desperate to run into her bedchambers and peer out the castle windows, but Noele's hand on her wrist stopped her. "Nay, you cannot go there."

"Roarke is in danger!" she cried. "I felt him. He reached out to me to tell me there was an attack."

Noele nodded, the expression on her worried face telling her that she knew already. "Aye, I felt it, too. But putting yourself in danger is not what he wants, Solara. Not right now. You need to bring your magic forth—we all do," she said, looking to Elise and Mina. "Roarke needs our help now."

Calm down. Force the panic aside. Noele is right. Roarke needs your magic right now, not your fear. She nodded, closed her eyes and took several deep breaths. It began to build within her, gaining strength, filling her with power. Once gathered, she sent every bit of magic she possessed to Roarke.

Their connection was instantaneous. So much that she traveled along with her magic. She merged with Roarke and found herself outside the gates. They were one now, as if she physically lived inside Roarke's body. She saw what he saw, felt what he felt, knew the same sense of hopelessness that he experienced. The battle was fierce and intensifying by the moment. They were outnumbered. They were going to die.

"No!"

She felt hands squeezing hers gently, felt the pull from her sisters to return to the castle, yet she would not leave him. If she could do nothing more, she wanted him to know that he was not alone.

If he needed eyes in the back of his head, she would be those. If he needed strength to wield the sword, she would give him all she had. If he was going to die, she wanted to be with him when it happened.

Wizards surrounded them, evil, twisted caricatures of beings, more skeletal than form. Yet their strength belied their appearance and they thrust with swords heavy enough to slice a man in two.

Roarke's incredible strength of will filled her as he thrust and stabbed a wizard, making a rapid turn to slice through another coming up behind him. She held on to his mind, not distracting him in any way, not letting him know of her worry, but giving him her hope and encouragement.

You will win, Roarke. Your will is stronger than theirs. They are but soulless demons with no heart. Stay strong and do not give up.

If her words penetrated, he did not acknowledge them. Nor did she push further other than to call forth the magic of the faerie, take what her sisters offered, and add to what the elvin people had already delivered to their warriors—their belief that the garrison outside the castle would win the battle they fought.

All around them the sounds of steel clashing with steel resounded in the air.

Arrows rained down as the guards inside sprayed the wizards from the tower battlements. Piercing screams resounded as the arrows penetrated the black hearts of the wizards. Each time one fell, Solara felt a joy she never knew she was capable of. Celebrating death was not in faerie nature, and yet these creatures had been a thorn in the side of the faerie and elvin people for too long now. Murderers, they not only killed and stole lands that did not belong to them, but also the very souls of the elvin and faerie people. The sooner they were all dead, the easier life would be for all of them.

The battle wore on for what seemed like hours. And yet, the longer it went on, the more it seemed as if the garrison had taken the upper hand. Solara sensed when the tide turned as she looked around and found a few of the Winterland guard on the ground, yet many more of the wizards.

They were winning, pushing the demons back toward the forest, advancing as the wizards retreated. She willed her strength even further into Roarke's arm as he hefted the sword above his head and decapitated an approaching wizard.

Soon, the attackers were turning and running into the forest. Leaving their horses behind, their thin, black-clad bodies slipped through the thick trees.

It was over. They were safe. No harm could come to—

A painful burning sensation in her side had Solara

doubled over, dropping to her knees on the ground. Her movements mimicked Roarke's. She saw him reach for his side, saw the blood covering his hand as he moved it in front of him, felt his disbelief as he turned and saw a lone wizard with a sword held over his head.

"No!" she screamed in her mind, knowing they were about to die. But one of Roarke's guards caught the wizard from behind, sinking his sword deeply into the creature's back. The wizard screamed an unholy sound, then dropped to the ground in a lifeless heap, the sword landing with a thud on the dirt.

Her heart lodged in her throat, she turned inward toward Roarke. She felt his strength ebb as he fought for consciousness. Dizziness assailed her and she had to squeeze her sisters' hands hard to keep from falling into the darkness.

She opened her eyes and stood, orienting herself to being back in the hall. "Roarke is injured. We must get out there now!"

Without waiting to see if they followed, she ran out, shouting for help along the way. She opened her wings and sailed through the doorway and out into the courtyard, hurrying toward the gate.

The archers who had fought from the battlements inside had already reached the drawbridge and were lowering it by the time she got there. They'd no more dropped it over the moat when she went flying across it, still mentally connected to Roarke, knowing exactly where he was.

Thankfully, he was not too far from the gates. Still on his knees where she had left him mentally, still staring at his blood-soaked hand. Several of his men surrounded him, but parted when she approached. She dropped to the ground as soon as she reached him, sweeping his hair away from his dirt-streaked face. His eyes were filled with pain—dull, nearly lifeless and half-closed. The normal sun-darkened color had left his face, replaced instead by a pallor that made her worry her bottom lip.

"You stayed with me," he whispered.

Solara fought back the tears that threatened to tear her apart. "Of course I did. I could not leave." She moved his hand, taking a thick cloth one of the villagers handed her and pressing it against the wound at his side. Blood flooded the cloth immediately and she replaced it with another, pressing hard despite his wince of pain.

"You shouldn't have seen all this. Blood, carnage, death…"

"Shhh," she whispered. "I did not fear what I saw. You needed all our magic to defeat the wizards. You and your men performed admirably."

Roarke offered a half-smile, then reached his blood-soaked hand out to caress her cheek. "Thank you, my faerie. You gave me strength."

Before she could respond, he crumpled against her and passed out.

Roarke's men picked him up and carried him inside, depositing him on the bed in his chambers.

She pushed the physician aside, wanting no one to care for him but herself. She was more knowledgeable about medicines and herbs than the man who doubled as the castle's barber.

Thankful for the medicinal lessons she had received from her mother, she immediately stripped off Roarke's battle gear and tunic, then his boots and breeches. Isolde and Noele stayed with her, helping to remove his clothes.

Neither said a word about Solara being in the room while Roarke was completely undressed. If they had, she would still have refused to leave. They did not know that she had seen all of him, and at this point it did not matter what anyone knew. The only thing that mattered was stopping the flow of blood before Roarke died.

Already it had soaked the cloths underneath him. If possible, he was even more pale now than he had been on the battlefield, his face as ghastly white as the wizards he had fought.

Solara cleaned the wound, a long gash at his side which bled much, but did not appear to be too deep.

"It does not appear that any of his organs were affected," she said, cleaning inside the cut. "But he has lost much blood."

Isolde sewed the wound closed, then Solara applied medicinal herbs, covering it with a clean cloth. At least the blood had stopped flowing now.

"All we can do is wait and see how he recovers. If the wizards poisoned their swords, infection could set in."

Noele voiced what Solara knew to be true. "We can only pray that such is not the case."

"He needs rest, Solara, as do you," Noele said, placing her hand on Solara's shoulder.

After securing the bandage with strips of cloth, she pulled the covers over Roarke, then turned to Noele. "I need no rest. I am not the one who fought a battle and was wounded."

"You expended much of your energy propelling yourself into his mind as you did. Giving up your strength, your magic, is exhausting."

Solara smiled at Noele. "You are the one who should be resting. Garick will have my head if something happens to you or the babe."

"There is nothing wrong with me. I am as fit as can be and have more than enough energy for both me and the baby."

Solara frowned. "I thought you were ill."

Noele's eyes widened. Isolde coughed and turned away.

"What I meant was, I'm feeling much better now. I believe the worst of the initial illness is over."

Something wasn't right, but Solara did not have time to ponder. "Either way, you need your rest, and Isolde is needed to watch over you. Go. See to the others who have been wounded. I will sit here with Roarke awhile, and then I promise to rest."

After Noele and Isolde left, she sat on the bed next to Roarke, constantly feeling his head to check for signs of fever. He slept soundly, not even moving once all through the night.

Solara did not sleep, nor did she leave his side. She could not, would not, until she was certain he would recover. Part of her wished he would awaken, yet the logical part of her knew that while he slept, he healed. As long as his skin remained cool to the touch, he would be fine.

If only she believed her own thoughts.

What would she do if Roarke didn't recover? No, she refused to think about that possibility. She stood and paced his bed, watching for any signs of flushed skin or delirium. Clutching her arms around her middle, she pondered all that had happened between them.

There was no doubt that, physically, she wanted him. He called to her in ways she was convinced no other man would be able to. But there was more than that. His honor, his sense of duty and loyalty, the way he cared for her. All of those things made him the man she...

Loved.

The word she had tried so hard not to think about stood front and center in her mind. And because she loved him she had been blinded to his need to see to his duty. She had asked him to sacrifice his honor for her. She sat on the bed and held his hand.

"Oh Roarke," she whispered, "What have I done? I have given my heart to you, my very soul, and look at the havoc it has created. How can I say I love you and at the same time put you through such torment?"

Isolde brought her food late in the evening, but she felt no hunger.

How could she feel anything but guilt? If it were not for her and her insistence on tormenting Roarke, he would not have felt it necessary to leave the castle grounds and patrol.

She had literally driven him from the safety of Winterland in an effort to flee from her and her foolish seduction.

The wizards had obviously been waiting for an opportunity to attack, and because of her the garrison had been left vulnerable. They had lost six men today, not a very large amount considering the number of wizards that had attacked, yet six men lost their lives who shouldn't have.

All because of her childish notions of love and desire.

If she had left Roarke alone and stayed committed to her fate to marry Braedon, he wouldn't be near death right now.

Nay, she would not leave his side until she atoned for the sins she had committed.

She would not leave until Roarke was awake, for she had much to tell him.

Chapter Twelve

ɛ͡ɔ

Roarke's eyes would not open. He fought, willing them to open, yet his struggle was for naught.

'Twas as if something pressed down on his entire body, a heavy weight that prevented him from moving his limbs.

He could still see, although the visions were distorted.

Sweeping colors of the sky. A meadow, a rainbow of sensual delights surrounding him, yet he could not lift his arm and touch that one elusive thing he wanted more than anything.

Solara.

She stood in the middle of a field of green, dressed all in white. Riotous colors spread out like a carpet of flowers at her feet. Yellows, purples, blues, like a sudden burst of springtime. Solara's feet were bare, her wings spread wide, hair unbound and flowing to her waist. Her golden green eyes gazed directly at him, dark lashes fluttering against her cheek as she blinked.

Her smile was warm and welcoming.

"Come to me, Roarke. I need you."

He started to move, but could not, the endless weight holding him back. Opening his mouth to speak, he found no sound forthcoming, despite the shouting of his voice in his own mind.

Solara frowned. "Roarke, why do you tease me so? Can you not see how much I want you? How much I need you? Please, come to me now." She spread her arms, beckoning him to her.

And still, the heaviness upon him held him at bay. He struggled mightily, but found he had no strength left in his body. So he touched her the only way he could — with his mind.

"I cannot come to you Solara. Something binds me."

"I need you Roarke. Please, before it is too late for us."

Too late? How could it ever be too late? From the moment he first saw her, he knew in his heart that she was his fate, that she was meant to be his. And yet an invisible wall kept them apart, preventing him from reaching out to her.

Frustration mounted, building with every passing moment. She was so close, and yet 'twas as if she stood miles away.

Now her eyes filled with moisture, tears streaking her face. Her bottom lip trembled as she pleaded with him. "Roarke, I do not have much time. You must come to me now, or we will never be."

Hopelessness filled every part of his being as he fought against the invisible bonds. "I cannot, Solara. Something keeps me from you."

She began to fade right in front of his eyes. The colors surrounding her muted, becoming hazy, brown, lifeless. Her white sheath turned black, her hair disappeared, her skin sinking into itself.

"It is too late for us Roarke. You should have come to me sooner. I must go."

"No! Wait!" He fought until his skin burned from the struggle. But as he did so, a part of him knew his efforts were for naught. She was nearly gone, no more than a shimmering cloud.

"Too late for us, my love. It is too late. You waited too long." Even her voice had lost its melodic beauty, her tone flat, sadness evident in every word.

He was a fool! He should have tried harder, done something, anything to break the bonds so he could reach her.

And now she would never be his.

Solara was gone.

* * * * *

Solara wiped the cool cloth over Roarke's feverish brow, her heart wrenching at the sound of his incoherent mumblings.

The fever had started early this morning. She had left him for only a moment to bathe and eat, and when she had returned, Isolde had told her that Roarke had worsened.

Not many survived the fever of the wizards. A poison in the blood, it spread quickly.

There was no known cure. No herbs, no medicines, nothing would help. Nothing but prayer and hope that Roarke was strong enough to withstand the effects of the toxin trying to destroy him.

For hours he had battled, his body shaking uncontrollably, nearly unintelligible words spilling from his lips. She had held him down when the convulsions threatened to send him catapulting off the bed, finally having to resort to magic to hold him still so he would not injure himself.

She kept his skin moist and cool with frequent bathing. Noele and Isolde stopped in frequently, but they knew as well as Solara did that there was nothing that could be done for him. He would either live or die, and they could not control what would happen.

"Witch," he mumbled. "You left me, faerie. You left me when I needed you. Do not go. Do not leave me."

His words made no sense. Witch? Faerie? She did not know of whom he spoke.

Until he said her name. "Solara, I cannot come to you. I have tried, but it holds me back."

She forgot to breathe as the anguishing pain in his words squeezed her heart. "Roarke, I am here."

He shook his head vehemently. "You are gone. I have lost you. I cannot come to you. I cannot."

Bathing his fevered face and neck, she whispered against his ear. "Roarke, do not fight it so. You need to rest, you need your strength."

"I have no strength. I have nothing. I could have...I almost took that which was not mine to have. My honor...'tis nothing without your love. But I have duty. Must not..."

His words faded again. Yet Solara knew what pained him.

It was her. He struggled within himself, wanting her and knowing he could not have her.

She caused his pain, both physically and emotionally. Her selfishness in wanting something she could not have, had brought Roarke to this state.

And now he might die. None of this should have happened, would have happened, if she had done what she was destined to do.

"Roarke, listen to me." She grabbed his shoulders, closed her eyes and entered his world. She took the risk to herself, knowing that giving him a vital part of her magic might well save his life while destroying hers.

Yet she had to do it.

'Twas like entering the gates of hell. Fire greeted her, the licking flames attempting to hold her back. Undaunted, she walked through the inferno. Roarke stood there, naked and glorious like some kind of god. He looked around as if he were lost. Then he saw her, and smiled.

"I have been looking for you, faerie," he said, his voice hot, husky with desire. His cock sprang to life, engorging, lengthening.

"You have found me, Roarke."

"Come to me."

She stepped forward, mindless of the blaze burning around them, unable to feel any other heat except the flame of his need for her.

He did not know he existed in a dream state, and she would not tell him. When he woke, when he was healed, he would know what had happened. But now, she would let him believe that they were together, that this was reality.

His naked skin scalded her when he pulled her against him. "I have waited a lifetime to touch you, to have you in my arms."

Her breath was lost as her heart pounded against her breast. "As have I. I am yours now, Roarke. I have always been yours. I always will be. No other will have my heart."

She knew that later he would recall what was said and done here in this magical state, yet she wanted him to know. After she was gone, she wanted him to remember that she had given him her heart.

"And remember, when you are far away, that my heart will be with you. I should not tell you this, but I cannot help myself. You are mine, Solara of D'Naath. You have been from the moment I greeted you."

She squeezed her eyes shut in the hopes that he wouldn't see her tears. Yet his thumb brushed her cheek, swiping away the one drop that escaped. When she opened them, she saw him smiling down at her.

"I might not live through this. I need you, Solara."

He knew where he was. She should have realized his force of will would push past the fantasy in his mind and accept that they could only touch within the boundaries of this dream.

Refusing to think beyond this moment, beyond this time when he still had the strength left to give her his thoughts, she touched her finger to his lips. "We will not speak of what may be, only what is now."

"Then let me love you now. The way I have wanted to for so long."

His mouth met hers and he gathered her close, wrapping his arms around her waist. His tongue grazed the seam of her lips and slipped inside, finding hers and gently stroking until she whimpered her need for him.

What started out a gentle kiss intensified. Roarke's fingers dug into her hips as if he were marking her as his own. His mouth seared her lips, her throat, blazing a hot trail over her shoulder.

There was not air enough to fill her lungs. His passion overwhelmed her, and yet matched her fervent desire for him. He moved his hands over her waist, her ribs, cupping her breasts and grazing her nipples with his thumbs.

"Yes, touch me, Roarke. I need your hands, your mouth on me. Everywhere."

Desperation tinged her every word. She did not know if she had the magic to heal him, but would give up everything to ensure his safe return to health. In merging with him here, she would forever lose some of her power, and yet she willingly gave it up to him.

"I need to be inside you, my faerie. We've waited too long already."

"Aye. Hurry."

He laid her on the soft ground of the misty darkness, warmth enveloping her as he pulled her legs apart and settled between them. Tension knotted the muscles of his arms and she squeezed them, reveling in the feel of his strength.

A sense of urgency surged within her. She fed off Roarke's hunger, knowing they did not need slow caresses or gentle play. Her pussy was moist, opening and inviting him to enter. She was ready now.

She reached for his shaft, its life pulse surging against her hand. He let loose a groan as she stroked him, pulling him towards her cunt, lifting her hips in a wordless sign of her desire.

No, this was not real, and yet it would feel the same as if they were actually making love. This would be her only chance to bring him inside her, to become one with him, and she wanted the memory to hold onto almost as much as she wanted to heal him.

She guided him to her entrance and removed her hand. Roarke took over, leaning over her, moving forward, the tip of his shaft brushing her slit. Her juices poured from her, the small quakes inside her only the beginning of what she knew would be a magical journey.

"Now, Roarke, please."

"Aye, faerie. Now." With one quick thrust he embedded himself within her, so deeply she felt him in her womb. She cried out and wrapped her legs around him, holding him close. Her body surrounded him, squeezing his rigid length.

Solara focused on his face and opened herself up, letting her magic and her love pour into him.

He shuddered over her, rocking back and forth. With every thrust she tightened more around him until he let loose a groan.

She felt his strength begin to grow as he drove into her over and over, taking what she willingly offered. Afterwards she would be weakened, but now she drew on his growing power, giving back what he gave.

Faster and harder he thrust within her until she shrieked her pleasure. A part of her mind begged for reality, but this would be all she would have. She pulled Roarke closer, wanting to feel every inch of his body against her sweat-soaked skin. She caressed his arms, his shoulders, drawing his head down to her mouth to capture his lips in a kiss that bound them forever.

"Come for me, faerie," he said through clenched teeth. "Come on me. I want to feel your nectar pour over my cock."

His control was admirable, yet she did not require it. She had held on only long enough to restore him, but now she could not hold back the torrent. Gripping his back, raking her nails along his skin, she cried out as the pinnacle reached her, lifting her hips so he could drive hard into her one last time before letting out a deep cry and pouring his seed inside her

They stayed within each other's arms for as long as t magic allowed. When she felt the connection breaking, s. gazed deeply into his eyes, memorizing every line, ever feature, knowing she would never be this close to him again.

The words she wanted to say would have to stay withir her. She would not pain him more than she already had. With a feather light touch of her lips against his, she broke the connection, finding herself lying next to him on the bed.

She felt his head, pleased to find his temperature had broken and his skin was moist and cool.

The magic had worked. Exhaustion overcame her, and she went in search of Isolde, asking her to sit with Roarke. She entered her chambers and climbed into bed, so weak she could barely pull the coverlet over herself.

Part of her magic was now forever inside the man she loved. Perhaps it wasn't what she had most wanted to give him, and yet it would have to do. He would recover now, and she took some satisfaction in knowing that she had helped.

For the first time in days, sleep overtook her.

Chapter Thirteen

လ

Roarke healed much faster than even he anticipated.

Much of that, he knew, was because of Solara. He felt the magic of her that she had left within him while he was feverish, remembered every moment that she shared herself with him.

He survived the attack because of her unselfish giving of her magic to him. That had cost her dearly, something she would never be able to retrieve. And yet he would not reveal to others what she had given away.

He only wished he could give something back to her.

Since he awoke the day before, he had not seen her. Surprisingly, the wound at his side was nearly healed, and he did not require any time to rest. 'Twas if he had gone to sleep whole and had awoken in the same state.

Resuming his duties immediately, he had stayed busy, not once seeking out Solara., knowing she needed time to rest. And yet he missed her smile, missed seeing her at meals, missed working with her. Stars, he even missed arguing with her!

For two days he had allowed her time to recover. Now, he wanted to find her, to thank her for what she had done.

Soon, Garick and Trista would return from Greenbriar, and Solara would be leaving. He had to see her one last time before she left, had to tell her what her gift meant to him.

Dawn cast a magnificent glow over the day. Rolling clouds tinged with pink strolled slowly over the castle. Roarke dressed, hurrying so that he could find Solara.

A knock came just as he finished fastening his tunic. He

opened the door, surprised to find Solara standing there.

Each time he gazed upon her his heart pounded. Her hair was pulled back from her face, her eyes widening as she looked at him.

"You look well, Roarke," she whispered.

He motioned her inside and shut the door. "Thank you. I feel quite fine."

"I am glad." She wrung her hands together, her back turned to him.

He felt awkward, did not know what to say. But he had to begin somewhere, had to tell her what her gift meant to him. "I was going to find you this morning, to tell you—"

Before he could finish she turned around. "I will not see you again before I leave."

Roarke frowned. "What do you mean?"

"What happened to you out there...everything that happened, was my fault."

"No, Solara, 'twas not your—"

"Let me finish, please. Yes, 'twas my fault entirely. I behaved foolishly. I should have left for Greenbriar when it was my time. Instead, I thought...well, it does not matter now what I thought. The truth is I have been playing a terrible game with your affections. One that was not mine to play. I drove you through the castle gates and put you and the other men in harm's way."

She was wrong. He did nothing that he did not want to do. He had to tell her. "Solara."

But she held up her hand. "Please, Roarke. I came to tell you that I will no longer come to you, will no longer tease and torment you with something we both want but know we cannot have. I have much to do to prepare for my departure in a few days, and I will stay out of your way. You need not worry that I will say or do anything to embarrass you or cause you to dishonor yourself. I will do my duty to my people. I will marry Braedon of Greenbriar."

The words he wanted to say to her did not come. She was right. They had to stay apart He knew it, but it left a bitter taste in his mouth. "Thank you for saving my life."

"'Twas the least I could do. Now, if you will excuse me, I have duties to attend to."

She turned away and hurried out the door before he could say anything more.

Truly, what would he have said? Despite his assurances to her that he had done what he wanted to do, he knew that they had both been at fault. It was time he realized it, for she certainly had. And yet he had wanted to pull her into his arms and tell her that she did nothing wrong, that the fault had been his.

This is what he had wanted all along. Distance between him and Solara, her promise that she would do nothing to compromise the vows they both held dear.

And yet, now that she had affirmed what he himself believed in, his heart clenched painfully in his chest. He would no longer see her, no longer touch her.

Damn the stars! This was not what he wanted at all!

Noele watched Roarke and Solara avoid each other, and wondered what had happened to cause the rift between them.

They belonged together. She knew it as surely as she knew her own destiny lay with Garick. 'Twas simply good fortune that had led her to love with her own husband.

But for Solara and Roarke, such was not the case. Yet the visions persisted, still too murky to make out, more like a feeling, a certainty that Solara's fate was not tied with Braedon of Greenbriar, but rather with Roarke.

It would seem the two of them could not come to that same realization on their own. Perhaps they needed a little more pushing in the right direction.

As Roarke went about his duties in one part of the castle, Solara went in another. Deciding to put an end to their separation, she began with Roarke, following him to Garick's office.

"I would speak with you alone," she said, closing the door behind her.

She should not interfere, yet something told her that Roarke and Solara would not find their happiness without her help. She sat down with him on a long sofa and took his hands in hers. She smiled as she felt part of Solara's magic within him. She knew her sister had brought Roarke back from near-death, which only convinced her even more that her sister and this elvin warrior shared the same fate.

"Is there something wrong, my queen?"

"Nay. I wish to speak with you about Solara."

His brows knit together. "What of her?"

"Tell me how you feel about her."

Roarke drew his hands from hers and stood, his eyes widening. "I feel nothing for her!"

Noele laughed. "You forget we are linked together. I know exactly how you feel, despite your attempts to hide your emotions. You love my sister."

"I do not."

"You do. Admit it, if not to her, then at least to me. 'Tis no crime to admit you love someone, Roarke."

His shoulders slumped and he sat back down, studying her face. Finally, with a long sigh, he nodded. "Aye, I love her."

Warmth filled her at the thought of the happiness her sister could have with Roarke. "What are you going to do about it?"

He turned his head and looked at her as if she had gone daft. "Do about it? Nothing. What can I do? She belongs to another."

"Do not be so certain of that fact. Sometimes our destiny is clouded and may not actually lead down the prepared path."

"She is betrothed to a king. She is a princess of D'Naath. You know the customs."

"Aye, I know. I also know those customs can be circumvented."

His eyes widened. "You would have me dishonor my king, your husband?"

His duty to Garick was admirable, but Noele refused to allow that to alter the course of his destiny. "Of course not. It is not a dishonor to love someone, Roarke."

"'Twould be for me. To take what is not mine is an unforgivable offense."

"But what if she *is* yours? What if you two are fated? Would you walk away from that?"

"If I were a king and she was betrothed to me, I would never let her go. But I am no king and she is not mine."

"Tell me, Roarke. What does your future hold?"

"I know nothing of the future. My powers do not include the foretelling of what is yet to be, and neither do yours."

Actually, her powers told her some of the future. The rest was obvious. "True enough. But envision your future. What do you see?"

He paused and looked straight ahead, as if the colorful tapestry on the wall would reveal his fate. "I see myself doing what I do now. Protecting Winterland, and serving you and Garick."

"Beyond that. To a wife, children, a family of your own. What do you see?"

"I see nothing like that."

"What if you could have those things? Who would you see then?"

"Solara."

He had said it so easily. "Then what stops you? Solara does not wish to marry Braedon. Petition Garick for the right to ask for her."

"I will not. 'Tis important to all our kingdoms for Braedon to marry a D'Naath princess."

"Solara is not the one for him."

"You know this to be a fact?"

"I feel it."

Roarke stood and walked to the window. "What you feel has no bearing on what is. Feelings are nothing more than foolish wishes."

Men were so stubborn sometimes. Roarke reminded her of Garick. Once his mind was set on something, 'twas difficult to change it. She stood and walked to him, stopping behind him to lay her hand upon his shoulder. "Roarke, love is never foolish. If you want Solara, then tell her. Fate will find a way."

"'Tis too late. She will leave soon."

She turned him around to face her. In so many ways, she loved Roarke. Not with the same all-consuming passion she felt for Garick, but a fondness that came from being linked to his soul. Caressing his cheek, she smiled. "No, 'tis not too late. Listen to your heart for once instead of your head. 'Tis your heart that will lead you to your fate."

* * * * *

Roarke thought of nothing else but his conversation with Noele. Had he been wrong in allowing custom to rule his actions? Was he possibly walking away from his own destiny by letting Solara go?

What would happen if he claimed her for his own?

No. They were not meant to be together. Even Solara admitted that her fate was with Braedon. He would not interfere.

Scrubbing his hand over the back of his neck, Roarke

231

tood and paced his chambers, tired of battling the demons that cursed him. The sun had long ago set on what had been a terminally long day. The castle was quiet, and he had been the last one about, finally giving in and entering his lonely bedchamber.

All day he had watched and waited for Solara, hoping to catch a glimpse of her, and yet she had remained true to her word and had not crossed his path. He ached to see the bright smile on her full lips, the way her eyes twinkled like the sun flitting through the leaves of the trees, the sexy way she moved that inflamed his desire.

And with those came visions of her lying in the arms of another man. An image that filled him with jealousy.

Hell's damnation. He *did* love her, and he did not want another man to touch her.

Which begged the question of how far was he willing to go to see that no other man ever had her? Was he willing to give up his honor, his position? Was he willing to change not only his life, but hers?

Roarke had never dishonored himself or a woman before. From the moment he and Garick had been bonded as children, he knew he would always remain faithful to his duty. Could he turn his back on everything he believed in for the chance to love the woman who haunted his every moment?

Noele's words still pounded away at the logic in his head. Should he, for the first time in his life, follow the dictates of his heart?

By all that was magic, he did not know what to do!

* * * * *

Solara shifted in the middle of the bed, then sat up and stared at the only light, that of the moon filtering in through the window. Sleep would not come tonight, she knew it. She drew her knees to her chest and wrapped her arms around her legs.

The night creatures called out through the partially open window, singing a wailing lament that echoed the stirrings in her heart.

She missed Roarke. It had only been a day, and she longed to see his face, gaze upon his magnificent body. Just to be in the same room with him filled her with peace and contentment. Apart, she was only half of a whole.

A strong urge to go to him made her ache all over. But she promised she would not. No matter how difficult it was, she would see it through.

The knob on her door startled her as it rattled. Raw fear crept into her throat, her heart slamming against her ribs. Wizards had not entered the castle since Noele had been abducted. Surely elvin and faerie magic was still able to keep them at bay.

But the door opened with a slight squeak. Thoughts of screaming out occurred to her, but she remained silent, hoping it was only Isolde or one of her sisters. The light streamed in from the window, shining upon her. She had never felt so exposed, so vulnerable. Whoever stood at the doorway could see her clearly, yet they were cast in darkness.

"You take the very breath from me, faerie."

"Roarke," she whispered. Instead of calming, her blood pounded, her body trembling at the thought of what reason he would have to be standing in her bedchamber.

The door shut, followed by the sound of the bolt. He had locked them in.

He moved across the room and stopped next to her bed. The moonlight filtered over him. He still wore his breeches, though they were partially unlaced. His shirt lay open, his broad chest and firm abdomen beautiful in the silver light. She clutched the coverlet in her hands to keep from reaching out for him.

Curiosity mixed with an elemental excitement. She was almost afraid to ask him, certain he came here for some other reason than the one she wished. Yet she had to know. One way or the other, she had to know. "Why are you here?"

He waited before answering, as if he struggled with his response. But finally he said, "I can no longer stay away."

It took a moment for his words to make sense. "But I thought—"

"Does not matter what you thought, or what I thought. We are fated, my faerie princess. Or damned. I'm not sure which. All I am certain of is if I don't take you into my arms and make love to you tonight, I will regret it until I die."

Her heart soared with love, knowing what it cost him to be here with her. What would happen after, she did not know. Whatever happened, she would accept the consequences willingly.

She let the sheet fall, baring her body to the waist. Pulling the coverlet aside, she moved over, leaving room for him in her bed.

"Come to me, Roarke. Make me yours."

Chapter Fourteen

෨

Roarke paused, waiting for the guilt to wash over him, the sense of hesitancy that had held him back before.

This time, it didn't come. Only a drive to finish what they had started before. Being here with Solara felt right, as if he'd finally found light in a darkened cavern.

She was his freedom, and his heart soared.

Her nipples were already puckered, thrusting outward like the peaks at the top of a mountain, waiting for his hands, his mouth, to claim them.

"This time, there is no dream, there will be no stopping before we consummate. Tell me now that you do not want this, and I will leave."

Without hesitation, she answered. "You know what I want, Roarke. What I've wanted since the first day we met. I want you to make love to me, in every way possible. I am yours for as long as we can be together."

Relief washed over him, as he had feared he was already too late. He slipped off his breeches and shirt, then climbed into the bed, gathering her against him. Her skin was silken, her legs long, her breasts small and perfectly shaped. She was his magic, his fantasy, and the only woman he would ever give his heart to.

"I want to touch you everywhere tonight, kiss you, take you in every way you can imagine, and even some you can't. Are you ready for this, my faerie?"

Her encouraging smile was all he needed to see. He dragged her on top of him, loving the freedom to stroke her back, her buttocks. Her hair spilled over his chest, the scent of her like wild summer roses.

"You are the most beautiful woman I have ever known."

She traced his bottom lip with the tip of her finger. "And you are the most beautiful man my eyes have ever beheld." She nipped at his lip with her teeth, tugging lightly. His cock surged against her pussy, her juices seeping over his balls.

"You are wet. Have you been thinking of me?"

"Aye. I think often of your heavy cock, how hot it feels in my hand, how it pulses in my mouth. Sadly, I have yet to feel it inside me."

Rolling her over onto her back, he grinned down at her. "Oh you will feel me inside you this night, my princess. But not yet."

He captured her mouth and she met his fervor with an equality that never ceased to amaze him. He had been with many women, and yet never one as passionate as Solara. Her breasts brushed his chest, her hardened nipples teasing him. He shifted and took one globe in his mouth, laving the crest with his tongue. She whimpered and moved her hips against him. The scent of her arousal filled his nostrils, and he slipped down between her legs, nestling his nose against her soft, red fur.

"Roarke." She breathed his name in a throaty whisper, winding her hands into his hair to direct him. He let out a low chuckle and took a long swipe of her swollen nether lips. Her nectar was sweet, musky, the scent of her never failing to make his cock pulse with need.

He lapped her juices, alternating tugging on her clit with his mouth and thrusting his tongue deep inside her slit. She bucked off the bed, tearing at his hair and shaking her head from side to side.

"Roarke, please, now," she begged.

He ignored her pleas, swirling his tongue over her sex, taking in the juices pouring from her. When he inserted his finger inside her and captured her clit between his lips, she tensed, cried out and flooded his hand with her climax.

Barely giving her time to catch her breath, he slipped two fingers inside her soaked pussy, gently at first, then harder as she recovered. He watched her face, the way she wrinkled her nose and closed her eyes when she was in the throes of ecstasy. He took her close to the edge again until she was crying out, begging him to fuck her.

He wanted to take her over the cliff so many times tonight that by morning she wouldn't be able to move. He wanted to delay the moment when he plunged inside her, not because he felt any semblance of guilt, but because he wanted to arouse her past the point of reason.

Trouble was, he could not wait. It had been too long already.

"Aye, my princess. Now I will give you what we have both wanted for so long." He rose over her, nudging her legs further apart with his knee and settling against her.

This was the moment, the point at which he could not return things to the way they were. Solara watched him, waiting, not saying a word, as if she knew how much he struggled with his decision.

Only this time there was no hesitation. He knew exactly what he wanted, what he had to have, and nothing would change his mind.

He eased the head of his shaft between her slit, watching the flecks in her green eyes turn a molten gold. He poised, waiting, his cock pulsing as her cunt grabbed onto it, drawing it deeper.

Solara's lips curled into a sensual smile. He leaned down, captured her mouth and plunged inside her, drinking in her gasp. Her legs wrapped around his waist and held tight against his back as her body fit itself around him.

Always and forever, she would be his.

She was so tight, hot, wet, that he feared completion before he even had a chance to move within her. Why had he waited so long for this? Her body was made for his, accommodating his length and width perfectly.

Roarke's eyes drifted shut and he tilted his head back, letting out a sigh. "Ah, yes, this is how I knew it would be."

He moved against her, gently at first, pulling out and sliding deeply inside once again. She began to move with him, lifting her hips and meeting his thrusts until they developed a rhythm, a sweet dance with the only partner he would ever need.

Small sounds escaped Solara's throat. Whimpers, whispered cries of delight, the love song of pleasure that took him ever higher on the climb to fulfillment.

He was lost inside her, this magical faerie that he loved with all his heart. Pleasuring her became as paramount, as necessary as his next breath.

He slipped his hands underneath her, cradling her buttocks and drawing her closer. When he moved, he brushed her sensitive clit, and she moaned into his shoulder, nipping lightly with her teeth, then harder as he thrust deeper.

"Roarke, I cannot...I'm going to..."

Her words trailed off into unintelligible comments. But he knew. She did not have to speak the words for him to know what was happening. Her cunt tightened around him, squeezing, coaxing the seed from his knotted balls. She let out a keening wail as her climax washed over her. He took her mouth, driving his tongue inside in the same way he drove his cock into her pussy. With a groan against her lips, he poured his release into her.

They lay there for awhile afterward, panting, stroking each other's skin, murmuring soft words to each other.

"I do not know what to say," she whispered against his ear.

He leaned back and smiled at her. Her hair was disheveled, a wild array of scarlet spread over the pillow. Her cheeks were flushed, her lips swollen from his deep kisses.

Truly, he had never seen anything more erotic in his life.

"There is nothing you need to say, faerie."

"I want to thank you, Roarke. I know that you struggled with this, that you —"

His finger against her lips silenced her. "Nay, do not speak the words. Tonight is only about the two of us. Nothing else exists. And we are not nearly finished yet."

She arched a brow. "Is that so?"

"Aye. I told you that this night I would have you every way imaginable."

Trailing a fingertip around his shoulder, she said, "I can imagine many ways, my elvin warrior."

"Would you care to tell me about them?"

She shook her head and grinned. "Oh no. I am but an inexperienced maid. I will rely upon you to teach me all that there is to know."

He kneeled on the bed and drew her up against him, her breasts flattening against his chest as he crushed her tightly to him. "Then you will not rest tonight, my faerie, as I have much to teach you."

"I do not require any sleep," she said, drawing his face to hers and licking his lips.

He pressed his mouth to hers, reveling in her heated passion. Again his cock stirred, ready to take her. Would he ever tire of this magical faerie? Would he ever survive losing her?

No. That he refused to think about. He turned her away from him and pushed her down until she was on her hands and knees on the bed, then backed away, taking his cock in his hand and stroking it as he admired her backside. Her slit was open to his view, juices seeping from her, and he caressed the swollen tender flesh, drawing some of her nectar onto his fingers, then spreading it between the twin globes of her buttocks.

She gasped, then leaned forward onto her elbows. His breath caught at the sight of her puckered rosette.

"Do you know what I want, Solara?"

Her answer was a panting breath of excitement. "Aye."

He caressed the hole with his moistened fingers, his other hand reaching underneath her to stroke her silken flesh. She shuddered.

"Is this something you do not wish me to do?"

"I want you to possess all of me, Roarke."

Her willingness to accept him astounded him.

"Then relax. I will not hurt you." He caressed the entrance to her ass, then slipped one finger partly inside, waiting for her body to accustom itself to the invasion. All the while he stroked her clit and petted her pussy until she was writhing against his hand.

Her movements drove him to the brink. If he did not take her soon he would explode. He positioned himself behind her, taking his cock in hand and guiding it to her slit. He teased her pussy, rubbing his cockhead back and forth until she squirmed and cried out. Then he dipped his shaft inside her cunt. She tightened around him immediately, pouring more of her nectar over his cock and balls.

Immediately he withdrew and positioned his shaft at her puckered entrance, slowly forcing it past the tight barrier.

"Tell me to stop at any time and I will."

"Just fuck me Roarke, please."

He laughed, his wicked faerie proving an equal match for his desires. Gently, he pushed the head of his cock further, holding still when Solara gasped.

By all that was magic she was tight! His balls drew up against his body, and he knew he was ready to shoot come deep inside her. But he waited, easing inch by inch deeper inside her until he was buried to the hilt. Then he leaned forward and caressed her clit, moving gently back and forth.

"Stars, Roarke," she cried, backing her buttocks against him as he thrust inside her. Her clit swelled against his questing fingers, her juices running down her legs when he caressed her slit. "Please make me come again."

"Your wish is my command, princess," he murmured, kissing her slender back and driving hard against her buttocks. He increased his movements against her clit, feeling her tense against him.

"Yes, like that!" she cried, his faerie now a fierce wildcat. She arched her back and slammed her ass against him. He met her thrusts with equal fervor, driving so deep his balls slapped against her cunt. She mewled a whimper and tilted her head back, her wild hair tantalizing him. Winding it around his fist, he tugged until she groaned, then rode her hard and fast until she screamed with her climax.

He followed her into the abyss, emptying his seed into her tiny hole, then collapsed on top of her. Rolling off, he pulled her against his chest, sweeping her hair away from her face and kissing the fast-pounding pulse at her throat.

He held her and stroked her, memorizing every inch of her. He knew that no matter what they both wanted, come tomorrow they would separate, never to be together again.

The thought kept him up the remainder of the night. He did not close his eyes until the first light of dawn sent its rays pouring into the bedchamber's window.

Chapter Fifteen

ॐ

"Solara, wake up. Garick is arriving!"

Solara blinked, forcing one eye open, the voice barely registering in her sleep-foggy mind. "What?"

A hand shook her shoulder. She tried to throw it off, but it persisted.

"Solara! Wake up now!"

The voice was louder, finally pulling her into reality. She turned and pushed the hair from her face to see Elise frowning down at her.

"It is midday, lazy faerie. Time to be up! Garick and Trista are returning!"

She quickly looked to the other side of the bed, not surprised and yet disappointed to realize that Roarke was no longer there.

And Garick was returning. Her heart fell, realization dawning that she had spent her last moments of freedom in Roarke's arms, but they would never be together again.

"Aye. Give me a few moments to dress and I will be down."

After Elise left, she climbed out of bed, stretching and releasing her wings. A pleasurable stiffness permeated her muscles, and she allowed a smile, remembering the time she spent with Roarke last night.

Another soreness presented itself between her legs. She was no longer a virgin, having freely given her gift to Roarke.

Tears pooled but she forced them aside, splashing water on her face and brushing her hair back. She dressed and went downstairs, joining the crowds gathering in the courtyard as the drawbridge was lowered.

She searched for Roarke, but did not see him among the assembled guards.

If only he had woken her this morning before he left. She wanted…

What? To hold him one more time, taste his lips upon her own, tell him that she loved him and never wanted to be apart?

What good would any of that have done? 'Twould change nothing of their fate.

She spied Roarke just as the drawbridge was lowered. He rode in with Garick, his face set in a grim line. He must have gone out to greet the king upon seeing his approach.

Garick led the procession, immediately dismounting and reaching for Noele, who stood near the drawbridge. Gathering her close, he pressed a warm kiss upon her lips and held her tight to his side as he motioned for Roarke to follow him. Noele beamed up at her husband, and Solara's heart swelled at the palpable love between the two of them.

The crowds milled about welcoming back the rest of the guards. Amidst all the confusion, she was jostled in the melee and lost sight of Roarke and Garick. And where was Trista? She did not recall seeing her sister ride in.

By the time the crowds had dispersed, she could not find Noele, either. Perhaps she had followed Trista to her bedchamber? Deciding to meet them, she headed up the steps, but stopped short when one of Roarke's captains motioned to her.

"King Garick wishes to speak with you in his office."

A cold dread formed in the pit of her stomach. She wished she could find Noele and Trista. She had a feeling she would need her sisters' support.

She knocked on the door to Garick's office. His gruff reply gave her permission to enter. When she stepped in, Garick's angry face greeted her.

Roarke and Noele were also in the room. Roarke's face was grim and Noele could not even look her in the eye.

They knew. They all knew what had happened.

Panic addled her mind and she could not think. She forced herself to clear her head, for the one thing she knew for certain was that Roarke would not suffer because of this. She would not let him lose his honor, knowing how much it meant to him, nor did she wish to be the cause of altering his standing with his king.

"Come in Solara. Be seated. I need to have a word with you."

What could she do to stop this before it happened? How could she make Garick understand that none of this was Roarke's doing?

"I need to speak with you, Garick. Alone, if I may."

Garick cast her a puzzled look, then shook his head. "Not right now. I have something important to discuss with all of you."

"This is important too, Garick."

Noele moved to her side. "Not now, Solara," she whispered, taking her hand and squeezing it gently.

Roarke looked at her and shook his head. He knew she wanted to say something about the two of them.

This could not wait! She had to find a way to speak. Could she defy a king to be heard?

"This is about Trista."

Garick's statement stopped her panicked thoughts. "Trista? Where is she?"

"If you'll sit down, I will explain to you what happened at Greenbriar."

His words filled her with dread. She sat in the chair and reached for Noele's hand, a sense of foreboding make her shiver.

"Upon our arrival in Greenbriar, Trista asked for Solara to

be released from her betrothal to Braedon."

"She did what?" Solara could not believe she heard Garick right. "Why would she do that?"

"Because it's Trista, and she has her own mind about things. You and I know how she is, Solara."

Noele was right. Trista always had a scheme, but for her to be bold enough to ask the southern king to release her was unthinkable. She could only imagine Braedon's reaction.

"So? Are you going to keep us in suspense or are you going to tell us what happened?" Noele asked.

Garick smiled at his wife. "Braedon indicated he did not care which faerie princess he married, so he chose Trista instead."

Solara stopped breathing, her gaze flitting to Roarke. His expression did not change except for the lifting of his brows.

What did all this mean? In an instant her entire fate had been changed. "Did Trista accept?"

A smile curved Garick's lips. "She was not given much choice considering she finally admitted to manipulating the whole situation with your disappearance. She took the note you gave her and hid it away instead of giving it to Noele as you had instructed."

"That explains much," Noele said.

Garick nodded. "Your father had accompanied us, and he accepted the betrothal of Braedon to Trista. The wedding will take place in one month's time."

"Poor Trista," Solara said, more to herself than anyone else. "I wish I had just gone to Greenbriar as I was destined to. Then none of this would have happened."

She refused to look at Roarke as she said it, knowing he wished the same thing.

"Does not matter," Garick explained. "As far as Trista, what's done is done. As for you, another king will be chosen for you to wed."

Solara fought the trembling of her lower lip, the thought of going through this charade again more than she could bear. "I cannot marry anyone," she said, keeping her eyes focused in her lap.

"Why is that?" Garick asked.

"Because I have compromised her and taken her virginity."

Her head snapped up at the sound of Roarke's voice. Roarke stood, his face like stone, his lips set in a grim line. He looked directly at Garick.

"You did what?"

"I took Solara's virginity."

She waited for Garick to speak. Anger hardened his features, more so than she had ever seen. She had to say something before Garick spoke.

"'Twas my fault, Garick. I lured him, tempted him, until he could not resist. Truly, I made it impossible for him to say no. This is my doing, my responsibility, and I should be punished accordingly, but Roarke should not be blamed."

"Ridiculous," Roarke interrupted. "I need no woman to stand up for me. I made the decision on my own and I will be held accountable for violating a faerie princess."

"No!" Solara stood and faced Roarke. "I will not have you stand in judgment as if this was your doing. You fought me every day, keeping your distance. 'Twas I that forced you into this."

Roarke smiled, his eyes gentling. "You are hardly able to force yourself upon me, faerie. As you can see, I am much stronger than you."

She looked to Garick, desperately grasping at anything that would release Roarke from punishment. "I put a magical spell on him, forcing him into it."

Garick rolled his eyes. "Enough. Leave now. I cannot think with the two of you arguing over who is at fault. I will call upon both of you later when I am ready to discuss this."

She was loath to leave, yet she had to follow the king's orders. With a bow of her head, she and Roarke left the room. Noele stayed behind, offering her a sympathetic smile as she closed the door.

As soon as the door was closed, Roarke asked her, "Why did you do that?"

"Because I could not stand to see your honor besmirched because of what I have done."

"You are not to blame in this, Solara. I came to your chambers last night, remember? You were the one who vowed to keep your distance."

She shook her head. "Does not matter. This is my fault, and I will not have you punished for it."

He reached for a tendril of hair and slid it through his fingers. His eyes darkened and he smiled at her. "I would accept any punishment for having had a chance to taste your delights, my princess. Do believe me when I say that you were worth any cost."

Her pulse skittered, blood roaring through every vein in her body. Oh, what she would not give for a moment of privacy, a chance to touch him one more time. "And I will accept any punishment as well, for I did not wish to go the rest of my life wondering what it was like to lie in your arms."

Roarke sucked in a breath. "We had best separate before Garick comes out and finds us together."

She nodded her agreement, but did not want to leave him.

"I know, faerie. I feel the same way. I want you in my arms so badly right now I am willing to risk death to defy my king."

"I need you Roarke. I am cold without the warmth of your arms around me."

He looked both ways down the hallway, then pulled her

into a dark corner, gathering her into his arms and taking her mouth in a kiss that spoke of a thirst that could never be quenched. Her heart ached, soaring with joy and plummeting with the realization that they could never be together.

Roarke rained kisses on her cheeks and neck, murmuring, "I wish so many things, Solara. I wish we were fated, I wish I was noble enough to ask for your hand, but I am no king, and therefore unworthy of you."

Now she could not hold back the tears. "You are my king, you are everything I have ever wanted. From the time of my youth I imagined a dark-haired man who would love me with his heart, not for what I could bring to his lands, but because he wanted me."

He smiled and wiped the tears from her cheeks. "And I do love you, Solara, although I do not think I have ever said the words."

"You did not need to. I love you, too. I have felt in my heart from the first time we met that we were fated. But our fate ends here, this day. Oh, Roarke, I cannot bear to lose you!"

He gathered her against his chest and stroked her hair, whispering words of love. Words she had wanted to hear from him.

But they both knew that despite the words they spoke, their love was not enough to ensure their future together.

Chapter Sixteen

80

Noele paced Garick's office. There was much she wanted to say to him and did not know where to begin.

He had been silent since Roarke and Solara left. Normally, she would not disturb him while he was deep in thought. But she felt that now she must, because she did not want him to make the wrong decisions.

"Garick, I must have a word with you."

He stared out the window into the courtyard. She stepped behind him, laying her hand on his shoulder. When he turned, she knew the pain that Roarke and Solara's admission had caused him.

But for her, he smiled, lifting her hand and pressing it to his lips. "I have missed you, my faerie queen. The first thing I wanted to do upon returning was to sweep you into my arms and carry you into our chambers, where I could make love to you throughout the day."

His words heated her, driving her nipples to hard peaks beneath her shift. Forcing thoughts of pleasure aside until later, she said, "I understand, for I have missed you greatly. My bed is cold at night without you next to me. But first, we must talk about Roarke and Solara."

His smile died and he turned away. "'Tis a decision I must make alone, and you know that."

"Aye, but I have thoughts too and would ask you to hear them."

He sighed and turned to her, leading her to the chaise. Taking her hands in his, he nodded. "Speak, then, for I must make a decision today."

"Roarke and Solara are fated. I feel it, have felt it since the moment the two of them met. The same day I was introduced to you."

He arched a brow. "I felt no such thing that day. Then again, my mind was filled with thoughts of the faerie princess I was to marry."

Caressing his cheek, she leaned in and pressed a kiss to his lips. "For that I thank you. But trust me on this, Garick. They are meant to be together. You cannot blame them for giving in to their desires for one another."

"'Twas forbidden for Roarke to touch Solara."

"True. But when two souls are fated, allowances must be made."

"There is no room for allowances in the laws and customs of our lands."

"Then perhaps it is time to change a few of those laws and customs."

His eyes widened. "What are you saying? That the laws of the land set down generations ago should be altered because Roarke could not keep his dick in his breeches?"

'Twas his frustration causing him to raise his voice, and she knew his conflict was great. Roarke was like an actual brother to Garick, and Garick would not make a decision on his future lightly. "No, that is not what I am saying. What I suggest is that you think about what would have happened had you met me and we bonded, and yet you were forbidden to have me."

He opened his mouth to speak, but Noele pressed a finger to his lips. "I know what you would say, but stop and think. Yes, we were lucky enough to be betrothed and to fall in love. But what if we had not been? What if I had been presented as betrothed to another man? Think before you answer me, Garick."

To his credit, he did. But it wasn't long before his warm grey gaze met hers. "I would have walked through the fires of hell to have you by my side."

His words seared her very soul. "And I would have done the same. I would have committed any crime, done anything, honorable or dishonorable, to make you mine. Now, think of that when you make your decision on Roarke and Solara. Your logic is sound and the laws are clear. But think with your heart, too."

He nodded and she turned to leave, knowing he needed time alone to make his decision. But then she hesitated, remembering her wonderful news. Before she left, she had to tell him, as she would be unable to contain her joy much longer.

"Before I go, Garick, one last thing?"

The way he looked at her, the love in his heart shining on his face, gave her a sense of contentment that she had not thought possible. "Yes, my love?"

She paused for only a second, then grinned. "I carry your child."

* * * * *

Roarke waited impatiently in the hall, oblivious to the stirrings of the castle inhabitants behind him. He only had eyes for Solara, who also stood in front of the two chairs set aside for the King and Queen of Winterland.

They awaited Garick and Noele's arrival. Many hours had passed between their meeting with Garick and this moment. Agonizing hours that Roarke spent wondering what his fate would be.

Garick was fair, had always been so, and yet he could not allow Roarke's violation of Solara to go unpunished. There were laws in the elvin and faerie kingdoms. When those laws were broken, the punishments were severe.

He could be banished, stripped of his position, dishonored publicly, or even imprisoned. As far as Solara, Garick would not punish her, but find her a king willing to accept a faerie princess who was not a virgin. Chances were she would not be taken. But then again, what man would be fool enough to resist her? Her scarlet hair curled wildly down her back, her wings of matching color fluttering slowly open and closed. Her skin was soft as butter, her green eyes reflecting golden pools of passion.

Nay, there would be a fight among the kingdoms. Many would want to claim her.

But she would always be his. No, he would not ask for her. He did not want her to suffer the dishonor that would be bestowed upon him tonight. Nay, he would give her up to a forthright and honorable king before he would allow her to be shamed.

Solara did not know this, but Roarke had spoken privately with Garick before the evening meal, making sure that Garick understood he was more than willing to accept his punishment, but that he wanted no harm to come to Solara.

Garick was strangely silent, but nodded at Roarke's request. He had not spoken to Roarke since, a fact that caused him much pain. He would miss his bonded brother greatly.

A hush went over the hall when Garick and Noele entered. The king's expression gave away nothing of his thoughts, and neither did Noele's. They sat, as did the rest of the people gathered in the hall.

Roarke and Solara were directed to seats in chairs provided for them in front of the crowd. She was so close he could smell her sweet scent. He longed to reach for her hand and reassure her that no harm would come to her this eve, yet did not dare touch her.

For as long as he lived, he would remember her scent, the silken feel of her skin, the warm gold flecks in her eyes and the love in her heart.

Garick cleared his throat and began, first giving the people of Winterland a summary of what had happened in Greenbriar. Gasps were heard when he told of Trista becoming the bride of Braedon. Roarke felt eyes on the back of his head, and no doubt Solara felt them too, yet no one said anything.

"Roarke, would you stand please?"

He stood, looking only at his king.

"Garick, I wish to speak."

The crowd murmured as Solara stood.

"You do not have permission to speak, Solara. Sit down."

"But you do not understand, Garick. I have been trying to tell you—"

"Sit down now or I will have you removed!" Garick bellowed.

Solara sat quickly. Roarke chanced a glance at her, his heart twisting in knots at the sight of her head bowed, fat tears falling onto the hands clasped tightly together in her lap.

Her attempts to protect him were admirable. If he could, he would kiss her for her unselfish willingness to bring dishonor upon herself on his behalf. But he could not.

"And now, if I may be allowed to continue with no more interruptions," Garick started, looking at Solara as if expecting her to object. When she didn't, he nodded and inclined his head to Roarke. "Roarke, please come forward."

He did as his king asked of him, approaching Garick.

"It has come to my attention that there have been some changes while I was gone. This has led me to reevaluate your position here at Winterland."

Roarke listened intently. Not even a sound was made behind him.

"Since the day we were bonded as children, your loyalty to me and to this kingdom has been above reproach. You have been my protector, my friend, and have never failed in your duties."

Roarke inhaled, fighting against the guilt as Garick recited the list of qualities he found admirable. Truly, he did not deserve this, even though he knew what would come after.

"Time and again you have proven yourself equal to the kings of any land. You have fought to protect all of us, your willingness to lay down your life for our people evident. You fended off yet another of the wizards' attacks a few days ago with honor and a warrior's strength. I commend you for this."

Roarke bowed his head, no longer able to meet Garick's eyes.

"Because of your loyalty, your bravery, and because of many other things that have come to light since my return, I am removing you as captain of my guard and releasing you as my protector."

A low murmur reverberated through the crowd. Roarke ignored it, knowing it was about to get much worse.

"Kneel before me, Roarke."

He dropped to one knee as was required, resting his hands on his leg. 'Twas in this position that he would receive his king's decree.

"Be it known throughout our lands that I, Garick, King of Winterland, do hereby bestow the title of King to Roarke. A parcel of my lands to the east will be cordoned off, and forever known as the lands of Roarke, King of Boreas."

Roarke's head snapped up to see Garick taking out his sword and gently placing it over Roarke's shoulders. Cheers resounded throughout the hall, the cacophony of sound blocked out by the blood roaring through his ears.

He stood, unable to fathom what had just occurred. Had he heard correctly? Surely this was some sort of dream, for 'twas not at all the outcome he expected.

Garick clasped him tightly and leaned back. Roarke shook his head. "I…I do not know what to say."

The grin of his old friend shined on his face. "Say nothing. You are now a king."

"I cannot accept this Garick. I do not deserve to be rewarded for an act of dishonor."

Garick arched a brow. "You will insult me if you do not accept. And that would be an act of dishonor. Loving a woman as you do Solara is no shame, Roarke. My own lovely wife reminded me that if our positions were reversed, I would have let nothing stand between me and the woman I loved."

'Twas all too much, only half of it sinking in. A celebration had already begun behind him, but all he could see was his king, his friend, and his beautiful wife, her silver-sparkled face beaming back at him.

"Thank you. I am deeply honored by your generous gift."

Garick nodded. Noele threw her arms around Roarke and kissed his cheek, then took his hands. "As a new king, your first duty should be to select your queen."

His queen. He was a king, still a term he would never think to identify himself. His gaze moved to Solara, who stood near him, smiling. Elise and Mina flanked her, their youthful, exuberant grins evident. Roarke moved to Solara, and Elise and Mina stepped back. He took Solara's hands in his, then dropped down to one knee.

The room fell silent as all eyes turned to them.

Solara placed her hand over her breast, trying to quiet the pounding of her heart. The emotion of the moment was almost more than she could bear. And now, to have Roarke on his knees before her was something she could have never imagined.

"Solara, faerie princess of D'Naath. You are the sun that rises in my heart, your soul is my soul, and I would be honored if you would agree to join with me for all eternity. Will you be my wife?"

The words she thought she would never hear from Roarke's lips made her heart soar. She fluttered her wings excitedly, then nodded. "Yes. Oh yes, Roarke. I love you with all my being. I would be honored to spend the remainder of my days at your side."

At her acceptance, the chorus of applause and shouting

was near deafening. Roarke stood, gathered her in his arms and kissed her. He held nothing back, pouring out his love in a public display that had her laughing with joy. When they parted, she ran and hugged Noele.

"You said something to Garick that made him change his mind."

Noele kissed her cheek. "Nay. Your love is fated, my sister. I had to do nothing but ask my husband to decide with his heart."

Solara looked to Garick, reaching for his hand and squeezing it. "I will never be able to thank you enough for what you have done."

Garick grinned. "'Tis enough that my wife will have her sister nearby when our baby comes. She will need much help, I think."

She hugged her sister and brother-in-law, then turned to Roarke, flinging herself into his arms and raining kisses all over his face.

"We must marry soon, my faerie," he said, nuzzling her neck. "I cannot wait until you warm my bed every night."

"'Twould be my honor to marry you at the day and time of your choosing. Oh, Roarke, I am so happy I am without words."

Winding his arm around her waist, he led her into the throng of celebration. "You will not need words very soon, my princess. You can show me your joy in acts without words."

The promise in his voice spread desire throughout her body. "Let us hope this celebration is a short one, then, for I have much to say."

The festivities lasted well into the night. Plans were made to refurbish Castle Boreas, which had lain dormant since the death of the previous king. They would begin immediately. Splitting up Garick's lands would create a stronger defense on the northern territories, making a more powerful force against the wizards.

Many of the villagers were eager to make their homes with Roarke. Some of the unprotected villagers outside of Winterland would be welcome in the new castle.

As Roarke and Garick sat and poured over plans, Solara stood watch, smiling at the pride on her soon-to-be-husband's beaming face.

In the end, his honor had stood strong, as had the man behind it. Solara eagerly anticipated her new life as Queen of Boreas, but more than that, as wife of her fated love.

Enjoy an excerpt from:
SUMMER HEAT

⠃⠕

Aidan led Melissa to his office, watching as she unloaded her laptop, presentation folders and notepad, lining them up neatly on his conference table.

He resisted the urge to laugh. He'd be lucky to find a pencil somewhere in his office. Having a near photographic memory helped, considering he rarely wrote things down. He had a secretary to enter important dates and information on his computer, not that he'd ever look at it.

When it was time to design a marketing plan he'd drag out the laptop and printer and go at it, pulling forth all the vital information he'd stored in his brain. Other than that, he kept it all within handy reach of his memory.

Apparently Melissa did things differently. She slid a neatly designed binder in front of him. "Now, if you look at the presentation folder in front of you, I've developed a initial marketing plan as a starting point. Open to your suggestions, of course."

"Of course." He quickly scanned the contents, impressed with her expertise. Then he closed it and looked at her, enjoying the way her green eyes flashed whenever they made eye contact.

Melissa Cross might insist she was all about business, but Aidan had a sixth sense about these things. And his sense told him underneath her cool Bostonian exterior beat the heart of a wildcat. The sudden urge to peel her frosty layers away piece by delectable piece had him hardening painfully.

"That's it? You're not going to look at it any further?"

The play of emotions in her expression was priceless. Shock, then indignation soared across her face. Her pert little nose wrinkled and she crossed her arms.

"I read it. It's good. I'll have more to add. There are a few changes I'd like to make, specifically on page four, paragraph three of the marketing plan. I think we need to play up the background of the two companies more, as well as identify the strategic marketing concepts in a bullet point presentation to make it clear what our primary goals are."

Her eyes widened. "How did you do that?"

"Do what?"

"You know what. You barely glanced at the binder, which has over 100 pages. And yet you pointed out an exact page and paragraph and knew precisely what it contained."

"I read lightning fast and have a photographic memory. No magic involved."

At her arched brow he nearly cringed. Why did he have to say that? Magic was an intrinsic part of his life, but he rarely mentioned it outside the family. Although the thought of using some magic to heat up Melissa Cross had already crossed his mind more than a few times. In fact, right now might be a good time. Maybe a little play and that was all. Just to see how she'd react—gauge if his intuition about her was right.

He rubbed his index and middle finger together, the warmth beginning deep inside. The singe of heat lightning was never painful, only a tingling excitement that never failed to arouse him. The air swirled, charged with electricity, centering in his middle like a gathering storm.

He opened his hand and let the magic sail across the table.

Oh, yeah. An invisible breeze wafted Melissa's hair and her eyes widened. Her creamy cheeks blushed pink, and she opened the top button of her blouse, shuddering when the warm air crept inside.

He leaned back in his chair and felt her, the heat buried deep inside her, and knew right then there was something different about this woman. No one had ever reacted instantly to the slightest bit of magic from him. No one had ever fired the heat waves back toward him, letting him experience exactly what he'd sent out.

Hot damn, that was exciting.

"Something wrong?" he asked, trying to sound innocent.

"Don't you feel it?"

"Feel what?"

Blowing out a quick breath, she said, "It just got really hot in here."

"No kidding. I didn't feel a thing."

She fanned herself with her hand. "I don't know what's wrong with me. I guess I must be more unaccustomed to the New Orleans heat and humidity than I thought. Mind if I take off my jacket?"

"Go right ahead." *Take anything off you like, darlin'. Jacket, skirt, panties and bra, anything.* He shifted to accommodate his burgeoning erection, welcoming the heady ache that came with arousal.

Why an electronic book?

We live in the Information Age—an exciting time in the history of human civilization, in which technology rules supreme and continues to progress in leaps and bounds every minute of every day. For a multitude of reasons, more and more avid literary fans are opting to purchase e-books instead of paper books. The question from those not yet initiated into the world of electronic reading is simply: *Why?*

1. ***Price.*** An electronic title at Ellora's Cave Publishing and Cerridwen Press runs anywhere from 40% to 75% less than the cover price of the exact same title in paperback format. Why? Basic mathematics and cost. It is less expensive to publish an e-book (no paper and printing, no warehousing and shipping) than it is to publish a paperback, so the savings are passed along to the consumer.

2. ***Space.*** Running out of room in your house for your books? That is one worry you will never have with electronic books. For a low one-time cost, you can purchase a handheld device specifically designed for e-reading. Many e-readers have large, convenient screens for viewing. Better yet, hundreds of titles can be stored within your new library—on a single microchip. There are a variety of e-readers from different manufacturers. You can also read e-books on your PC or laptop computer. (Please note that Ellora's Cave does not endorse any specific brands.

You can check our websites at www.ellorascave.com or www.cerridwenpress.com for information we make available to new consumers.)

3. *Mobility.* Because your new e-library consists of only a microchip within a small, easily transportable e-reader, your entire cache of books can be taken with you wherever you go.

4. *Personal Viewing Preferences.* Are the words you are currently reading too small? Too large? Too... ANNOYING? Paperback books cannot be modified according to personal preferences, but e-books can.

5. *Instant Gratification.* Is it the middle of the night and all the bookstores near you are closed? Are you tired of waiting days, sometimes weeks, for bookstores to ship the novels you bought? Ellora's Cave Publishing sells instantaneous downloads twenty-four hours a day, seven days a week, every day of the year. Our webstore is never closed. Our e-book delivery system is 100% automated, meaning your order is filled as soon as you pay for it.

Those are a few of the top reasons why electronic books are replacing paperbacks for many avid readers.

As always, Ellora's Cave and Cerridwen Press welcome your questions and comments. We invite you to email us at Comments@ellorascave.com or write to us directly at Ellora's Cave Publishing Inc., 1056 Home Avenue, Akron, OH 44310-3502.

erridwen, the Celtic Goddess of wisdom, was the muse who brought inspiration to storytellers and those in the creative arts. Cerridwen Press encompasses the best and most innovative stories in all genres of today's fiction. Visit our site and discover the newest titles by talented authors who still get inspired - much like the ancient storytellers did, once upon a time.